T0099729

# Her Ghost Wears Kilts

KATHLEEN SHAPUTIS

Crimson Romance
New York London Toronto Sydney New Delhi

Crimson Romance
An Imprint of Simon & Schuster, Inc.
1230 Avenue of the Americas
New York, NY 10020



ISBN 978-1-4405-7216-6
ISBN 978-1-4405-7215-9 (ebook)

*To the bubbly and bubbling Eva Shaw*

*Who began this yellow brick road of fun for me*

*Long ago and far away.*

# Acknowledgments

This is not the first book I've written, nor will it be my last, so the road to completing *Her Ghost Wears Kilts* was filled with many familiar faces and some delightful new ones. I want to thank Crimson Romance for accepting this wonderful story and my editor extraordinaire, Julie Sturgeon, who made my pages sing.

Many knew this by an early working title, *The B&B Mystery*. Helping with early critiques: In Southern California S. Kay Murphy and Laura Slattery, who linked me to Graeme of which I am grateful. In Olympia, Becky Durkin and Jane Brooks were there for me. My initial readers who read the full first draft: Shani Bruce (who may not forgive me for using Bruce as the villain); Bob Shaputis, my incredible husband; and Sara Hooker of Irish Alana, a favorite place of mine.

I will always be grateful for my dedicated cheering sections, which come in various sizes and dimensions. Sherry Scranton Morales, the best sister ever; Jim Verstraeten, my wise older brother; Peggy Johnson, my cousin of many creative talents; Colleen Hill, my BFF; Christina Willis, Tana Propst, and many, many more not mentioned but cherished and appreciated.

Of all the stars in my heavens, here are a shining few whose love and encouragement I miss every day but know they are always in my heart: my mother and father Ruth and Fred Scranton; Grammie Baillie; my wonderful aunts, Margie and Marie; brother Bob; and the phenomenal Jean Butera.

# Chapter One

The cat flattened itself to the carpet near the front bookcase, ears lost against its orange-striped head, frozen in fear. A terrified hiss leaked through his open mouth and, slinking backward, the cat spun and ran toward the back of the store.

Catching a brief flash of orange out of the corner of her eye, Baillie shook her head. "Now what's gotten into Sebastian? Must be a mouse." She fanned her painted fingernails along the spines of books stacked on the shelf beside her. Listening to the hushed clicking sounds of her nails against the bindings as she walked down the aisle, she inhaled the intoxicating aroma of paper and leather around her. She loved opening her bookshop every morning, where antique classics, used and new volumes of various sizes filled the shelves around her. Framed paintings by local artists dotted the walls between the bookcases.

"Morning," Baillie called to the previously owned hardbacks without the slightest apprehension of appearing insane. She talked to inanimate objects all the time—great audience, no heckling. *Besides, I'm alone in here unless you count the cat, and you can't count on that spoiled feline for anything. Where did he dash off to just now in such a hurry?*

A thin volume of poems lay exposed on a shelf. "You don't belong here," Baillie said, sweeping it up to reshelve. She hesitated; the book cover felt cold in her hand, the worn leather chilling her fingers, sucking the warmth from her fingertips in seconds. She quickly shook her head to keep her thoughts from running amok. Of course the book was cold; in the Northwest, things always seemed cold.

"I swear someone helps themselves around here at night. The least they could do is put the books back where they belong when they're done." She turned and pushed a ceramic bookend aside and placed the wayward book next to the others as a quick chill shivered down her spine.

"Hey, Einstein, ol' buddy." Baillie grabbed an ornate feather duster from a brass umbrella stand nearby and took a few housekeeping swipes against the framed lithograph hanging on the wall. "Dang, I'm looking more like you every day." She checked her reflection in the glass. "Tell me, did you see who moved Robert Burns's book of poems last night? Maybe I need to borrow your glasses—going blind in my old age and missed putting it away after closing."

Baillie turned, whistling the theme song from *Fame*, at the end of the aisle. She missed seeing the slow, deliberate movement as the same book silently shifted out from the shelf. The dark brown edition slid away from the other poetry books, hanging suspended for a moment, then lay back on the empty surface of the shelf. The ceramic bookend moved, closing the empty gap.

The front door of the shop opened with a tinkling of metal chimes. "It's just me," yelled a female voice as she came in.

"I'm in the north quarter, Sally. Would you turn on the computer?" Baillie responded from somewhere behind the walls of books. "Time to open up, I guess."

"No problem, boss." Sally dropped her purse under the counter.

Baillie knew her assistant's routine by heart: She'd click the black toggle switch on the power strip with the toe of her shoe, sending juice to all the electronics at the same time. Baillie heard the calculator, printer, and credit card unit each create its own hum as Sally pressed the power button.

"How are the hot flashes this morning?" Sally asked.

"Midlife under control, thank you very much young whiner." Baillie dusted another shelf with a few fast swishes. "You can kick the personal heater on for a while."

"Just a little damp for June this year, you know. Some of us don't have the benefit of hormonal heaters," she taunted.

"I heard that!" Baillie continued up and down the aisles, swishing the duster back and forth. Suddenly, a bitter cold swept around her, sending a blinding chill through her body. She gasped from the icy shock. Baillie couldn't catch her breath as the splash of numbing cold flowed into her heart and out again, pounding inside her chest. The reddish blond hairs on the back of her exposed neck stood on end. Her teeth chattered against the chill, like Lucy Ricardo locked in the meat freezer.

"What the…?" She leaned against the shelving for support. "Whoa." Baillie blinked rapidly and focused on her right hand, more specifically the beige metal shelf under her crimson-painted fingernails. The metal felt warm, warmer than her soul at the moment. Goose bumps traveled up her bare arms and under her short-sleeved blouse. Titles describing Scotland and its clans stood in military straight rows in front of her.

As quickly as it had struck, the air around her trembling body returned to normal temperatures. She took a shaky breath, mentally searching for some logical explanation for the bone-chilling cold. "Who turned the air conditioner on?" she whispered to herself with mock confidence. Looking around the cramped quarters of bookshelves as she moved away, the store seemed peaceful. She dropped the feather duster into a stand with a soft thud.

Baillie walked with determination toward the front of the spacious lobby, checking from one side to the other—for what, she couldn't imagine. As she walked, her hand came up and absent-mindedly played with an escaped tendril of hair from the casual bun she had pinned on the back of her head. A habit from childhood, she twirled the soft hair around her finger in concentration.

"Sally? Did you play with the thermostat just now?"

"No, my heater's on low; haven't touched the wall unit." The twenty-seven-year-old assistant bent her head over the index card file she'd been sorting. Locks of dark, straight hair fell across the gold-colored, wire-framed glasses on her face.

Baillie leaned against the polished oak counter, spotting a few morning customers already settled in overstuffed reading chairs or studying the latest local art hanging in the lobby. Baillie even noted a crusty old weekly regular absorbed in the newspapers of the Puget Sound. All seemed normal at Pen and Pages.

"Too weird." Baillie rubbed her hands together, trying to forget the icy anomaly, and grabbed a stack of new books waiting for shelving. Her arm wrapped around the volumes as naturally and lovingly as a mother cradled a newborn baby.

The entryway of Pen and Pages smelled of remodeling from recently installed rose-patterned carpet and coats of fresh paint on the walls to match the mauve in the threaded petals. Baillie took a deep breath and exhaled to the count of six. She felt her pulse slow back to normal. *I'm not alone.* The company of customers felt like a warm knitted wrap over her shoulders. She tightened her hold on the armload of books, hesitant to move from the security of the counter and Sally's presence.

"Is everything all right?" Sally stared at her, holding her finger inside the small white cards to mark her place. Though Baillie kept the shop's sales, billing and cost accounting on the computer, she insisted the shop keep a manual file of certain art forms on consignment, a throwback of her childhood delight in handling 3 x 5 index cards and endless searches in the old card catalogs at the local library. Sally didn't mind the odd recordkeeping.

"I'm sure it's nothing. I just felt this bizarre rush of cold air while standing in the travel books. Not a blast really; I mean, nothing stirred or moved I don't think. You didn't feel anything, right?" Baillie chewed on her lower lip as Sally shook her head.

"Dang, it felt like I was standing on top of Mt. Rainier for a moment or two."

Sally crossed her short but shapely legs and tucked loose strands of hair behind her ear for the tenth time in an hour. "The Queen of Menopause suffering from chills? That's a new one," she teased with gentle affection.

"Excuse me." Baillie stared at the young woman across from her with mock surprise. "Your turn will come sooner than you think, Ms. Generation X. Don't make fun of my freakishly early passage into mature womanhood."

"Maybe your Aunt Fran's upset over the remodeling. This was her house first."

"Wha—?" Baillie felt the blood drain from her face. "You think it was a ghost?"

"I'm kidding! I didn't mean it. Seriously," Sally stuttered at Baillie's scared reaction. "My grandma used to say something crazy like if you got a chill or shiver down your back that someone's walking over your grave."

"I knew you were just pulling my chain, Sally," Baillie said, aiming for nonchalance in her tone. *Get a grip, you're freaking out the hired help.* "You know, I don't plan on having a grave for anyone to tromp over." Baillie fiddled with a stack of Post-It notes, avoiding Sally's brilliant blue eyes behind the gold-rimmed glasses, the ghost idea still making her heart race. "I'm going with a bake-and-shake process when I die. Someone can spread my ashes across the Sound or inside some potted plant for all I care. I won't be here."

"Baillie, that's morbid. And probably illegal. Don't they have laws about interring cremated ashes?"

"Me, worry about breaking stupid laws? I'm an orphan, for gosh sake, with no relatives anywhere. Who'd worry about me? Sebastian? Anyone gives him a bowl of tuna and he'd forget me in a minute, the fickle old feline. I intend to leave my worldly goods to Wolf Haven with a clause that my orange buddy be given a good home with some lady who will continue to spoil him rotten. Where is that darn nuisance anyway?"

The phone rang, and both women jumped at the sudden intrusion and laughed nervously at their dual reactions. Sally picked up the receiver, and Baillie pushed herself away from the counter. These books weren't going to sell themselves.

"Hmm, what *will* I do when this pitiful body quits?" Baillie mused. She stopped in the first aisle of fiction and shoved two books apart. "Hell, at fifty-four, I've got twenty, thirty years to figure out something." She added the top book from her stack and then read the author's name and title of the next book. "Guarantee me the Angel of Death who comes to take me to the other side looks as good as Andrew on *Touched by an Angel*, and I'll put my request in early. God, was he gorgeous or what?" she said to no one. *Okay, I'm losing it worse than usual. No more talking to myself; there are customers around.*

Floor-to-ceiling bookcases filled various rooms like a fractured maze from Lewis Carroll's *Wonderland*, with hard-covered beauties or glazed pottery works adding to the colorful personality of the old house's first floor. Walking among the mismatched bookcases, some painted eggshell white, some collected from going-out-of-business sales of other stores, Baillie focused on moving and shifting the volumes, making room for the new additions. For every book she added, she automatically checked if one or two volumes might be out of alphabetical sequence.

Baillie was born a librarian her maternal grandmother had always told her. "Black ink flows through those veins of yours," Grammie often said during her visits when Baillie was a child. Baillie would curl up with a book in the corner of the couch with her Grammie during most of her visits and had kept a stack of additional books waiting by her bed.

She agreed with her grandmother's assessment. She'd wanted to be a librarian since she was a little girl proudly carting her first library card in a tiny, white wicker purse. At least she had until she noted the job requirements during her high school years. Who decided it took a master's degree to organize books? What a high-priced concept, enduring years of advanced schooling to memorize the numbered file system of Dewy Decimal. Only after sweat and thesis could you work for low government wages under a maniacal boss *just* to do what you loved most in the world. Sounded like a Dilbert comic strip to Baillie.

Books held magic and knowledge that broke her loose from the sterile home life she had been raised in. Granted, being raised in Southern California held nothing of the descriptive seasons she found in the printed pages of Beverly Cleary's books long ago. Her characters lived in neatly packaged, tree-lined neighborhoods where it snowed in the winter, and woolen underwear was a necessity for walking to school. At least Ellen Tibbets had to.

Baillie was probably allergic to wool. Who wore anything other than cotton and polyester in Southern California? Her only-child household had sat in the middle of a cement and asphalt suburb. The constant sun blazed from season to season. If the temperature dropped below sixty degrees, Baillie felt frostbitten and crabby. Cold was nasty and unforgiving back then. *Beezus and Ramona, eat your paper hearts out.*

Cold. Baillie found herself turning into aisle three, the frozen section from earlier. She stared down the familiar aisle as seconds ticked by. Nothing looked out of the ordinary. She felt her heart slam against her chest in a jarring beat. *Snap out of it, this is ridiculous.* Smiling at the superstitious fear, Baillie focused on her work, though her knuckles whitened around the books in her arm.

Scenes from the haunted forest in the *Wizard of Oz* ran through her mind as she stared down the aisle. "I do believe in spooks, I do believe in spooks," the Cowardly Lion had cried as he held his tail between his paws. "Nonsense. It's probably nothing. I haven't eaten breakfast yet; maybe this is just low blood sugar. More likely a miserable draft I'll be spending a fortune to fix. There's no such thing as spooks."

Baillie found that her body wouldn't move. Her feet were firmly planted on the carpet as if long roots had sprouted through the floor. She looked down at her sensible black pumps with irritation. "I have work to do," she muttered under her breath. She lifted her right foot with every intention of taking a step forward. Nothing happened.

A lilting sound tickled her ear, faint notes of a melody. "The CD player's broken. There's no music playing in the shop," she said out loud to herself. "Has been for days; it still has my favorite Jimmy Buffett disc inside." *Maybe someone's MP3 player is turned up too high.*

Nothing. Silence. Only the fast beating of her heart and a hum of conversations in the front of the store could be heard. She slowly placed her foot, still dangling in midair, back on the carpet. Straining her ears, she tried to decipher what she thought she'd heard. There it was again, more audible this time, a handful of notes like a flute or pipe played. *A Celtic sound*, she thought, as it faded away.

She moved a short inch down the aisle.

The same set of lyrical notes from a Celtic pipe started caressing her ears. *Definitely Celtic; this is not someone's iPod.* "What the—" she started, a slight chill ran down her spine, a tingling bolt. Not the invasive full-body freeze as before, but a chill squeezing her wildly beating heart. She glanced around, alone in the aisle. Goose bumps speckled her minimally tanned-from-a-bottle forearms. "It couldn't be." She slowly forced her head to turn toward the neatly packed shelves. Titles of Scotland filled her vision.

"Lassie, ye be cracking up around these books of ye ancestors." Baillie melted against the bookshelves for support, her legs like wet strands of pasta. *Am I having a stroke?* "Get over it, Catharine Anne Baillie. Ignore the dark fairies of the glen trying to frighten life out of ye and get ye wide-burdened butt back to work." Baillie laughed shakily at her pitiful attempt at a Sean Connery brogue. Breaking the invisible hold of fear, she wobbled off to find a place for the last two books in her arm.

# Chapter Two

"Whoa." An older man dressed in a perfectly tailored jacket and flannel slacks leaned against his Jaguar, the silver-blue paint matching the color of his cold, calculating eyes. He raised his arm toward the man and horse riding toward him. "What a handsome mount there, lad."

"Thank ye kindly, Sean. He be my youngest, brightest star o' me stables." The younger man reigned in the magnificent seventeen-hand steed alongside the expensive car parked underneath an old withered tree. He reached out from his saddle to shake the familiar man's hand in greeting. The handshake was firm, quick.

The green Scottish hillsides shimmered around them in rare brilliant sunshine. The rolling slopes looked like bolts of dark green velvet carelessly draped about, scattered clusters of gray boulders now and again breaking up the hues of green. The sky of azure blue canopied over the two men.

Age had been kind to the man standing, with few wrinkles and dark hair showing only dapples of distinguished gray at his temples. Sean reached into the outside pocket of his navy blue jacket and brought out a couple lumps of sugar. "Would you mind? I haven't the room nor time to tend a stable myself these days."

"Nay, I'll wear the sweets off him."

Careful not to spook the horse, the older man stretched his flattened left hand toward the stallion's nose, offering the white treats. With his pale right hand, he rubbed the smooth damp skin of its neck. "He's mighty fine."

"Man should'na be too busy to take part in animals and nature. 'Tis grand to see ye step away from that iron chain of ya desk, man." The rider, a decade younger, leaned down and stroked the neck of the horse. "What brings ye out to this open area of God's country?"

"I had to check on a piece of property just past here, and I saw you galloping up the road. Has everything gone well in your new manor? Have'na seen you in months," the driver asked with a concerned smile.

"Aye, quite well, thank you. A few boxes left to unpack, but time will handle the lot." The horse whinnied and impatiently pawed at the dirt. "He needs his morning run to quell the devil in him on a day like this. I'll not hold up your business any further." The man tipped his cap and spurred his heels into the soft sides of the horse.

A few wisps of dust settled back to the damp earth as the driver watched the horse and rider, as he had secretly for the past few weeks. Sean walked around the back of his low-slung car and opened the door, seemingly in no hurry. The pair had already disappeared around a curve by the time he bent his large frame into the car and started the engine, shattering the silence of the area with a precision growl. The brittle corners of the man's mouth fractured into a rare smile, as the car rumbled a continuous purr. He turned the car around easily on the wide dirt road and drove off.

• • •

The young bachelor pulled gently on the left rein of the stallion, heading them in a comfortable canter toward the sound of the sea. It felt good to be away from the dreariness of the castle and the unending task of emptying crates and barrels, though the inherited staff had been more than generous in their attention and help. The wee angels had smiled down on him bringing his Baillie bloodlines to this honor of land baron.

A tug on his tweed cap pulled it snug to his head, as he didn't wish to lose it with the now fierce rush of sea air. Waves crashing against the jagged rocks somewhere ahead created rhythmic sounds in his ears, gulls overhead cried in sad harmonies. The air had a bite of salt to it.

Breaking out of the comfortable rocking stride to a trot, the horse's footing slipped in the muddy grass. The stumble jolted the man in the saddle.

"Easy, lad. This terrain inna as smooth as she looks."

Beneath him, the animal's breathing felt labored and erratic. *Impossible*, he thought. As they crossed the meadow, a second stumble worried him like the flick of a red flag. The horse's neck broke out in a pattern of thin froth, a veil of white against the black hide, though they'd only been out a short time. The man's ruddy face wrinkled in concern.

His mount's dark, gentle eyes suddenly went wild, showing large amounts of stark white. He had no time to react to the earthquake of tightened muscles under him as the horse lunged ahead at a full, powerful speed. An experienced rider, he strained to get control of the runaway without success, his arms aching with the pressure against the reins as the horse failed to acknowledge he was astride him. Jagged cliffs rushed toward the pair, the edge of land moving closer at frightening speed. The man's frantic pleas against the leather straps meant nothing to the crazed animal.

The area was empty of any other living soul; the thundering hooves reverberated only to the desperate rider. At the last merciful foot of muddied earth, the dark-stained horse reared to an abnormal height, pawing the air with gigantic hooves, screaming into space, a sound that chilled the man to his very core. Before the echo faded in the wind, his own high-pitched scream hit unknown notes as the horse twisted violently and he was thrown from the saddle over the last inches of earthly sanity. The reins, the man's last link to life, cut through his fingers before being torn away completely as he dropped fifty feet onto the sharp, jagged rocks below. A wave of frigid water and tangled vines of kelp splashed across his body as it shattered on impact.

The horse bolted back into the field, away from the edge, kicking his hind legs viciously at an invisible attacker. The stirrups, empty of their rider, flapped wildly in a frenzied dance, inciting the horse into more bizarre behavior.

At the bottom of the cliff, a broken neck had cut short the man's pain from a crushed face, broken ribs, and a right leg twisted at an impossible angle. The ocean arrogantly crashed over the limp specimen, splashing against the still warm skin, coating the black rocks in a layer of seawater and blood.

Skidding into a stand of ancient gnarled trees, the horse's wet skin rippled in fear. It shook its majestic head again and again, clanging the bit and reins. The silent sun beat down on his empty back, frozen to the spot in terror.

# Chapter Three

"Hey," Sally snapped her gum while entering yesterday's receipts into the computer. "Is everything, you know, behaving in the back of the shop?" Baillie stared at her as Sally crossed her arms in a pretend shiver. "You know, Aunt Fran's ghost? The new freezer section?"

"Uh, yeah," Baillie tried to snicker and shrug it off. "Probably a draft or something I've never noticed before kinda thing." *But how would I explain spooky soundtracks from some Celtic Casper to Sally?* She felt nauseous remembering the icicle blasts and invisible bagpipes over the last few days.

"Do you need to lay down, boss? You're looking a little green. Maybe you're coming down with something. You know how many colds and flus are going around," Sally said, concerned. "Couldn't possibly be you're working too hard," Sally threw at Baillie over her shoulder before switching gears with a brilliant smile, waiting on a young man in front of her. He held a framed watercolor against the counter. "What an excellent choice. Is this for you and your wife?"

Baillie shook her head at her employee's chameleon emotions.

When Sally finished the sale, she rushed to Baillie's side. "Did you see the guy who bought Montelongo's *Riverside Drive*? Wasn't he a fantasy in tight jeans? No wedding ring tan line, either." Sally poked her elbow into Baillie's side. "I asked; he's single."

"Excuse me, Miss Fix-Up-the-Spinster. He was twenty years younger than me." Baillie smoothed loose strands of hair up toward the knot, feeling her cheeks flush a bright red. "Don't push me into the arms of eligible male customers, you Dolly-what's-her-name from that Streisand musical." *God knows how long it's been since I've been out on a date, blind or otherwise.*

"Levi, Dolly Levi. And Carol Channing also played the part, which you would remember except for these senior moments you keep complaining about." Sally ducked the glare Baillie shot her. "Sorry, just trying to help. That was one of your favorite paintings, you know. Maybe you should make sure it got a good home. I have his address on the sales slip if you, ah, want the exact location." She laughed as she walked toward the shop's bathroom in the back.

"A Montelongo painting always finds a good home," Baillie snapped at Sally's receding figure.

"Are you coming to Casie's game Saturday?" Sally asked later in the day.

"You know I wouldn't miss it, and Gillian's opening the shop for me. Who schedules Little League for eight in the morning? What happened to kids sleeping in on weekends?" Baillie complained.

"I'm thankful she only had a couple during dawn's early light this year."

"Guess it was a good thing that I couldn't play growing up if you had to be at the plate before a decent breakfast. Casie has a terrific arm; you must be so proud." Baillie pretended to grasp an imaginary bat. No girls were allowed in baseball during her pre-Title 9 youth. "Maybe it'll lead to a scholarship."

"Wouldn't that be great? Kids are so expensive," Sally complained while smiling. "I'm getting carpal tunnel from opening the checkbook or swiping the debit card every five minutes."

"Are we whining?" Baillie asked. Sally's life held a variety of ordinary facets that, when piled together, compressed into a radiant jewel of chaos and family joy. Baillie loved hearing the stories.

"That's my job; I'm a mom."

"And a darn good one."

Sally flushed at the praise. "Your children live here inside these walls, safely tucked nice and neat on bookshelves. You need a personal life," Sally threw out. "This is a business, not a shelter for hermits, Catharine." With the last word, she dropped behind the counter.

"You're on thin ice, Little Grasshopper," Baillie raised her hands in a karate stance, "for calling me Catharine. Do not fall into icy water below and drown." She sniffed. "I have a good life, thank you very much. I leave the shop and go home on a daily basis."

"Big friggin' deal. Your home is upstairs. And I've often wondered if you don't sneak back down and open up the store again after I've gone."

"What a great idea. I could have moonlight sales for insomniacs."

"Get serious," Sally laughed.

Baillie smelled victory as Sally lost this battle, but Baillie knew she'd never give up the war of pushing her into meeting people, specifically male, outside the world of books and this house.

"Is it a crime to like your job? I'm self-employed; I'm supposed to be a workaholic. It's the law of survival." Baillie scratched her nose, hiding a grin. "I have Sebastian, a freezer stocked with great selections of Lean Cuisine entrees and a case of Diet Coke. It's the simple life for me."

"Sounds like something from some Rogers and Hammerstein musical my mom's always watching. What about dating?"

"Dating. Hmm, is that anything like fishing off a tiny boat with a piece of string in the middle of the ocean? Doesn't sound interesting."

"Stop it. You joke about any reference to the male species, girl. They can be fun if you give them half a chance."

"I have Gillian if I want fun."

"Right, I said male." Sally snorted with a laugh. "That flashy, mirror-obsessed piece of 'fairy tail' is not exactly what I'm talking about. He's a facade you hide behind once in a while."

"He makes me laugh," Baillie defended Gillian Nation, a drop-dead gorgeous hunk of late twenty-something gayness. A computer genius by day working north in the land between

Amazon and Microsoft up the I-5 freeway, Baillie loved tagging along on various entertainment ventures with him.

She'd met this Adonis of minimal testosterone more than a year ago. With Baillie's luck running true to course, the first time in a decade her encased-in-stone heart had melted for something in the men's department, it turned out he knew more about how to catch a good-looking man than she did. Once she delicately wiped the lustful drool from her chin and enjoyed the view as well as his company, they'd become good friends. A walking directory of any and every entertainment event held around western Washington, he didn't mind taking an independent, older woman out into public when Mr. Popularity's calendar had a vacancy.

"Hmpf," Sally slammed her palm against the stapler then readied another set of papers, tapping the edges with a little too much force on the desktop.

"Meow. The lady will have a saucer of milk to go, please. You're just jealous because he's cuter than your George. It's okay," Baillie dramatically raised her hand to her forehead. "I can handle the vicious attack against my choice of companion. I'll loan you a photo of Gillian for 1-900 fantasies any time."

"Oh, puh-leeze." Dragging the last word out to two syllables, Sally laughed. "You're right, I'm being completely jealous. I don't have a pop-up muscle beach card to play. Gillian has been a good friend to you. At least the flashy cretin knows how to do that much.

"And," Sally hung her head, "he *is* a great salesman, I hate to admit. When he's minding the shop, the receipt book always shows an increase in sold slips. I don't want to know what goes on during his trysts here. And he does get you out socially without too much kicking and screaming. I should be grateful somebody can force you into some kind of personal life, even a barren, platonic one with him and his girls."

Baillie nodded with a smile and a wink. "Atta, girl."

• • •

"Ready to call it a night?" Sally suppressed a yawn. The sun, now behind the tops of fir trees, left the shop's interior bathed with the warm glow of its various lighting fixtures.

"If we must." Baillie was still bent over an inventory list, oblivious to the passing of time.

Sally walked to the back of the shop and started checking the various rooms for straggling customers.

Baillie listened to Sally's movements while neurotically chewing on the end of her pencil. Her shoulder muscles were clinched as tight as a concrete block wall as Sally passed through the aisle of books on Scotland. Not a startled gasp or squeak from Sally—nothing as she moved by the books.

Of course nothing. They were just used books about Scotland and its clans. Inanimate objects. Could she be going through some middle-aged hormone hallucinations, Baillie wondered, a nasty taste of eraser in her mouth. Maybe an ancient Scottish curse no one had told her about caused mental fatigue after fifty. Baillie had avoided that area of the shop for any reason. She'd taken a wandering route along the back walls when she needed a bathroom break or left for home. Bizarre, unexplainable incidents at the same spot had her more than a little on edge. *I'm becoming afraid of my own shop.*

"What?" Sally asked as she passed by the desk and turned over the hand-painted closed sign at the front door.

"Huh?"

"You should see your face. What could possibly be putting wrinkles in your brow at this time of day? It's time to go home and relax, enjoy ourselves."

"Just thinking about the, uh, draft I felt this week and what it's going to cost me."

"Geesh, I forgot about your spooks."

"Who said anything about spooks?" Baillie's voice squeaked, edging on a plea for reassurance.

"I'm kidding, though I never felt anything out of the ordinary in the shop. You're not worried, are you? I was joking about your aunt being a ghost. Try getting a good night's sleep once in a while. You remember sleep, don't you? Laying your head on a pillow with the lights and television off?" Sally shook her index finger. "Stay away from the ancient movie channel when you get upstairs."

Baillie shot her a guilty smile as she shut down the shop's computer. She watched Sally reach along the wall and turn off the overhead lights. Sally knew how much she loved the oldies on cable, classics of the forties and fifties with a few Technicolor sixties ones thrown in for balance. The musical background scores set the scene and mood for her even if Baillie grabbed a snack or drink in the kitchen. Yes, she was addicted to films and film stars of the past. Not a bad habit if you had to have one.

"Hey," Baillie said, "I have other love interests. A few cable channels let me relive my prime time television adolescence whenever I want to."

"Shoot, I gotta run. George will be making God-knows-what for dinner, and Casie will lock herself in her room. Tomorrow." Sally grabbed her purse and went out the front door, locking it from the outside.

"Goodnight," Baillie whispered, still standing at the counter. *I better be alone in here.* Her mouth felt parched.

Baillie usually enjoyed the shop after a busy day. Tonight her heart pounded as she held her breath, listening. Silence enveloped her. Her palms started to sweat, and the route from the front of the shop to the back door seemed endless, like it stretched into a hall of mirrors. She wished Sally had waited. Waited for what, she couldn't say. Baillie tried to kick herself out of the tension. Pushing herself away from the counter, she bent over and dropped the master keys in a drawer, wincing at the loud clanking, and closed it. "There's nothing to be afraid of," Baillie admonished herself. *This is my shop, my home, the same old family house, right Aunt Fran? Anything you're trying to tell me after all these years?*

Nothing convinced her, though. She took a hesitant step in the familiar gloom and then another. No frigid blasts of cold air slapped her in the face. Another step. It was just her, a fifty-something crazy woman scaring herself before she got upstairs to dinner and a nice hot bath.

Baillie forced herself to walk through each of the rooms, took one last look around and turned off the various shaped lamps added here and there for warmth in shadowed areas. Antique mirrors were strategically placed between paintings in different positions on the walls around the house to add a feeling of depth as well as security. She could easily see into rooms or around corners as she walked quicker than usual tonight on her daily rounds.

She froze as faint, faraway strains of a bagpipe reached her. The melancholy notes locked her spine like the Tin Man without his can of oil. The notes sounded familiar, the same song from before. Baillie broke out in a nervous sweat, closed her eyes, and quickly walked with stiff legs to the back door, refusing to break into the run her hammering heart desperately demanded.

# Chapter Four

"Ya dinna notice the stallion came back alone? Half out of its wits, he was."

Putney drew her arthritic right hand quickly in front of her in the sign of a cross. She looked around the ancient smoke-gray walls of the familiar kitchen. "What wretched evil lives in this house? The very bricks of its walls are held together in pain."

"Barnaby said they found the body following the screams of gulls circling above."

"The new owner was so young."

"What matter his age, woman? The curse continues in these barren halls." The old gentleman wrinkled his pale brow in frustration and swept tired fingers through his gray hair, making it wilder than before.

"Dinna think we would lose this one so soon." Putney dabbed a corner of her worn cooking apron at the tears in her eyes. She sniffed and let go of the material, slapping her hands to smooth it against her dress. "That worthless Rogue. I seen her standing there by the barn door jus' staring off, she was. Like she dinna understand the direness to us all of his death. The pitiful likes of her, she probably loosened the poor horse's straps herself. She be the devil's own kin, coming with him from nowhere, without a reference of her own. How the master let her stay as part of the family is ne'er going to be answered now."

"Woman, be quiet," the old man slapped his hand on the wooden table with force. "The young lass would'na harm a hair on that man's head. She lived and breathed in gratitude to the man. He gave her shelter when no one would open a door to her."

"Not any longer, she doesn't," Putney turned her stiff, bowed back to the old man. The heat radiating from the stove wrapped around her, shielding her body from the damp Scottish air. She grabbed a worn, scarred ladle and stirred the steaming pot of stew, their midday meal. "Humphf. She'll not be inheriting this place from winning over his heart, I tell ya, may his soul rest in peace. I ne'er trusted the likes of her, not from the day we laid eyes on her shivering on the doorstep behind him like he were her da."

The hand-hewn chair creaked beneath the man as he leaned toward the woman. "Whatever the horse saw out there, the girl had no part of it. They are of kindred souls. I dinna live this long for you to tear apart a youngster's first charity at happiness. This has torn her heart to shreds, I tell ya."

"We'll see, old man."

# Chapter Five

Baillie unlocked the shop's back door of the office, her trembling hand making it difficult to insert the key. She usually enjoyed the cool draft of the dim stairwell, an air-lock transition between work and home. Tonight she looked over her shoulder before walking up the brief flight of stairs. As the sixth stair creaked through the thin carpet, Baillie touched her heart and made a wish for good sales tomorrow. A silly habit, she knew, but the normalcy comforted her as she stepped into the kitchen.

Baillie checked her answering machine on the white tiled counter across from the door, its red light blinking at a rapid pace. She slipped off her shoes as she punched the play button. The first two were hang-ups; the last was Gillian.

"Hello, darling. Have you checked your calendar lately, and please tell me it's not some dreadful Garfield thing on the wall. I'll accept no excuses, my lady. You promised you'd attend the Renaissance Faire this year with me, and the time has come to cash in on that delicious promise." The voice crackled; he must have called from his car. "I expect you to come up with a totally fabulous costume to wear—I do not play in the Elizabethan era without everyone in proper wardrobe. You must call me. *Ciao*, darling."

The Renaissance Faire? She'd forgotten about her forced promise eons ago. Gillian Nation, her dear but extremely spoiled friend, had twisted her arm last winter and planned a future play date to some annual carnival among pretending heathens and royalty. This could be fun, though; Gillian raved about prior years he and his friends had attended. Baillie's tag-along invitation was probably suggested as a royal mascot, a token female in a group of twisted testicles dressed in velvet and lace.

Baillie grabbed a bottle of water from the refrigerator and smiled at the memory of her first encounter with Gillian. It had been late, almost tropically warm for the South Sound, when she had headed over to the Barnes & Noble on the west side to scout the latest titles.

• • •

Bright florescent lights made her squint as she stepped out of the spring night's soaking rain. The smell of fresh pages differed from the musky perfume of her shop. She shook her wet locks, like a drenched puppy flipping droplets from its fur. Her shopping trip ended in the celebrity biography section. Her fascination with actors and actresses did not end with film or television—she had built a personal collection of bios and profiles on her favorites filling a wall of bookshelves in her living room. As she reached for a new volume, her hand collided with a young man's meticulously manicured fingers reaching for the same book.

"Pardon me. Please, take this one." A young Fabio-like creature, tall, with twinkling blue eyes, let go of the volume.

"Uh, thank you," stuttered Baillie.

"I've heard it's scandalous; wouldn't you die if it's true?" The man had the most incredibly white teeth against a too-perfect tanned face. *In Olympia in May?*

Baillie barely nodded as her eyes dropped toward the book in her hands, but not before she noticed with pleasure the open-throated white shirt, neatly tucked into beige slacks she'd only seen in glamour magazines at Irish Alana when she got her hair cut. His outfit alone probably outpriced her entire closet. Including shoes.

He tossed a strand of long, luxurious hair over his shoulder as he grabbed another copy off the shelf. "Could you imagine how many calls she must have made to lawyers trying to block this book?" The blond locks fell in soft, thick waves behind his back.

Baillie self-consciously tucked a stray hair behind her ear as she lusted over his most likely natural curl. Men were unfairly the more chosen ones when it came to hair and eyelashes in the world of nature. Baillie would kill for hair like his.

"How rude of me, rambling on without proper introduction." The twenty-something male turned to her and stuck his hand out toward her dazed look. "My name is Gillian Nation, and yours?"

"Oh, Baillie, um, I'm Baillie," she said. Taking his manicured hand, she noticed how soft and warm his skin felt against her own. Baillie washed her hands often at the store, hoping against leaving fingerprints on the books, but it left her hands chapped and dry. She self-consciously pulled her hand back.

Shaking off the intensity of this gorgeous man and regaining some sense of composure, Baillie flipped through the first few pages of the book. "I heard she tried for an injunction against the author, but the judge denied the case." She hoped her voice wouldn't squeak.

"Oh, my girl, the fur flew into quite a scrumptious cat fight," Gillian leaned against the bookcase and filled in detail after juicy detail of the scandal.

"Would you like to, uh, if you have time, sit at Starbucks for a cup of coffee?" Baillie stuttered the invitation. "I'd love to hear more, and we could, um, sit down right near here." *Why does this guy take my breath away? He's young enough to be my son, if I had one.*

"Actually, I'm horribly late getting home."

"Oh, sure." Baillie dropped her eyes to the floor, and she knew a flush of color painted her cheeks.

"But what's a few more minutes?" His hand flew lightly in front of her face. "I've had such a ghastly day at the office. You do realize I don't live here in this mecca wanna-be, right?" Gillian gathered a short stack of books in his other arm and led her toward the cashier, talking all the way.

"You don't think of Olympia as a city?"

Gillian graced her with a spectacular smile. "You can hardly call the capital building a skyline, darling." His face barely shifted. "A dear friend was in crisis—of all nights—bringing me down from the Emerald City. You can't imagine the trials this day has been."

Baillie grinned at his energy level this late in the evening. She stood meekly in line beside him, absorbing the rantings and ravings of his day, ignoring her brain as it tugged at her with warnings to not waste her lust on a man who obviously played for the other team.

"You're staring," he paused. "Am I being a cretin? Don't tell me, don't tell me." He pinched the bridge of his nose with those perfectly manicured fingers. "You live out here. No, not just live out here; you love it here."

Nodding, she felt winded from his enthusiastic complaining.

Gillian looked her up and down as Baillie, finger-fluffing her damp locks, wished the ground would swallow her up. "Hmm, but there's something about you; you're not a purist of the Northwest," he started. "I'm originally from Southern California, Orange County. I came up here about five years ago on a software-development carpet ride." Gillian tilted his head ever so slightly. "I can't place the aura, but the bemused look on your face is truly giving you away."

"I'm originally from Southern California," she giggled, "too." The last word squeaked as she'd feared it would. It was not fair for one man to be this attractive.

"Ah-ha, see? The radar doesn't lie. You do have Disney dust in your soul."

"Sort of. Born and raised a few counties over from Disneyland, in the Ontario area."

Gillian raised his perfectly shaped left eyebrow. "Horrors. So was my former boss, Lord love her. When did you migrate up here?"

"Close to ten years, I guess. My aunt passed away and left me her home and inheritance. I've always loved this area from childhood visits. So I stayed."

"What do you do with yourself?" Gillian slowly fanned an advertisement flyer while gazing over the top of her head, scouting the room.

Baillie tightened her shoulders, standing large in defense. "I own a used bookshop not far from here."

"Down, girl," Gillian laughed. "You'll get neck strain; relax. Such a noble profession for a single, white woman, so don't get your Dewey Decimals in a tizzy. Ah, finally, my turn. Meet me in line at Starbucks when you finish," and he waltzed to the counter and pulled an eel skin wallet out of the black zippered pouch he carried casually over his shoulder.

The rest of the night blurred in laughter and cappuccino lattes, beginning a wonderful, unique friendship for Baillie. Over the past year, Gillian had wound his charm into her life. During flings of merriment and splendor, when Gillian deemed her worthy or needy, he enhanced her life with his presence and forced her out into the world.

• • •

Baillie moved away from the now silent answering machine with a sigh. Gillian, *mi amore*. She snagged her water and crossed the carpet to change her clothes.

Baillie had inherited the antique clapboard house from her Aunt Fran twelve years ago and had turned the lower half into Pen and Pages. Nestled between a popular mini-mall and an old three-acre cemetery, Baillie lived alone in the top floor of the gabled house. Tall fir trees canopied the small parking lot where the front yard used to be. Maples and oaks dotted in between the evergreen branches, acting as bird condominiums with a variety of colorful feeders hanging on the lowest limbs.

A kaleidoscope of miniature rooms covered the top floor; the total square footage above the store felt perfect for one person. She'd remodeled as she could afford, starting with deep forest green carpeting in the main rooms and heated wood flooring in the kitchen and bath.

The master bedroom held a queen-size bed and vanity dresser with minimal room to move around. One major addition she'd made was installing oak French doors where a decrepit sliding glass door had originally opened onto a slender wooden balcony. She loved the soothing burgundy and beige designs she'd picked out for her room.

She opened the efficient walk-in closet and pulled a navy short-sleeve sweatshirt from a hanger. Slipping out of her dress, she did a few bends and stretches before donning comfortable sweats and knee socks. What wonderful person had invented fleece material? She'd Google it later for fun. Details make life so interesting, Baillie mused.

Finishing her water, she slid across the kitchen floor in her stocking feet and dumped the empty bottle into the recycle bin. Baillie pushed play on her CD player, and a fast-tempoed Village People tune filled the room. Moving to the disco beat, she picked up the cordless phone. Quickly hitting speed dial, she listened to the ring.

"Hello, my bedraggled store monger."

"Gillian, it's…I hate caller ID. You messed me up. What am I supposed to say?"

"That you're trying to kill me with whatever racket is blaring in the background. Immediate volume control, please, I have sensitive ears, and those cretins are not worth losing my precious hearing."

"Are you saying you never listen to disco?" Baillie walked over and clicked off the music.

"My sweet pet, disco was dead and buried before I was born. It would stay six feet below ground, yet you alone resurrect the bohemian crudeness."

"Gillian, don't hold back, tell me how you really feel about my music." She laughed.

He ignored her. "You should drive up to Seattle, and we'll both pick out our costumes for the upcoming faire. I'm giving you ample time for your selection."

"I don't have a clue what I'm supposed to wear. This is my first time, remember?"

"Ah, yes, my Renaissance virgin, you will be delighted to discover that the peasants, clad in dreary rags, come in droves, mingling among the Queen and her royal subjects, such as myself, in velvet and trimmings. Your heart may choose anything from barbarian to authoritarian while you frolic at the faire."

"Barbarian? You're kidding?"

"And colors. We must pick out something a bit bright for your dull pallor. Have you heard of getting out in sunlight, darling? Surely your quaint city has a tanning salon hidden somewhere."

"Don't start on me." Baillie grabbed a dinner entrée out of the freezer and pulled one of the cardboard corners back. "Pale is in style, what with all the published accounts of skin cancer in Baby Boomers." She popped the box into the microwave and tapped four minutes on the front panel.

"There's a distinct difference between baking hideous facial wrinkles by staying out in the sun for a living and letting the sun rays paint a healthy blush on those cheeks of yours." Gillian let out a disgusted sound. "What *is* that irritating noise?"

"Dinner."

"What awful chemicals are you putting in your body this time? Have you learned nothing in my presence, nothing at all?"

"Tonight it's fettuccini with broccoli or something like that. I like my frozen food delights, thank you."

"That's not food; that's heresy."

"I don't have a muscular live-in chef like you, Gillian. I make do with my own culinary talents." Baillie chuckled, cradling the phone on her shoulder. *Gillian's caviar and champagne tastes to my cardboard-boxed entrées and Diet Coke are quite a stretch*, she thought.

"Which amounts to absolutely zero, darling. I'll not think about it; you'll ruin my evening. Poof, it's gone. Let's plan to talk tomorrow at the shop, putting our thinking caps on for your outfit when you're back from the runt's game. Since I'm making a special run into the South Sound just for you, let's use it for good."

"You always think you're slumming when you come down." She shifted her feet. "Gillian?"

"Ooh, do I detect a change in tone? I'm intrigued."

"Have you ever noticed a…draft—a chill—in the store among the shelves when you've worked there?"

"No-o-o," he replied, drawing the word out into three syllables.

Baillie chewed her bottom lip. She jumped when the microwave beeped. Her heart skipped in a fast tempo in the brightly lit kitchen. "Would you, uh, check around aisle three for me tomorrow? I don't know what it was, but I thought I felt a weird, cold, drafty kind of thing this week."

His voice took on a bored tone. "A draft. Really? That's the big deal? I must run. Until tomorrow. *Ciao, bella*." Gillian blew kisses into the phone before he hung up.

# Chapter Six

Saturday morning blossomed into a breathtakingly sunny day, forcing back gray clouds. A chill saturated the air, while rays of brilliant light broke through budding branches of maple trees and plowed through thicker branches of the firs.

Pulling into the parking lot of Pen and Pages after the baseball game, Baillie noticed cars of various makes and models lined up in front as she parked next to the building. Looked like a busy Saturday already. She pulled off her fleece gloves and scanned the outside of the house. Nothing looked out of the ordinary, no broken window or siding missing that might account for the draft. She grabbed her purse and headed for the front door, checking out the few potted plants around the front entry. She pulled a dead leaf off one before opening the door.

Gillian looked up from behind the counter. "Ah, the cat returns, and the well-groomed mice will have to behave themselves." He finished with the customer in front of him. "How was the game?"

"Casie was awesome. I'm hoarse from yelling, 'He's going!' and 'Turn two, turn two!'" She removed her jacket and set her purse under the counter.

"And I'm supposed to understand this strange language? You come back from these soirées with the oddest verbiage." Gillian sniffed.

Straightening her shirt, Baillie headed over to the cart for a cup of tea. "Uh, have things gone smoothly this morning?"

"As always," Gillian nodded at a group passing between them. Every chair held a young student or patron, the majority under thirty, male and good-looking.

Baillie tilted her head, looking around. "Do you send out postcards letting people know when you'll be here?"

"I spoil them with a jug from Starbucks and pastries, what can I say?"

Baillie chewed her bottom lip, absently stirring a red plastic straw in her cup.

"But great coffee isn't the point of this conversation." He walked toward Baillie and twisted his shoulder close, protecting her with a look of patient, friendly concern. "What's really making the double-line highway between your eyebrows?"

"It's nothing."

Adding fresh coffee to his cup, Gillian said, "I may not be an expert in feminine wiles, but I do know *nothing* is the matriarchal code for *something*."

"Did you get a chance to check out aisle three? You know, the drafty thing I mentioned?"

Gillian tapped his buffed nails against his cup. "I walked the shop during my rounds and found no temperature variants in aisle three or anywhere else. I doubt you have a global warming crisis in the shop."

Baillie closed her eyes. "Could you check again for me, please?"

Gillian shrugged and arched away from her. Baillie noticed most of the customers turned their eyes toward his fleeting, smooth figure.

"How can one man look so good?" Baillie whispered before a sharp shiver, like a blast of Freon, spilled down the back of her neck. An icicle of cold stabbed through her as she gasped for air. She had both hands wrapped around her cup, hoping no one noticed their sudden shaking. Her stomach felt like the floor had dropped out in a high-speed elevator, the sting of single-digit temperatures, a sudden lurch, yet she stood where Gillian had left her. An endless moment later, warmth enveloped her again, the cruel ice sensation gone.

Gillian strolled back toward her as if on a fashion runway in Paris, his left hand in his pocket, while his right flipped his long hair off his shoulder. "Nothing as far I—" He stopped a foot from her. "Baillie, what's wrong? Are you all right? You're pale as milk toast." He grabbed her upper arm and helped put her cup on the cart, knocking an errant book to the floor. Both of them automatically looked down. The gold foiling read *Robert Burns Complete Book of Poems*. Baillie's mouth tried to form a word, but nothing came out before her legs went limp. Gillian braced his arms around her, keeping her upright.

People crowded the area, and an old gentleman closest to the cart looked over and murmured, "Is she okay?"

Leading her carefully behind the counter, Gillian raised his head to the customers. "She'll be fine. Too much excitement at a Little League game this morning, I'm sure." He bent over, creating a cascade of blond hair in front of her, dropping his voice. "At least I hope so. You look dreadful. Confess, what's really going on?"

"The cold." Baillie's teeth chattered as she tried to explain. "The, the draft again." She took a breath. "It's like a January cold nothing Mother Nature has ever blasted through the Sound. Like I felt in aisle three, it clenches my whole body like an electric bolt of ice right through my heart." Her voice shivered. "It's insane." She rubbed her crossed arms and mumbled, "Why would it hit at the cart? Is nothing safe around here?" Something nagged her thoughts, just out of reach, like she should remember something, but she couldn't catch the details.

Gillian grabbed her shoulder as he straightened up. "Most extraordinary, Baillie, but whatever you felt, it is not a draft. No one else, nothing else, seemed different to me or the customers."

A young man appeared at the counter with a stack of books. Gillian smiled at her briefly then turned to help the customer. A lively conversation progressed.

Pushing back the office chair, Baillie stood up carefully and shook off the cool sensation. She felt embarrassed at being caught by the customers with a deer-in- headlights stare. Maybe she was hormonal, the opposite of a hot flash? *Maybe I should Google the symptoms. Who gets ice flashes?* But in her soul she knew whatever *it* was, it wasn't her estrogen levels.

Gillian glanced over at her, a questioning look in his eyes.

"I'm fine," she mouthed back and bent over the receipts.

"It is most curious," Gillian said after the customer left. "You looked like the disposable character in a horror movie."

"Must just be me. Maybe I need a checkup or something."

Between customers Gillian filled her head with costume ideas, helping to keep her mind distracted.

Late in the afternoon, Gillian gathered a tray of used coffee cups as he headed toward the back of the shop. He picked up the fallen book of Robert Burns's poetry near the cart and tucked it under his arm. Baillie watched Gillian walk by with the book, startled to her core, as a breath of cold breeze blew her hair off her shoulder.

• • •

Monday morning, a cool eeriness saturated the inside of the shop. Darkness lurked beyond the mottled sunlight creeping from the front windows. The serving cart stood unattended, cold, no delicious aroma or hot water ready. Baillie was bent over the computer and didn't notice the front door opening.

"Hello?" Sally whispered. "Baillie? Anyone here?"

A guttural response came from behind the counter. Baillie barely looked up, her hand glued to the mouse in front of her. "What's the matter with you?"

"I was expecting bloodshed or mayhem. The shop's dark." Sally let out a shaky breath. "You scared me half to death." She moved away from the front door. "Are you okay? Do you want me to, uh, open up?" Sally stumbled over her words.

"Geesh, what time is it?" Baillie almost slipped off the desk chair when she rolled it away from the computer. "Good grief, I had no idea it was morning. Gillian updated the computer's speed, and I was just looking up a few things last night." Baillie ran her fingers through her thick hair. "A few hours ago, I guess."

Relieved, Sally dropped her purse behind the counter before heading for the teacart. "We have a timer for Casie, otherwise she hogs the computer for homework." Sally bent her fingers in air quotes on the last word.

Baillie stood and stretched her arms to the ceiling, hearing things creak and groan before rushing through the divided rooms to switch on the table lamps. Baillie couldn't believe she'd lost the whole night on the stupid computer. One minute she was looking up some out-of-print title, and the next Sally was freaking out at the front door like it was a crime scene. Turning a corner, mumbling to herself, Baillie banged her ankle against the corner of a bookcase.

"Ouch, darn it." The throbbing pain set her teeth together as she limped down the aisle. Baillie was using the shelves like a crutch when a sudden frigid blast of cold air struck again. "Not again." Each strand of her hair felt frozen in place. She hadn't paid any attention to where she was walking; only the agonizing pain helped her focus on the books—books on Scotland. *What is Burns doing over here?* she wondered before squeezing her eyes shut against what seemed a devastating arctic storm. Her pounding heart competed with the throbbing ankle. The air inside her nose felt frozen as she tried to inhale.

"What is this? What do you want?" Baillie's teeth chattered. "Seriously, you're giving me pneumonia with these flash freezes."

Baillie strained, pulling herself away from the too-familiar draining cold, using the bookshelf for balance. She forced her way out of the Scottish section toward the protective lobby and Sally. "Get thee behind me, devil," she gritted between her teeth. "I've no time for you this morning. Unless you've got pain medications in your bag of tricks, back off and leave me alone." Her skin quivered as the killing cold held for a last second then stopped as suddenly as it began.

"Thank you," she stuttered, to what she didn't know. The hair on her arm prickled in goose bumps as Baillie limped away.

Sally finished up starting the coffee on the cart. "The Emerald City prince graced you with a visit? Gillian's a magician with a computer."

"Digital magic; I like the sound of that. I love the new speed, but you know I'll be whining in days about having to wait for something to download." Baillie leaned against the counter and bent over to rub her ankle. Her hand couldn't stop shaking. Thank goodness Sally wasn't looking.

"What happened to you?"

*She noticed?* "Uh, whacked my foot taking a corner too sharply back there."

Sally nodded as she poured the water into the second machine. "I hate when that happens. Hey, did Gillian get a chance to upgrade the store's website, too? Didn't you ask him months ago to tweak the shopping cart page?"

"Yeah, he did. Better late than dead, I guess."

Sally stared incredulously at her boss, her hands poised over the water container. "Excuse me?"

Baillie looked up. "What?" She didn't like the look on Sally's startled face.

"Ewww, you said, 'Better late than dead.'" Sally turned too fast and dropped pink packets of Sugar Twin over the tabletop.

"I meant never; didn't I say never? Probably hallucinating from too-many hours on the Internet." *Why would I say dead? How morbid.* Baillie hobbled over to help Sally and hesitated. She'd hit a frigid zone there on Saturday. She couldn't make herself move any closer. Why the cart? She thought she remembered Gillian walking away from it with a book under his arm. Wasn't that the Burns book? She twisted her head behind her as if something were sneaking up on her from the travel book section, but the bookshelves looked normal.

When had she purchased the poetry book? Could there be a link between this recent Ghostbuster pabulum of cold and the book itself? Baillie chewed her thumbnail. No, the book was usually shelved in the poetry section.

Musical tones suddenly created a Celtic soundtrack to her thoughts. *Am I supposed to recognize this song? What?* The music stopped mid note. Baillie blinked, as she thought she heard a voice. *Impossible.* The cold wrapped around her shoulders almost like a caress, a shawl of ice. She couldn't be sure if she'd heard a voice over the loud pounding of her heart. "Who you gonna call?" Baillie whispered. "I need to get to work."

Still having a difficult time concentrating, Baillie was grateful when the store emptied of customers for a while to give her time to calm down. And there was nothing like sales stats for that purpose. Both women hovered around the computer during the lull, noses to the monitor.

"Have you embraced your kilt-wearing roots yet?" Sally rolled the last word in a phony brogue.

Baillie choked on her sip of tea. "My what?"

"You used to brag about being a Baillie, and last winter you were curious about your Scots bloodlines. Have you signed up anywhere with your family history? Check this out." Sally clicked the mouse and her fingers flew over the keyboard. "It's called Sign of the Clans. You can register online and check out historical facts, even find possible relatives."

"Why would I want to do that?" Baillie's voice came out sharper than she expected. Baillie closed her eyes. First the shop goes Poltergeist on me in the Scotland section and now Sally gets a harebrained, pushy idea. What in plaid is going on around here?

"It's fun. I do this stuff all the time, love the ancestry adventures. Look, here's the Baillie motto, *Quid Clarius Astris.*"

"Stop torturing that poor language," Baillie laughed. "Do they have a translation?"

"Yep. 'What is brighter than the stars?' Ah, how romantic. What if you found some cousin on your great-great-great-grandfather's side? You said you don't have any family left. Who knows? Maybe you do."

Baillie sighed at Sally's enthusiasm, dispelling the fear from earlier. "How many generations do you think I could go back? I don't know much about the nuts in my family tree, girl. Are there trees in Scotland?"

Sally sniffed. "Don't get sarcastic. You said Aunt Fran had a leather chest of old family correspondence up in the attic. Haul its expensive antique butt out here, and we'll climb whatever ancestral branches we can reach. It's quiet right now. Go get it, and I'll help type in the details."

"It's been forever since I've thought of that box." Baillie bent over, rubbing her tender ankle while avoiding Sally's stare. "I don't remember where I've seen it."

"Don't try that I-don't-know routine with me. That catalog you call a mind knows exactly where it is in this old house. Go." Sally wiggled her fingers back and forth at her boss. "Let me start the registration, you go get the dirt. It'll be fun. Really. Trust me."

With a sigh, Baillie pushed her chair away and headed without enthusiasm toward the back of the shop. Her ankle throbbed as she walked, a constant reminder of the incident in the aisle, like she needed one. Did she really want to stir up old relatives? What if that cold blast of air was a rotting spirit trying to do just that?

A loud thud somewhere in the shop broke the silence as a book fell from a shelf. "Shoot," Baillie jumped, clenching her throat. "Look, who or whatever you are, don't get all sensitive on me," she snapped under her breath.

Sally yelled across the room, "You okay, boss?"

"Just klutzy ol' me," Baillie shot back. *Why am I lying?* She lowered her voice to a growl. "Why don't you just advertise you're pissed?" A shiver worked down her back. She was talking to what? To whom? A nasty taste worked up the back of her throat. "My house is not haunted," she repeated as she walked. Who was she trying to convince, herself or the house?

• • •

Sally's hands flew between the mouse and the keyboard. "So we have your dad, Baillie, son of William, son of Josiah, and Isaiah, then son of Joshua." The clicking keys punctuated the room. "And Joshua's wife was a Bruce. Wow, two clans, girl. You are a double-kissed Scottish lass." The plastic tapping continued for a minute more. "Hey, look at this. Your aunt traced the family back pretty far, actually. This first name is huge. Some kinda lord. Who gives their kid that many middle names?"

"Where?"

"Here, this William guy." Sally pointed at the screen. "And he's a fourth, so a few more of your ancestors had this same insane string. I hope they were cute at least. William Andrew Kai Robert Baillie the fourth. Dang, he didn't live very long. Was twenty-seven middle age back then?"

Baillie kept reading the thin, yellowed papers in her hand. "A lord, huh? No, he seems to have died young. I wonder if it was in a battle somewhere on the moors." She leaned over, looking at the list of names. "Who'da thunk Aunt Frannie would have collected so much stuff?" Baillie carefully laid the faded correspondence in the pile nearest Sally. "Now what?"

"Well, if anyone recognizes any names and dates we've put in here as part of their heritage, they'll contact you by email."

"Clan stuff, huh? I'm born and bred West Coast, and most of my relatives were corn-fed Midwesterners from what I heard. I don't remember seeing any plaid among them."

"Between your maternal small part and all this lengthy stuff on your paternal side, there's a whole lot more to you than you think."

"You're going to get carpal tunnel from all this nonsense and sue me for workers' comp." Sally laughed as she kept posting data off the papers. "I'm American," Baillie said, leaving her chair to refill her empty teacup.

Sally snorted. "I've seen you wring six cups of tea out of one teabag, oh Thrifty One. You're of Scots bloodline whether you like it or not, Princess of the Thistles."

Baillie bent her head and curtsied deep to the floor.

# Chapter Seven

Rogue swiped a dirty hand across her eyes before stabbing the pitchfork into the hay. "I bet the curs blamin' this on me," she spit out. "They dinna care how I felt, just stared at me, they did." She threw another dry forkful into the stall.

A tear slid down her grimy cheek. This time she didn't stop it. How could he be gone? Leaving her here alone? Dead, the man who'd treated her like a lady and gave her a second chance at life. A roof over her head and warm meals in her stomach is what he gave her, instead of scavenging in the streets of Edinburgh.

All those early years in foster care, Rogue had fought against adults and authority. She ran away often from the tyranny of strangers inside their cold walls of different homes. Often dressed in drab, ill-fitted clothes with unraveling stockings and worn shoes, Rogue's temperament seemed her downfall, forcing her to handle the worst of the chores as punishment for something the day before. Her life had been a never-ending cascade of falling dominoes of cause and effect.

One overcast morning, she'd bolted from the latest house, ignoring screeches, her stoic expression set in cement. Once she realized no one was following her, Rogue had headed for the city.

• • •

Hearing a police whistle behind her, Rogue dashed into the street just as a truck and horse trailer came around the rain-slick corner. The driver slammed on the brakes, barely missing her, the heavy load of the trailer pushing the truck extra footage. Rogue remained still, her nose inches away from the hood of the truck, nothing registering on her face, but her breath came hard in white wisps against the cold.

From the trailer, a horse screamed in frightened anger, kicking at the sides of his confinement. A man leaped from the passenger's side, a cap pulled tight over his dark brown hair, and moved quickly to the front of the trailer. Rogue glared at the burly driver. She moved curiously a step to the right side of the truck, the horse's cries pulling her toward the trailer.

"Easy, my lad. Whoa," the man with the cap called into the trailer. Loud thuds echoed from the horse stomping the floor, rocking the trailer on its axles. She inched her way closer.

She climbed a fender well and found herself eye to eye with a gigantic stallion. She whispered into the dark stall, grasping the metal bars of the trailer for balance. The horse stopped beating the trailer floor, yet its hoofs moved in a tap dance of stress. Rogue leaned toward the cab window of the truck, ignoring the man near her, and called through the open window. "Ye must pull over and let him out. Now."

"Be serious, girl. Have you no sense? The bloody traffic will not ease his wicked soul," the driver said as he rubbed his chin. "Boss, you hear this kid? You want me to park here?"

"Aye," she said, staring into the driver's squinted eyes. She finally glared at the man on the ground, daring him to contradict her.

Putting the truck in gear, the driver moved them off the road and into a deserted parking lot. As soon as he turned the key, Rogue jumped off the fender well and walked to the back of the trailer. Sighing, the driver came around, cussing under his breath about witches, to unlock the back door. In a flash, Rogue slipped into the trailer before anyone could stop her. Both men stared at the open trailer.

Pushing the door wider, Rogue backed the enormous horse out. One hand held his bridle; the other cupped the air as she talked in a soft brogue. Seconds passed until the stallion's eyes rolled back showing white, yet a soothing ripple passed through its muscles. With bent head, the horse sneezed into the pavement. Rogue rubbed her dry, cracked hand between its eyes and down the smooth flat nose.

"Ye've a way with animals, a gift," the passenger spoke up. "He doesna take to just anyone." His arms crossed, Rogue couldn't see his clenched fists of worry.

Rogue ignored the man, keeping her gaze on the horse. Never before had she seen such a magnificent creature up close. The glide of her hand over its silky coat mesmerized her, the heat of its breath against her body brought her heart to life.

The man pushed his cap back and coaxed conversation out of Rogue as gently as she'd coaxed the horse from the trailer. The driver grumbled something unintelligible and climbed back into the cab. Still, the sun's glare registered with Rogue, though she never took her hands from the horse. She started to panic, feeling exposed in the open area—someone might see her, find her. She couldn't go back into the never-ending foster system. Sensing the shift of emotions, the horse snorted into the ground, stomping its right leg. Rogue broke free of her own concerns and laid her head against his neck, whispering soft nothings.

But the man had noticed her worn clothing and scuffed shoes, the haphazard cut of her hair. "Would ya come work for me, lass? I'm in need of someone to help with me horses. I dinna think I've seen the likes of such natural talent with a horse. Especially me Dougal here."

"I...I..." Rogue stuttered against a pounding heart. She looked around with quick jerks in an unconscious imitation of the horse's actions earlier. Before she could bolt, the man laid a hand on her arm.

"Could ya bear to leave 'im now, lass? Help me to get him back inna the trailer and come with me. I'm sure I can persuade the county powers to let ya work for me." A smile crossed his face.

Rogue dipped her head down, snuggled against the horse for a moment, and without another sound, grasped the reins. She moved toward the open door of the trailer, and the enormous black horse followed her.

• • •

Rogue leaned against the worn, wooden handle and buried her head in the crook of her arm at the memory. Sinking to the dirt floor of the stable, she felt her stomach tighten as the sobs wrenched deep from her soul. How could he be dead? The man so gentle and good, gone from this earth, leaving her alone in this morose castle without protection? Would she be sent back to the foster system? *I'd rather ta die, myself.*

She curled into a fetal position as her forehead grazed against her knees. She instinctively felt the horses move to the front of their stalls and stare at the mound of human wailing in the dirt and straw. Their ears flattened from the frightening sound.

• • •

"What becomes of us if there's no one to own the land?" Putney wiped her damp hands on a frayed kitchen towel. "Where does the bloody banker think we're ta live?"

"Aye, old girl. We may be looking for shelter elsewhere soon enough."

Rogue passed by the kitchen window, only the top of her head visible, her steps somber.

"The wee one has nowhere to go herself." Putney's heart twisted at the sight, the echo of Rogue's sobs etched in her soul. "She canna stop crying long enough to eat most days. Ye be right, old man, she loved him something awful."

"Aye," he chewed the end of his pipe, a slight pull of his mouth nearly came to a grin.

"Let's keep her close, Robbie." Putney laid a gentle hand on the man's shoulder. "She has little in this life."

The old man nodded.

The moon, forcing its way through the damp low clouds, pointed its thin pale glow against the bricks of the east wing. Moaning winds shoved the thickening mist across the sky and blocked what pitiful moonlight had ventured toward the castle.

"Woman, did he not have a great-grandfather that took hisself to America?" Robbie nervously chewed on the end of his pipe. "In the pitch of night he stowed away on a vessel bound to cross the Atlantic, story goes, aye? They ne're spoke of him again, not in the village."

Putney stirred the soup with a determined arm. "Hold your tongue, old man. No one knows if the wee devil made it to land or not in those days. My own mother wouldn't give a pence to that rubbish of a tale. And she worked for the family herself in those days."

"But what if he did?" the old man paused, a twinkle glinting from his dark eyes under pursed thick brows. He delighted in teasing her, creating a stir in her blood where such hadn't happened in a long time.

"Aye, if, old man." She stared at the steam as it curled and vanished, her thoughts twisting in the air. "A family heir to this castle in a country Satan hisself doesn't know about? Who would believe such an idea?" She turned her large body slightly back toward him. "An American? Lord, our Queen, save us."

# Chapter Eight

Pacing across the kitchen, Baillie ran her fingers through her freshly washed hair. She had to talk to someone. "This is getting ridiculous." She kicked a cabinet. "This house is my life, my work." She spun and walked in the other direction, her stocking feet silent. "Now it's scaring the soup out of me. Spooks in Olympia? Oh, please."

She grabbed the phone and dialed. "Gillian?"

"Baillie?" His voice sounded vague.

"Sebastian won't go into the shop anymore," she whined. "Maybe the cat knew something about this spooky cold before I did."

"I'm sorry, what?"

"It's been days. I can't throw him in there. If I do, he growls and slinks back through the door. He even hides under the bed when I first come home at night, totally avoiding me, like I have cooties."

"We're talking about the cat?" Gillian mumbled something to someone else in the background, and Baillie heard a rustle of material as he settled again. "You sure Sally never felt anything?"

"*Nada*. I've watched her and nothing. I brought up an air-conditioning problem, a draft, and she's felt zip in the shop. She thinks it's my Aunt Fran's ghost, which is just ridiculous."

Baillie heard static as Gillian cradled the phone to some place more comfortable. "Really? An auntie ghost? That hired woman of yours is droll. Besides, I should think you'd love these cool spells, Ms. Hot Flash."

"Cute. Do you trash all your premenopausal queens?"

"None of them are that old, girlfriend. They still freak about adult acne."

"Ouch." Baillie smiled at Gillian's dry humor. "Hurray, I'm your only one. Seriously, though, you didn't feel anything either on Saturday, remember?"

"You felt something, though," he acknowledged. "Quite the dramatic if I recall."

"You know, that's the only time I've felt it outside of aisle three, I think. Maybe." She rubbed her forehead. "But I remember seeing the Robert Burns book." Her voice faded.

"Hmm, you're right. I picked up the Burns poetry book off the floor by the cart and put it back in the Scotland section. You think there's a connection?"

"I don't know, it's bizarre. And don't get me started on the strange music." She slapped her hand over her mouth.

"Really? What else are you holding out on me? Does Auntie Fran's ghost have a thing for Glen Miller?"

"Cute. No, more like a flute thingy or bagpipes sometimes, very Celtic. Sometimes it's the same piece, same notes, but not always." Baillie bit her bottom lip. *Nothing like throwing it all out there. Gillian will be calling the men in the white coats any minute.*

"Aye, lass, 'tis the ancestors of the Highlands calling you home. Speaking of the Highlands, huzzah! My lady, are you ready to meet Queen Victoria?"

Baillie smiled, grabbing a Diet Coke out of the refrigerator. "Nice segue into something completely more pleasant. Yes, as ready as I'll ever be, I guess. Have you warned the guys—I mean, girls—to be nice to me? I'm feeling really fragile right now."

"Free-jally, you? Yes, I've given explicit instructions. Rafael and T-Cup know of your hysterics and have offered to share their Xanax with you." Gillian laughed at his own words. "Seriously, woman, practice walking like you're bred of royalty, not some street peasant." The conversation sailed on through velvet and lacy notes for the upcoming faire.

Moments later, Baillie whispered into the receiver, "Thanks, Gillian. I feel better."

"*Ciao, bella.*"

•••

Gillian bowed deeply to a passing hunk dressed as a lord, sweeping the dry grassland with the edge of his flowing sleeve. The young man dressed in royal blue brocade and flowing gray cape, touched the brim of his feathered velvet hat in appreciative silence. "God save the Queen," Gillian waved a long, white silk handkerchief in front of his face. "They grow more enticing every year."

A summer heat wave baked the crowded area. Baillie's outfit, once fun and luxurious when tried on in air-conditioning, now weighed heavy against her damp body. The layers of yardage rustled as she walked. Gillian had draped her in jewel tones of emerald and crème lace. Passing under a manmade balcony with turrets at each end, Gillian pointed out repeat visitors who were comfortable as various characters. The group stopped to listen to a rowdy conversation. Rows of vendor tents met them inside, as the decorated crowds split up across the fairgrounds.

Rafael paused a moment and canvassed the crowd. Yards of burgundy brocade accented her mocha latte skin, the corset and plunging sweetheart neckline. Saucy and sexy, Rafael usually channeled the life and personality of Jennifer Lopez during her night gigs as Jaello. "It's all in the padding," she'd said when Baillie had admired her act. Today, dramatic ivory combs held her wig's curls in a soft cascade down her back.

Next to Rafael, a foot shorter but no less impressive, stood T-Cup, a shaker of spicy pepper and sexuality in or out of drag. Baillie stared at the fluidity of her long painted fingers as T fussed with a ribbon of lace wrapped through her hair and dangling near her neck, flirting with anything good-looking close by. The tight bodice showed more cleavage than Baillie could ever dream of. T's dark eyes flicked among the males, and Baillie could almost see the swish of a cat's tail stalking its prey under her dress.

"You didn't say the girls were going to dress better than me," Baillie whined. A half beat later, she dug her fingernails into Gillian's arm with sudden force.

"My lady, thou art severing this good arm with your sharpened talons." Gillian tried wresting her nails from his skin without causing a scene. "What madness has caused this attack of my flesh?"

"Do you hear it?" Baillie's whisper shook with fear.

"Hear what, my stressed-out lady who's drawing blue blood this moment?"

"The…the bagpipes." She felt her knees go weak and leaned heavily against him. "Gillian, it followed me. From the shop. It's here!"

Gillian slipped his arm around her waist before they both fell. The girls materialized, fluttering around them in concern at Baillie's paleness. "Have you lost your God-given senses, woman?" Gillian hissed. "You're at the Renaissance Faire. Of course there are pipers playing around us. The Highlanders think they rule some of the Queen's own ground and play their obnoxious tunes from morn 'til dusk, I dare say. 'Tis nothing to rip into a poor man's arm over, my lady."

Baillie tried taking a normal breath. "I'm sorry. It's just that I heard bagpipes…at the shop."

Gillian interrupted her whining and unclenched his teeth. "I forgot about your apparitions. Forgive me, Baillie, how callous of me to ignore your pain, and I have now paid dearly for my lack of attention." He rubbed his arm. He turned to the girls around him. "My lady has heard the calling of her past. We must take her to the witches. 'Tis time this woman heard her fortune from the lips of the chosen. Come, girls, let us escort the Lady Baillie."

Gillian's duo of merry men, draped in lace and brocade, yelled, "Huzzah!" in unison and linked their arms, leading Baillie down a dirt path and across a short, wooden bridge. Ahead of them sat a row of brightly colored tents sheltered under spreading branches of ancient maples. The sun glared like a brilliant curtain behind the clothed cubicles of the psychics.

Gillian held up his arm. "We have arrived. Let those of you who do not believe leave us and find yourselves a wicked cup of ale to quench your sorry souls of this mortal earth." The girls dropped in deep, extensive curtsies to Baillie and laughingly headed toward the nearest beer stand yelling a bawdy, "Huzzah!"

"Do you want a good witch or a bad witch?" Gillian looked over at Baillie with an innocent smile.

"That's not funny."

Gillian feigned hurt. "I ask but your preference."

"Oh, sure, like I do this all the time." Baillie fussed at the tight bodice of her dress. "What am I doing here?"

"Let the forces of good and evil be revealed to you through a medium of the spirit world. In other words, let's see what kind of spook is haunting your store. Maybe one of these women can channel your ghost for you and we'll get some answers."

"Seriously?"

The pair walked toward the first tent, and a heavy smell of incense accosted them.

"Hardly. That stench will ruin your karma and settle into our clothes for the rest of the day." Gillian pushed her ahead.

The next tent advertised love potions and palm reading. "Nay." Gillian clapped his hands together. "Here, this will do." No one waited outside the entrance, cornered by well-placed hay bales, so Gillian pushed Baillie toward the purple and yellow opening draped with glass beads. "This is your destiny." Gillian bent grandly from the waist and pulled the strands of beads aside. They softly clicked against each other.

Baillie glared at Gillian's face before stepping inside.

An ornate iron sign read Lady Nell above the woman who beamed at Baillie. The volume of skin overflowing the scooped neckline of her dress exacerbated her paleness and barely kept her decent by Washington law.

"Come in, I'm here for you, my lady," she said, her voice low, with a gentle confidence that poured over Baillie like liquid Xanax. "Let me tell your future, your past, find your solution."

"How? I don't even know the problem." Baillie dropped like an anchor on dry land onto the bale of hay next to a table draped in fringed violet. Two striking gargoyles behind the woman stared back at Baillie.

"Give me your hands, my lady." Each of Lady Nell's fingers wore rings of silver and stones of different colors.

"Be gentle," Baillie said to be funny. "This is my first time, and I don't have a clue what I'm supposed to do or how this goes."

Baillie closed her eyes as the woman's warm hands enveloped hers. A soothing aroma of vanilla floated between them, even in the stifling tent. An energy level flowed between the hands, a bonding between the two women. Baillie exhaled as a single bead of sweat trickled down her chest, pooling against the bottom of her bra.

A second later, a blast of familiar chill attacked Baillie, snapping her shoulders back like a flush of ice water doused over her head. She stared at Lady Nell for assurance and watched the woman's head move in the slightest nod. Baillie didn't panic, nor did Lady Nell pull away. The power of the cold grew stronger around them, and Baillie clenched her teeth as the cold stung her flesh. Not a strand of hair moved, nor a hint of breeze inside the draped walls, just a soul-crippling presence of ice.

"He's trying to talk to you," the woman whispered with a shaky smile. Her sepia brown eyes focused beyond Baillie's head. Baillie could almost see her reflection in their darkness.

"He? You're telling me this is a guy, a somebody, doing this?"

"His need is important, but he doesn't know how to communicate from the other side."

"Who is he? I don't understand. These weird things go on at my shop. It's like a deep freeze one minute, off and on like a freaking switch, and I swear I hear bagpipes. This cold thing is really unnerving." Baillie rambled almost incoherently, her face numb from cold. "I don't understand what's going on." The woman's hands tightened around Baillie's and would have caused pain had Baillie been more cognizant.

"You are…" Lady Nell's voice came out breathy and low.

"What? I am what?" Baillie leaned forward.

"Beautiful." The woman actually blushed under the theatrical makeup and perspiration.

"Come again?" Baillie's voice squeaked. "Are you hitting on me?" Nice distraction, but it didn't explain the numbing cold still around them.

"No, that's what he said. His words are thick with a brogue and talking so fast that's all I understood." Their eyes locked across the table. "He thinks you're beautiful."

"Great. I've got a ghost with a crush following me around? Why does he need to talk to me? Can you find out anything else from him?" Baillie babbled along like she really believed this spiel. *This is nonsense; it can't be real.*

Lady Nell again looked beyond Baillie's shoulder, staring straight ahead. "Cattle—his accent is strong—no, that's not right," she listened. "Castle. Something about a castle, yes. Do you know anything about a castle?"

"Sleeping Beauty has one at Disneyland. It's rather small, quaint and incredibly crowded most of the time." Baillie squirmed on the hay bale, trying to ignore the stray stalks stabbing into her seat. "But that's probably not what you mean, is it?"

"Scotland," she sighed heavily, as if she'd traveled a great distance. Baillie noticed the woman's face had grown pasty, and beads of sweat appeared on her forehead despite the ever-present cold in the tent.

"Scotland? Shit—shoot, I mean. That's where I feel this freaking cold—this him—in a section of my store where I have books on Scotland." Baillie felt herself hyperventilating. "Seems my ghost friend plays a mean bagpipe, too. I couldn't really recognize anything, except he plays this one tune often. Why would I know it? It's not like I've ever been to Scotland. I've never been east of the Rockies." Baillie stopped for a breath. Then panic set it. "Uh, Lady Nell? Nell?" The woman's neck seemed made of putty, and she drooped over the table. Baillie yanked her hands out of the medium's grasp and immediately felt the afternoon heat overpower her inside the tent again. The temperature change felt as if she had stepped out of a freezer into the Sahara desert in one brief movement.

"Why did you do that? You broke the connection," Lady Nell panted with hoarseness in her voice. She picked up an ornate cup with a shaking hand and quickly grabbed it with her other hand. Her parched lips stuck to the ceramic rim as she tried to take a sip of liquid.

"You looked ready to faint, and I got frightened. Are you okay?" Baillie leaned forward and touched the woman's bare arm. An electric charge surged between them, and she jumped in her chair. "This is totally insane. What just happened? I thought you were going to pass out on me, talking about some guy and a castle."

"I could hear him." The woman lightly touched her face with her fingertips, disturbing the beads of sweat. "He's from the other side, Catharine, an old soul from the ancient moors. He's trying to contact you, tell you something."

Baillie froze. She hadn't given her name, least of all that horrid one. "How do you know my first name?"

"I didn't. That's what he called you when I could understand through the accent." Lady Nell took out an ornate paper fan and regained some composure by beating a quick pace for a bit of air. "It's incredibly strong, his connection to you, but he doesn't know how to communicate with anyone on this side. Half the time he was shouting, but I still couldn't understand the accent. Loud, but garbled in spirit, and Gaelic, though rugged like Sean Connery, a young Sean Connery. He's quite young, your spirit."

"Other side of what?" Baillie whispered.

"The other side of life, Catharine. His physical body died years ago, possibly hundreds of years, and for some reason his yearning to make contact with you is important enough he is trying to break through."

"I don't know anyone from Scotland." Baillie rubbed her eyes.

"What an experience! Trying to decipher through that thick brogue was a killer. Thank goodness I've paid attention to the fools that work this faire over the years. Some of them are skirted lads like your friend."

Baillie watched the woman gain strength as she talked. A twinkle came back to her eyes, and her lips parted into a crooked smile. "Your ghost wears the kilts. Could we try again?" Lady Nell placed her hands palms up on the table in front of her with authority.

"No." Baillie blinked at her, shrinking backward. "No. This is nuts. Whatever it is can go back where it came from."

"It's a he, Catharine. Please, let me try again. This is an incredible chance; he's channeling through me." Her face flushed with excitement. "He kept repeating castle but there was so much more I couldn't understand. Please, I'm not kidding. Don't take this opportunity away from me."

"Take what away from you? I'm the one with Jack Frost haunting my shop, scaring me half to death. Do you have any idea what it's like thinking you're losing your mind, let alone there's something out there following you around?" Baillie stared at the woman.

"What about tonight? The faire closes at dusk, and we could try to reach him again at your place—a shop you said?" Lady Nell took a business card and wrote her cell phone number on the back. Her rings flashed with the movement. "You could bring a friend or two along if you're worried. I just want a chance to connect with him again. Please let me try." Lady Nell leaned closer. "He's quite taken with you, you know."

"Oh, great. The first time in years a guy shows interest in me, and he's dead."

Baillie caught Nell's eyes, and they burst into hysterical laughter. The beads behind Baillie clicked together as Gillian stood in the opening of the tent. Lady Nell gasped, no doubt at his beauty filling her doorway.

"What cackling comes from this room of the spirit world?" he asked in mock authority.

Relief and reality set them both off giggling again as Gillian sniffed at their rudeness.

"Don't get pissed." Baillie wiped her face with a Kleenex from her beaded satchel. "I'm sorry, we're not laughing at you. She made contact with some kind of male ghost and wants to try again tonight, like a séance or something at the Pen and Pages."

"Oh!" Gillian clapped his hands together in pure delight, glowing in expectation. "Absolutely. You must, and I want to be there. The girls will be over the moon at something like this."

Lady Nell spoke up, her eyes never leaving his face. "I let Catharine know others are welcome to attend tonight."

Gillian raised his eyebrows. "Catharine?"

"She said it's what the ghost calls me." Baillie watched as the woman nearly batted her eyes at Gillian. "Forgive me, Lady Nell, may I introduce you to Sir Gillian Nation. Sir Gillian, Lady Nell."

Gillian graciously bowed in theatrical style with a flourish of arm movement. "My lady, your talents proclaim my appreciation." He paused. "It's a he? How randy, a gentleman caller of the netherworld. Is Ghost Boy cute?"

"Down, Gillian. We don't have many clues about him except he's Scottish and is trying to say something about a castle. I broke it off before Lady Nell got very far."

"Crude, Baillie. Your dating skills are definitely lacking finesse."

"He's dead, not that I want to date a ghost. There's no Miss Manner's book on this kind of thing. I thought Lady Nell was going to faint, and I yanked my hands out of hers."

"Then we must get him back. Ah, Lady Nell, what hour on this good night would you visit?" Gillian dropped to one knee before them. He clutched a hand against the ruffles on his chest.

"What about nine o'clock? I can drive down after the faire closes. You live at Pen and Pages?" She looked at the business card Baillie handed her.

Gillian nodded, his blond curls swayed. "She does, in this ghastly excuse of a garret she refuses to let me decorate, though it's above a divine little shop," Gillian sniffed, dotting his nose with his handkerchief.

"Perfect. Write the directions on the back of your card, and I'll meet you there at nine. Oh, I can't wait." Lady Nell fluttered her paper fan in front of her flushed face.

Baillie took out a pen and made a quick map from the fairgrounds to her house. She shook her head at the idea of having a séance—like his unearthly presence wasn't bad enough in the shop? But maybe they could find out what he wanted and he'd leave.

Gillian leaned against her shoulder, still down on one knee, fluttering his baby blues at her. "My darling haunted one, this is going to be a truly delightful night. I should have brought you to a psychic medium before this. Who would have thought you had your own adoring apparition?"

"Like I've known about this problem for a long time? And you told me I was being a little twinkle dust when I first told you if I recall."

"A mere mistake, my lady. Come, let's find the others and share this mystical adventure. Lady Nell, until tonight, we bid you adieu." Gillian stood, left a handful of twenties on the table and bowed toward the woman. He then held the glass beads apart for Baillie to make her way back out to the crowded faire.

The glaring sunlight caused Baillie to squint and pause at the doorway. The suffocating heat radiated from the packed dirt, and she found herself almost faint from the intensity in temperature. Gillian stepped up and tightened an arm around her waist.

"Come over here, let's get you something cold to drink. You look a little flushed after that delicious phenomenon from the afterlife. I could use my own cool glass of ale to wash down the thought of tonight's excitement. Won't this be simply grand? A séance in your own house! Tell me, has this charming, uh, Scots fellow ever been upstairs?"

"Ooh, seriously? I hope not. I've only felt the cold and music downstairs. This is too crazy. Really? Upstairs? Haunting my living areas? Eww."

"You are such a naïve little thing. Why would a spirit force not know everything about you, darling? Walls can't hold him back. Other than a little slow learning about reaching out into this physical world, I can't imagine him quarantined to just the downstairs."

Baillie leaned against the nearest tree, weak from the sudden thought of a nightly visitor as she undressed for bed. "Excuse me? You're saying this guy-thing could be hanging around while I'm in the shower? Getting dressed?"

"Well, remember a minor detail, Baillie, he's long dead. But if he's tried to get your attention only downstairs, then…" Gillian followed a well-chiseled lad with his eyes and slightly turned away from Baillie.

"Hey, lust on your own time. Hello? Will you pay attention to me and not your Victorian appetite?" Baillie slugged his arm. "I'm having a nervous breakdown and, according to her, I'm not having it by myself." A shiver ran down her spine. "While you're out here hitting on lords of the flesh."

"Sorry, darling, where were we? Oh, never mind. Tonight can be held wherever you'd like, but do let's get back to the merriment of today and the delicious, fun things to do here. The girls are probably a little restless from our dallying."

Baillie tugged on Gillian's sleeve and started to lead him into the flowing throngs of people. "Why do I always feel like I'm competing with you for the male flesh? I'm tired of sharing every gorgeous leather-strapped vision of manhood with you."

"You take the leather then, and I'll take the lacey ones. Tut, tut, child, don't lose your charm over a few young, healthy testosterone examples." Gillian melted toward a singularly attractive specimen that passed by.

Baillie lifted her skirt in one hand and continued to playfully drag Gillian with the other. "The girls are waiting for us. Wipe the drool off your face and let's go."

# Chapter Nine

"May I offer you a glass?" Gillian raised a bottle of chilled Zinfandel. Still dressed in costume, he tilted the opened wine and poured one for himself.

Baillie rubbed her arms as she paced in her shop's entryway, the emerald dress rustling as she turned. "Please." The clock above the counter said ten minutes before nine. What was she thinking inviting a strange woman into her business, her home, to make contact with…what? A ghost?

"You're fraying the hem of the dress," Rafael snapped. "Please go upstairs and get into something more comfortable before Gillian loses his deposit on the gown."

"Girl, listen to her, respect the dress." T flipped back the lace around her wrist. "This is going to be fabulous. Why does Baillie seem reluctant to meet her Prince Poltergeist?" She held her empty wine glass in the air, demanding a refill.

A tense sigh followed Baillie out of the room.

Pulling her arms out of the cap sleeves, Baillie chewed on her bottom lip. The frolicking downstairs was wearing on her last nerve. The day flashed through her mind in an unending video loop. *Can this be real? There's a Casper wannabe trying to make contact with me?*

A slight chill against her bared back made her gasp. She spun around and almost landed on the floor, her feet trapped in the yards of tangled material. "It's not a ghost. You're standing here practically naked. Get dressed. This isn't solving anything, and your butt's freezing," she said aloud. Baillie grabbed a pair of stretch pants and threw an oversized T-shirt over her head before dashing down the stairs.

Out of the corner of her eye, she noticed Sebastian curled up on a chair, the orange tail twitching in short snaps. "Seriously? You're mad at me? I didn't invite the spook siren—she invited herself. And once Gillian opened his painted mouth, all the girls wanted to be a part of the séance."

The cat sunk its claws into the cushion and pulled itself around, putting its back to Baillie. "Benedict Arnold," she mumbled, opening the door into the shop.

• • •

Headlights from a car flashed from the small parking lot out front. Baillie looked at Gillian with a mixture of fear and concern. "Help," she whispered.

A slight tap at the door roused them both, and Gillian stepped forward to answer it. Lady Nell bustled through the doorway, still in her velvet costume with a large carpetbag hanging from one arm.

"What a gorgeous house," Lady Nell said, craning her neck from one side to the other.

Baillie pushed herself away from the counter to greet her guest. "Thank you. Uh, can we get you anything? Something to drink?" Gillian hoisted his glass of wine like a sample. "We weren't sure what you'd need for tonight."

Setting her bag just inside the door, Lady Nell smiled. "A glass of wine would be lovely."

Gillian filled an extra glass. "May I introduce the rest of us, Lady Nell?"

She accepted the glass and nodded her head.

"Lovely ladies, please step forward when I call your name. Rafael. And T-Cup." Both stepped into full, graceful curtsies until T started giggling.

"Please, relax, everyone. I can work just about anywhere you'd like. I'm glad you took my call while I drove down here. It gave me a little more to expect. Though first, can you take me to the books, the area you said you first felt him?"

Squeals flew out of the ribbon and lace section. Gillian snapped his fingers. "Not that kind of feeling, girls."

*The woman doesn't waste any time, does she?* Baillie swallowed a large gulp of wine and headed toward the back of the store. She turned on a few lamps along the way, trying to reassure herself against...what? Evil spirits?

A train of Elizabethan wannabes walked in silence behind her. Baillie stared down the row of shelves and pointed out the area with a shaky hand, her feet glued to the floor. Gillian swept by her and fondled the books in question. Baillie watched him cock his head as if trying to feel anything different in front of the travel section of Scotland.

"Nothing, sorry, no change in temperature. And I certainly do not hear any noise."

T-Cup wiggled her Spandex way next to Gillian. "Let me, let me." She bounced in front of the bookshelf on her tiptoes. "Pick me, Prince, pick me. I'm heee-rrre," stretching the last word into multiple syllables. Her bottom lip extended into a perfect pout. "Nothing."

Lady Nell watched both men before she, too, ventured in a bridal gait down the aisle. Her pale cheeks looked damp. She carefully put her hands on the volumes, closing her eyes, feeling the cool spines of various books. She seemed interested, intent only with the row of books from the British Isles, her fingertips pausing now and then. Nothing happened.

"Can I ask a question?" Baillie's voice cracked. "Does anyone hear the bagpipes or is it just me?" In a different scenario, she might have enjoyed the soothing song. Right now it felt like the opening theme of the *Phantom of the Opera*.

Nell's face lit up. "You hear him?" She bustled back to Baillie's side and, taking a deep, slow breath, clasped their hands together. Closing her eyes for a brief moment, Nell gasped before her eyes flew open and stared into Baillie's. "I hear it. He's here, and the laddie's not bad on the pipes. I know this song. It's Scotland the Brave. The pipers play it often at the faire."

A single tear welled up and threatened to plunge down Baillie's cheek. She was not hallucinating. Everyone stared at Baillie, straining to hear anything in the silence.

"His lordship is talking a hundred miles an hour again," Lady Nell said, breaking free of Baillie's grasp. "Is there somewhere we can sit down, my dear?" Lady Nell laughed. "This afternoon took a lot out of me, I must tell you. You are like a solar panel, and your spirit friend is absorbing whatever energy I can create faster than light speed. I need a spot where I can be comfortable."

Baillie bolted toward the front of the store and a reading area of overstuffed chairs with a coffee table they could use by the teacart. Gillian grabbed the half-empty wine bottle, and Rafael moved more chairs into the designated area. T-Cup wrestled four large volumes to put under the legs of the table to raise it higher for the women.

Settled, everyone looked at Lady Nell. "Well, we know the gentleman from the other side is a Scotsman and unusually focused on contacting Baillie. He has zero interest in anyone else obviously, making no attempt to be noticed by anyone but you, my dear."

T-Cup nodded in quick, snappy succession. "I am so jealous."

"Does anyone have any questions before we start?"

Rafael's tan arm shot up. "Will we see this hunky Highlander while you're working?"

"No. Contact, if made, is verbal only and only if the spirit is strong, though this one seems very ardent in his passion to make contact." Rafael pouted. "Catharine," the medium continued, "give me your hands."

The expanse between them felt like the Grand Canyon—miles of open, barren space. Baillie rubbed her hands against her thighs before reaching out. She watched her fingers cross the table and meld into the waiting warm, fleshy ones.

The second their fingers closed, the room felt like a subzero freezer. Both women jerked from the shock, and the others flattened themselves against the backs of their chairs at their reactions.

"What's happening?" T-Cup whispered.

Her teeth chattering, Baillie stiffened with the now familiar intense cold as Nell said, "He's powerful, this one." T let out a nervous giggle, fanning his flushed face.

"Please, slower…Try, please," Nell flinched. "He's shouting, and his accent is fierce." Nell cocked her head to one side, nodding in slow motion. "Baillie, yes?"

Rafael and T-Cup suddenly grabbed each other's hands, mouths open. Gillian sat alone on the other side of the bridge of women and leaned closer. This name everyone understood.

"Lord Baillie. Yes, I hear you. That's better, thank you."

Baillie thought her heart would pound out of her chest. Lord? Nell had called him lordship earlier. Her ghost was a Scots lord? How could that be?

"Shh, it's okay, I want to help you. He wants…" Beads of sweat broke out on Nell's forehead. Her hands, clenched tight in Baillie's, felt like pockets of heat as the chill burrowed deeper into Baillie's soul. "He needs to warn you."

Bouncing in her chair, T-Cup fluttered, "Oh my god, oh my god, this is better than reality television."

"Wa…warn me?" Baillie started shaking.

"The castle…danger…he…must…"

Baillie watched the woman's mouth continue moving without a sound. A fresh blast of ice enveloped Baillie like a polar plunge, taking her concentration. The room darkened around her, and she thought she heard Gillian shout before she fell into a dark abyss.

# Chapter Ten

"No way!" Sally squealed as quietly as she could, though the store was nearly empty. She nursed a cup of Starbucks coffee behind the counter next to Baillie. "Start at the beginning and leave nothing to my imagination."

"I'm trying to tell you." Recounting the ghostly excitement at the faire to her assistant in the rational light of a Monday morning still seemed horribly unreal, and she wasn't going to mention the séance. She didn't want to lose Sally over some spook story.

"Seriously? What did you do?"

"Freaked, what else? I'm holding her hands and she's telling me I'm not alone and there is this guy trying to get in touch with me." Baillie frowned. Sally's mouth formed an O as she nodded like a bobblehead doll.

"I don't know, Sally, it was bizarre. She had me in this intense eye lock, holding both my hands while going on and on, talking about some guy who's supposedly telling her things."

"What kind of things?"

"I don't know, I couldn't focus. At some point she said he said I was beautiful." She knew she couldn't avoid looking embarrassed relaying that piece of news.

"You're kidding? A dead guy is hitting on you?" Sally quickly put down her paper cup, as she'd nearly squeezed it in half. "Where was Sir Gillian through all this?"

"He had his perfect nose pressed against the beads, I guess—he practically fell into the tent when it was over." The adrenaline burst at the memory kept Baillie searching for something to do with her hands. She sorted a pile of order forms and put the completed ones into neat little stacks.

"That would have been fun to see the Prince fall on his firm butt for a change," Sally snorted.

"Sally!"

"I'm sorry, it's true. Go on. Then what happened?"

"We took off to find the girls. I paid my money and got my fortune." Baillie touched Sally's arm, signaling her to take care of the young woman coming toward them.

While Sally handled the customer, Baillie bit on her thumbnail, lost in thought. She hated withholding information from Sally, but the whole crazy day was too bizarre to blab. Who was this Lord Baillie, and why was he trying to contact her through spooks and goblins? What could possibly be important enough for some lost soul to reach past the netherworld to contact her? Not just contact, but warn her. No wonder she'd fainted. Did she even believe in ghosts?

More than once her mother had told her stories while they sat at the scratched Formica kitchen table of her relatives from both sides who came to America from the moors, spending their lives in the flat plains and wild yellow grasses of the Midwest as ranchers. The eventual migration west brought stories of independent women and bullheaded men surrounded by herds of sheep and a few good dogs.

After growing up with Pet Rocks, surviving disco fever, and blossoming into a small-business owner, it was impossible to picture an ancient Scotsman of some royal level walking around in a plaid skirt with bared knees trying to contact her. A harsh blast of cold slapped Baillie on the side of her face. Baillie took a sharp breath, blinking hard against the sudden tears.

"Are you okay?" Sally mouthed as she helped another customer at the counter.

Baillie forced a smile and mouthed back, "Headache." She left Sally and walked toward the break room as if for aspirin. As soon as she was out of hearing range, Baillie grabbed her cell phone. "He's here," she whispered to Gillian, her breath shaky and shallow.

"Who's here?" Gillian drawled.

"Him, Lord Baillie."

"I thought we validated that Saturday night."

"No, he's loose. I was at the counter, nowhere near the travel books or a book of Burns's poems. It's like he's been set free in the shop, you know? Nell said he was having trouble making contact from the other world, and now I'm feeling the cold even at the counter. Should I be worried about Sally working here?"

"She hasn't felt or heard him before so I'd say she's safe, same as the customers. The psychic said he was focused only on you. Too bad she couldn't come back another night, but she had to make her plane. Pity."

"I'm being stalked by an ancient ghoul, and you're all pouty that she couldn't play anymore."

"Stalked is such a strong word, Baillie, if he's trying to be a superhero and warn you about something dangerous."

"Yeah, whatever this is, Lord Baillie doesn't feel evil, per se. Weird, but not ugly, you know? What would a ghost of a Scottish lord want with me?"

"I wonder, if he's free to roam now, will he be watching you upstairs?"

Baillie ran her fingers through her hair and twisted away at a stray curl. "Why do you keep going there? I don't know, I haven't sensed anything when I go to bed. I thought he was stuck with the clan books. But now in the lobby…I don't know anymore." Baillie paused. "Hopefully Lord Baillie's a gentleman spirit. Not like the wild hair and screamers of the Wallace clan, like in the movie…"

A loud thud toward the back of the shop startled her into silence.

"Did a customer just drop something? Are they okay?" asked Gillian.

Baillie blinked a couple times before answering. Her mouth was suddenly dry. "I think I just insulted my ghost."

# Chapter Eleven

Rogue viciously threw the curry comb against the back of the stall slamming it into the brick. "How dare that bastard of a banker claim to know what killed the man, hisself, and looking me straight in the eye with his devil words." She kicked her boot into the dirt and the gray horse whinnied at the straw flying.

She reached up and rubbed her dirty hands across the horse's neck. "Aye, it is he who should be a'frayd. The man is a banshee and should be dealt with by the likes of his own kind," Rogue spit out. "He best take care or he'll get his due one o' these days."

Whispering soothing sounds as the horse slowly lowered his head, Rogue buried her face in its freshly combed mane to hide the wave of tears. The animal stamped the ground, sensing the girl's emotions after having witnessed the large man blocking the stall door earlier. His conversation had been one-sided, short and arrogant. The air still reeked of his cologne.

Wiping her eyes with the back of her shaking hand, she patted the warm flesh and picked up her tools. "He'll not make me cry. None of 'em will ever see me cry. I dinna kill the man, and I'll not go quietly among them if they say so."

The black stallion kicked his stall and let out a scream of rage.

• • •

The old man shuffled into the kitchen, waving a folded sheet of paper, the rest of the day's mail under his arm. "Woman, go get the girl. She'll be needin' ta hear this, too."

Putney turned away from the stove, her eyebrows raised. "The meal is near ready and ya need me to drag the girl in early?" Wiping her hands on the stained apron around her waist, she asked, "And what is so bloody urgent I must risk the food being scorched this very moment?"

Sagging into the chair, he sighed. "The banker is declaring ownership of the castle." He dropped the official-looking letter on the table before setting the rest of the mail into a pile next to it. "He's saying he canna find an heir and the property now reverts to the Clan of the Bruce, making himself the rightful owner."

"The devil, you say," Putney whispered.

"Aye." He rubbed his forehead. "Never thought I'd live to see the day the land would fall to a Bruce."

"Isn't there something we can do?" She wrung her hands in the apron, twisting the material into a knot. "I canna leave our home to such evil after all these generations."

The outside door opened, and Rogue scuffed her feet before entering the kitchen. She headed to the sink, turning the handle, breaking the silence in the room with the rushing water. The old man watched her a moment, the young shoulders hunched over washing her hands, then looked at Putney.

Clearing his throat, he spoke up. "Rogue, I need you over here, please." He saw her body stiffen as she stopped the flowing water.

She turned in slow motion. Her eyes widened at the sight of the scowls on the older couple's faces. "What now?" Water dripped from her fingers, speckling the floor. She leaned against the counter.

"Come sit, child," he said. "We've got a bit of nasty news, and I donna feel like shouting it across the room." He watched her shove herself from the sink and hang her head, walking across the room. "The banker is spouting rubbish he's taking the castle because he canna find a blood relation."

Rogue stared at him with blank eyes as if he spoke a foreign language. She twisted her head back and looked at Putney.

"It's like the bloody fox is allowed to say who owns the henhouse, child. He's crowning himself the rooster, and we are forced to move out." Putney folded her arms across her chest.

"Can he do that?" Rogue's voice squeaked.

Putney plopped into a chair. "Old man, you hightail yourself into town and ask the powers that be if all nooks and crannies have been searched before the devil pounds on our door for eviction."

# Chapter Twelve

"How's Casie like her new teacher?"

"They all shine during the first week of school; it's hard to tell. Seems like we just finished Capitol Little League, doesn't it?"

"Did you get the mail?" A wisp of chilled air tickled the back of Baillie's neck, making her smile.

Lately she'd found herself comfortable with the incidental touches of cold, more frequent every day. No more shocking ice baths when she least expected it, the feelings of his presence were more restrained, gentle, but still insistent.

The melodic ballads he crooned in the mornings no longer frightened her. She was adjusting, sharing space with the unknown lord. She'd found herself welcoming his comings and goings, almost anticipating when she might hear a few notes to send her whistling through the rest of her day.

Baillie walked through the shop thinking of Lord Baillie's touches. In the mornings, the spirit opened doors for her downstairs if Sally wasn't at work yet. He left the book of Burn's poems open to certain passages for her enjoyment. Rain pounded against the windows, cloaking the shop in a gray veil outside, enhancing the warmth and coziness inside. She loved the sound of rain, autumn wetness drenching the earth. She moved to the reading area where the séance had been held and kneeled on the edge of an overstuffed chair, staring at the cascading water in the window.

The lamplight beside her cast a faint reflection of her face on the glass. The beads of rain trickled down in a continuous stream, hypnotic. Baillie watched the movement until it seemed there was more to the scene in front of her. She gasped as she focused on her watery image or, more specifically, the additional reflection next to her on the window. A taller, second outline of someone wavered in her view, barely noticeable, behind her. She strained to see more clearly, leaning closer, and the outline was gone.

Yet she felt his presence still beside her. With a sigh, she moved away from the chair and back to the counter. A smile pulled at the edge of her mouth.

The front door opened, jingling the little chimes. The FedEx guy in his familiar purple and black uniform walked into the lobby, dripping, and stopped inside the door.

"Hey, got a flat one for you. Seems too skinny to be a book," the guy joked.

"Better for you, but with all this rain it's a good day to curl up on the couch and read a book." Sally teased back as she signed for the package. She walked the thick envelope over to Baillie, her eyes glancing at the return address. "Boss, you maybe want to open this right away."

Baillie looked up to see Sally's mouth hanging open. She stuck her hand out and quickly read the label. Edinburgh, Scotland? The familiar chill surrounded her like a cloak of ice, strong, urgency drawing tight around her. She ripped the tab open and pulled out a sheath of papers. She felt herself lean against the cold as the words of the cover letter swam in front of her.

"Well?"

"Well, it looks like I've either inherited a castle somewhere in Scotland or someone's playing a very expensive joke." Baillie flipped through the pages. "This is a bank offering to buy the property from me for some bizarre amount in pounds. I need to Google the conversion rate—these pound things mean nothing to me." She turned toward the shop computer, mumbling, "Too many zeros, must be a mistake."

"Get outta here," Sally squealed. She grabbed the papers from Baillie's hand and stared at the lines of legalese. "You lucky dog. First Aunt Fran and now a castle?"

"Hey, that's my inheritance you almost tore in half." Baillie tapped in some numbers, took a short breath and screamed, bouncing on her toes in quick spurts. "I got a castle! Somebody left me a castle!"

The door of the shop opened, jarring the chimes, as a couple in their sixties stepped in. They stared at the squealing Baillie.

"Don't mind her," Sally waved the papers. "She's become a finalist in the Publisher's Clearing House sweepstakes." The two women leaned against each other, laughing, trying to compose themselves.

Baillie took the papers back from Sally. "Do you hear music playing?"

Sally laid her hand on Baillie's shoulder. "Yes, the CD player is on. Remember, we had it fixed." Her voice dropped to a low and eerie pitch. "Unless you mean your friend Casper's bagpipes, then no, I don't." Sally stopped herself, dropping her eyes. "Sorry, bad joke. Shouldn't tease your boss about ghosts. But didn't you say the psychic at the faire said something about a castle?"

Baillie stared at her assistant in confusion. "Huh?" Her eyes widened, and the pile of papers scattered on the floor. "Oh my gawd, a castle in Scotland! The witch woman did say something about a castle." A trickle of sweat made a path down her back. Baillie couldn't catch her breath, panting for air.

"I'm sorry, really sorry. Are you okay? I didn't mean to say anything about the ghost of Flanders or whoever; it just slipped out."

"Scotland," Baillie whispered, slipping into a nearby chair, her jelly legs useless in holding her up. A brush of frigid cold caressed her face, sending goose bumps down her bare arms.

"Could you help us?" The older couple beckoned from the back wall, and Sally avoided Baillie's face as she moved away from the counter.

Baillie rubbed her shaking hands together. An icy touch passed her face as she watched the pages flutter from the floor into a neat pile on her lap. The cold touched her soul as she grabbed the papers. She self-consciously tugged the bottom hem of her skirt lower toward her knees with a slight giggle. "You're still here."

"Uh, yes. I'd like to buy this painting."

Startled, Baillie let out a shriek and stood up, crushing the pages against her. Before her stood a gorgeous hunk of dark-haired maleness with a quizzical look across his tanned face.

"I'm terribly sorry. I didn't mean to frighten you." He leaned his tall, muscular stature even closer to her. "Are you all right? You look pale. Should I call 9-1-1?" He snapped his cell phone open.

Baillie figured she was blushing a dark crimson color at the animal arousal his GQ looks produced inside her. "Sorry, I guess I forgot where I was for a minute. You're ready to check out?" She fought to regain some professional control, setting the papers down and picking up the small, framed painting of an oak tree. "Give me a chance to catch my breath." She started to fill out the receipt and told him, "This is one of my favorites by Montelongo. She lives locally and has quite a talent with a brush and canvas."

The man reached behind and pulled out an expensive looking leather wallet from the back pocket of his khaki shorts, stretching the knit fabric of his T-shirt against his chest. "I admit it caught my eye."

Baillie forced her eyes away from the magnificent view of young hunkiness. "Could you fill out the top portion of this for me with your name and address while I wrap the painting?"

"And don't forget to fill in your phone number if you're single." Sally, finished with the couple, had snuck up to the counter unnoticed.

"Sally," Baillie spat out in a horrified whisper. "Please forgive the rudeness of the hired help, sir. She was just about to be fired."

Sally helped Baillie tape the heavy wrapping paper with a twinkle in her eye.

"Actually I just moved to the area a short time ago from northern Texas." The man turned the receipt book around and took a credit card from the back of the wallet to pay for the painting.

"Well then, you must come by the shop again soon," Sally's tone imitated a sappy imitation of a Southern drawl. "Baillie's practically born and raised here. She can show you—umph." A sharp jab into her ribs cut the sentence off in mid-breath.

"Mr.—," Baillie started, checking the receipt book, "Johnson, ignore the insane woman behind the counter."

"Gee, you inherit a castle and lose your sense of humor."

"Really, I…" The man quickly pocketed his wallet, took his brown paper package under his arm and stepped toward the front door.

"Ouch!" Sally quickly put her hand up to her forearm.

"Come again, Mr. Johnson, when the staff isn't quite so impolite. Welcome to Olympia." Baillie tried to breathe as the man left the building with a smile and a nod.

"You pinched me." Sally whined, rubbing the sore spot. "Hard, too."

"What were you thinking, carrying on like that?"

"He's cute. I was trying to help you out."

"You scared the man half to death. He may never come near a female again, let alone my shop. What's the matter with you?" Baillie gripped the counter. She wasn't sure whom she was more irritated at, Sally, herself, or the freaky things happening.

"Okay, so my social skills with single men are a little off," she pouted at Baillie's sharp tone. "I've been happily married a long time." Then, in an obvious attempt to change the subject, she added, "Tell me again what the letter says."

Baillie retrieved the crinkled sheets, smoothing them out on the counter with the side of her hand. A slight quiver of anticipation passed through her.

"'Dear Miss Baillie, you are hereby notified,' yada, yada, yada. It's just too weird, Sally. The bank guy of Scotland or whatever is suggesting I sell the property to them for *an expeditious settlement of my inheritance.*" She slapped her hands down on the top page.

"Absolutely. You sell, girl. What would you do with a drafty bunch of bricks on the other side of the world? Take the money and play."

"Play? Play what? Don't you enjoy working here? Isn't this enough for you? It is for me."

"Don't make me sigh. Play, another word for fun: Frequent Useless Nancystuff. Opposite of work. I don't think you're familiar with the concept."

"Don't go there." Baillie grabbed the feather duster, waving it over her head like a fairy godmother. "Poof, be gone. I own a castle now." Laughing, she flipped her hair over her shoulder, heading toward the back of the shop.

• • •

"My dear, of course you sell the bloody monstrosity." Sitting outside of a Tumwater Starbucks, Gillian kept both male and female heads turning for a second look. "Didn't you say you wanted to upgrade the shop? Or if you didn't, you should have. Here's a perfect financial opportunity—boom—dropped in your lap from out of the blue." Gillian sipped at his drink with the confidant air of new-money culture. He leaned back in the white iron chair, gliding into a perfect pose.

"But…"

"There's no hesitation, Baillie. I can't believe I hear doubt in your voice. This is the lost-relative lottery, and you've just won first prize. Again, these are astronomical odds. What are you waiting for?" Gillian pushed the envelope of papers back to her. "Sign and seal."

"Gillian, shouldn't I check it out? Shouldn't I see the property at least? What if it's worth a lot more than they're offering or something..." Her voice faded under his confident stare.

"Like their banks are going to tweak the deal in their favor? With the generous amount they're offering, who's to say what drafty castles are going for these days?"

"Your sarcasm is not appreciated."

"Okay, look at it another way. Do you want to spend ten thousand dollars to sightsee some run-down property to make maybe an additional twenty thousand when you close the deal?" The disdain in his voice was spread thick. "What kind of business head are you dreaming with? Is this relic from an old British movie worth traveling halfway around the world for?"

Baillie pouted into her coffee latte. "I like to travel."

"All the more reason to sell this thing quickly and go somewhere fun, exciting. Warm. You don't like walking down the frozen food section of a market without your parka. You hate being cold. Imagine island-hopping on the south end of the Pacific, getting a delicious tan, with just a portion of the money you'll get. And I could go with you, *mon ami*!"

"Nothing like thoughts of naked island boys to stir up the adrenaline, eh, Gillian? I don't know. I've never even been to Mexico. It does sound awfully tropical for a vacation."

"Hmm, versus catching pneumonia in some drafty castle you're probably going to sell anyway. Gee, pretty tough decision you've been given by the Choice Fairy." Gillian flipped his fingers in the air.

"I knew I'd get unbiased assistance from you. But tell me how you really feel."

"Don't I always?" he sniffed right back at her.

"I wouldn't ask if I didn't want honesty from you." Baillie tore a strip of the paper napkin in front of her. "Sally agrees I should dump the property and grab the dough. Sounds unanimous around here." She wiggled the manila packet. "I guess I should contact this banker guy."

"The sooner you sign, the sooner you can deposit the check, darling. Time is money, as the old cliché goes."

Baillie sighed and looked up through her short eyelashes. Time to play the ace card she'd held back from him. "What about Lady Nell from the faire?"

Gillian squealed and sat up quickly in the chair, bumping his knee against the table, rocking their half-empty cups. "Oh my gawd, I completely forgot about your little invisible friend. He's hung around so long he's just your musical shadow. The castle! That's exactly what Lady Nell foretold in your future. And the message came practically hand delivered, once we found you a medium to unleash his lordship."

Gillian started rambling. "I've never been so enthralled with a ghost story. Wait 'til I tell the girls! You really did have someone come through the veil of death, risking eternal tranquility of the other world, to reach out to you. They won't believe this." He brought his cup up for a long drink.

"I'm still not sure I do," Baillie mumbled, her head down.

"Darling, don't talk to the table instead of me. It's most unbecoming and extremely rude. I can't understand a single word you said."

"Gillian, when I opened the letter earlier at the shop, the ghost was…well, I felt him next to me and could feel his anxiety. I know I haven't said anything for a while, but Lord Baillie has been very active in the shop. He's like an invisible friend anymore. Yet this time I felt so vulnerable reading the packet, like it was a protective caress when he touched me. I swear on a stack of Bibles he picked the papers off the floor when I dropped them and placed them in a stack on my lap."

Gillian stared at her as if she had grown snakes in her hair. Speechless.

Baillie chewed on her lower lip. "Remember, I told you months ago? It was like Lady Nell broke him loose, and he's mobile now. He even opens the door to the shop for me."

"Really?" Gillian leaned forward, his typical bland expression now one of concern. "You've continued to, uh, experience the ghost, Lord Baillie? The girls all thought it was delightful entertainment that night, but no more. And I know you've called a couple times worried about your polter-guy. I'm sorry I didn't take your stories of your imaginary friend more seriously. How dreadful. You must think me a shallow cad."

Gillian reached out for her hand. "Didn't she say the ghostly prince was trying to warn you of a castle?" Baillie nodded. "See? Even *he* agrees you should sell immediately. I knew I liked this guy, spirit, whatever from last summer. This makes it abundantly clear. You must sell."

"But it's my castle, my legacy. My ancestors of yore came from the Isle of Somewhere, some place over there." Baillie rattled the papers with both hands. "I wanna see my castle."

"You're whining in public. Have I taught you nothing of decorum?" Gillian sighed, his blue eyes intense. "And it's one of your ancestors warning you against the castle. You're going, aren't you?"

Baillie nodded again.

"No matter what I say or how much money you'll waste over this folly?"

Her head still bounced up and down as she finished the last of her latte with a smile. "Because," Baillie bent down and pulled a second envelope out of her oversized purse, "the bank sent me a document showing family lineage, and somewhere in there are my predecessors." She pulled out a sheaf of papers and set them on the table between them. "Funny, Sally forced me to sign up to a clan site earlier this year and look what happened."

"I would hope they've researched to be sure you're in the bloodlines." Gillian sipped his drink.

"They also sent some history about the castle and, uh, I found a picture of Lord Baillie."

"Interesting that Sally would have been a catalyst to... What? You have a photo of *the* Lord Baillie, the old guy you say is haunting the shop?"

Baillie nodded her head, feeling a bit mischievous as she bit her bottom lip.

"Look at that face. What are you keeping from me? Spill it, spill it now." Gillian stuck his hand out, palm up, and wiggled his fingers.

"No, you won't give it back."

"Oh, now this is serious. Hand it over."

Baillie laughed and gave Gillian a copied article. She leaned forward and watched his expression as the intense blue eyes bore into the two-inch black-and-white photo of a painting with a caption that read, in part, "Lord Baillie." He pulled the paper close to his nose and then arm's length.

"Kinda cute, don't you think?" Baillie bounced in her seat. "What if that's my ghost, the guy trying to communicate with me? Look at that gorgeous thick hair. I'd kill for those waves."

Gillian pondered the photo. "Hard to get a good feeling other than he's young and manly. This looks like a copy of a copy, pretty pixilated image."

"But?" she raised her eyebrows.

"I'm pleasantly shocked." He handed back the papers. "Now I understand better what your sudden passion to visit the castle is all about. You do realize he's a ghost, a phantom?"

"Of course."

"Then go and get castledom out of your system. The sooner you sell the place, the sooner I can get my life back to normal."

# Chapter Thirteen

Baillie hung up the shop's phone with a soft squeal, pushing her office chair away from the counter.

"Did I just hear first class?" Gillian gasped with theatrics, hands to his chiseled cheeks.

"I'm heiress to a castle. Can't I splurge a little?"

Gillian sniffed. "How many times have I begged you about those very same words: 'splurge a little'? The queen of cheap is your middle name; you make nickels squeak. 'Never spend a dollar when change will do' I believe is your motto."

"I am frugal, not cheap. The airline gave me a platinum credit card with enough zeros to cover this and a whole lot more as a reward." Baillie brandished the card in the air. "I'm charging the plane fare and worrying about the bill when I get back. I'll have to sell some of my signed first editions. I guess this is the rainy day I've been saving for." She looked around the shop, her sanctuary against reality. No politics argued within these hallow walls, no reality television or gang wars. "If I come back, that is," she giggled. "I'm going to Scotland."

"Don't let Sally hear you talk like that. She'll hunt you down and drag you back. Cushy jobs like this don't come along every day. She's taking today off?"

"Yes, something about Casie and a school meeting." Baillie tucked her travel papers into a folder. "You know, I haven't left the store in years."

Gillian sighed. "What have I been saying? People do not live by work alone."

"This isn't just work. I'm selling dreams and passion. I sponsor Little League teams and support the local economy. I love it here, except for the few eco-freaks who rave about their eReaders, thinking eBooks are saving thousands of trees when the environment is taking its licks from the manufacturing of the reader equipment." Baillie reached over for a book under the counter. "Besides, I can flash one of these at 'em, my 1954 library edition of *Half Magic*. Reading a book is one thing; holding your childhood memories in your hand is another."

Gillian shrugged and made himself comfortable.

"How can downloading an eBook replace standing in line for hours waiting until the magical stroke of midnight to purchase the latest craze like *Harry Potter*? Granted, the *Potter* era was probably a once-in-a-lifetime extravaganza. I don't imagine we'll see the likes or levels of excitement like that again. It's rather sad."

"And now you're going to Scotland. Maybe the castle is a mini Hogwarts."

"Full of spooks? Is that what you're implying?" Baillie's eyes widened, laughing.

"Just a little castle joke." Gillian flipped his ponytail over his shoulder.

Faint notes of a bagpipe began behind her ear. Baillie tilted her head as the strains of phantom music became familiar. "Excuse me?" Gillian asked. "Were you singing?"

Baillie said the first thing that popped into her head. "Just a song I remembered from an old Disney movie."

"Real-ly." He stretched the word into multiple syllables. "No coincidence the tune is from Scotland? Your *mi amore* serenading you again? Your face is practically glowing."

Baillie sighed. "Yes, since I've made the decision to go, his attention has ramped up tenfold. Sometimes the music is more intense or the cold will sting with a fierceness when I know he can control it."

"He sounds worried, oh stubborn one. He's come far to warn you away, and you shove his efforts aside. I'm surprised he's still here. I'd have told you good luck and bolted back to the homeland."

Leave? Baillie chewed her bottom lip, moving away from the counter. She rather enjoyed having his attention now and again. She hadn't thought of him leaving her. Really? He's all upset at her for ignoring the warning? A chilled nudge pushed her down an aisle out of sight of Gillian. Baillie looked around. "What? What do you want?"

Baillie watched as books moved slowly on the shelves in front of her. "Lord Baillie, I don't mean to be disrespectful, but I've never been to a castle. And I really want to go." The urge to stomp her foot was great. "You can't make me stay here."

A tornado of cold blinded her, a pressure forced her against the shelving behind her. She raised her arms over her face, shielding it against the invisible biting storm. "Knock it off," she hissed, and the air around her settled back to normal. A stack of books were haphazardly piled on top of each other with the spines facing her. Titles of death and murder filled the pile.

"Seriously? If I go over there to see my inherited castle, I'm gonna die? That's what you're trying to tell me?" *There's never a good psychic around when you need one.* "I don't believe it. I am going. Case closed."

# Chapter Fourteen

Baillie rubbed her eyes, feeling the grittiness from lack of sleep as the wheels of the plane touched down in Heathrow. She'd spent hours watching newly released movies until she'd fallen asleep somewhere over the Atlantic. Pushing up the plastic shade, she saw rain trickling down the plane's window. "That must be one big cloud out there—El Niño on steroids. It was raining in SeaTac when I left."

Baillie stayed cuddled in her sleeper cubicle, in no hurry to dash away with the rest of first class as she watched the mass of plane-mates shuffle down the aisle. What struck her most was that the majority were men, a slow-moving river of dark business suits rippling between the seats. Grays in charcoal, granite, with a few blacks and navy thrown in—no designer imagination in this bunch.

While the sea of humanity continued, Baillie finally stood and listened to her body creak and groan. Why couldn't this inheritance stuff have come around twenty years earlier?

She stepped into the Heathrow airport. "Why did I let Gillian talk me into spending the night in London? I wanna see the castle." Baillie eased into the crowded flow of people heading toward arrivals.

The lines through customs flowed steadily. Holding her documents tightly, she stepped up to the glass window. The person glanced at her landing document and passed it back. "Address of your destination, mum."

"Um, it's the Castle Baillie in Scotland. I have no idea what the address is." She dug into her shoulder bag for the three-ring notebook of details she'd created. Flipping through the first pages of her flight information, everything in sleeve protectors, Baillie set the notebook on the counter and pointed to one of the documents the bank had supplied. "I'm going here after tomorrow."

The man jotted a few notes, and Baillie heard the resounding thump of the stamp on her passport. She was officially in England. Time to grab her suitcase and find a train to downtown London. Strains of the Petula Clark song now filled her head. Gillian had her staying somewhere close to the famous Harrods department store.

Her purple suitcase sat alone on the moving carousel. She must have been one of the few Americans on board or the only one who actually brought something other than carry-on. She grabbed the handle and followed the signs. Buying a ticket for the underground train, she handed her credit card over and took a moment for a deep breath. She couldn't remember Gillian's tutorial about green lines and yellow lines while he used words like *underground*, *circular* and *tubes*. Maybe she should have paid more attention. Throngs of people quietly moved through the area, a mass of humanity focused on getting to their destinations.

The train car was fairly empty, modern and comfortable. Pleasantly surprised, Baillie plopped her suitcase in the marked area and dropped into the second row. Plucking a large laminated safety card from the seat pocket in front her, she used it for a fan. The weather was indeed similar to Olympia's, and walking indoors through the terminal she was grateful she'd worn short sleeves. A slight sheen of perspiration on her upper lip reflected the exertion it took to get through the airport. Where was her ghost when she needed a refreshing cold breeze?

As the view changed from industrial around the airport to more residential, Baillie stared at streets of row houses made of brick with multiple chimney stacks. She pinched herself on the arm. This was no Hollywood movie but truly London. She absorbed details, soaking in the view of England outside her window. She felt like a small-town girl heading toward the big city sitting in the train. A cloak of exhaustion wrapped itself around her as Baillie stepped from the train in the bowels of underground London. The hotel Gillian had suggested was supposed to be a short walk from the station. A long nap sounded like a luxurious idea as the stress of travel wound down the last of her resistance. Tomorrow would be here quick enough.

Looking around for an escalator or elevator, Baillie couldn't believe the amount of people around her for morning rush hour. Hoards of men and women either getting off a train or waiting to get on a train made walking the platform quite difficult, like an errant salmon swimming upstream. She got to the end of the platform and looked up at steep stairs. People merged around her stopped position, not saying anything, but obviously she was holding up the flow of traffic.

She turned around and headed toward the other end of the platform. Surely there was a handicap route to the surface she could use, being older and more out of shape than the dark-clothed masses surrounding her. She saw nothing except more stairwells every few yards. Gripping the handle of her luggage, she took a deep breath and started up a set of stairs.

Step, pull the bag up. Next step up, pull the bag. Trickles of sweat dripped down her back and the sides of her face. The congested walk of the platform had already depleted her pitiful dregs of energy. Flights of stairs were cruel and unjust punishment, undermining the start of her trip. Her breathing became labored by the third stair.

A large male hand reached over hers for the handle. "Let me help you, mum." And a black-suited gentleman lifted the stuffed suitcase like a weightless bag and moved at a brisk pace up the crowded stairs.

Too exhausted to yell anything like "slow down!" or "stop, thief!" Baillie took a ragged breath and tried keeping up with the man. Sweat dripped off the tip of her nose, the sides of her face, drenched. At the top of the second flight of stairs, he set the bag down and made sure she was nearby before blending into the seething crowd of commuters. Gone.

Her hands shook as she wrapped her fingers around the handle, too tired for gratitude. *I'm going to die right here, and there's no room for an ambulance gurney.* Baillie shuffled into a corner, getting out of the continuing waves of people. *I can't move anymore.* She leaned against the cool, painted wall. Propping her shoulder bag on her suitcase, she searched for a napkin, anything to wipe her dripping face.

A man and a row of gray kiosk gates stood between her and the outside world. She watched people poke tickets or hold passes at them to open the way. Where'd she put her ticket? Crap. She dug in her shoulder bag for what seemed like an hour and finally found the golden ticket of escape. Snapping up the handle after a few more moments, Baillie stuck the ticket in the machine and headed into the grand open area of the station.

The first beacon of hope she saw was a Burger King in a line of small shops and cafes, like an oasis with a familiar logo of salvation: Diet Coke. Huge billboards of train arrival and departure times filled her vision next. Making her way to the tiny tables out front, she threw her coat over one chair and fell into another. *Stairs, seriously!* her mind screamed. *Do I look like someone who takes stairs? Where are the warning signs: Do not get off at this stop unless athletically fit?*

She fished out a wad of pound notes she'd ordered from the bank back home and ordered a deliciously quenching large Diet Coke, a gift from the gods. She fanned the notes like cards and offered the clerk to pick one. He gave her back a handful of strange coins with her order. Gillian was going to get an earful next time she talked to him. *'Oh, you must visit London, my foot.'*

• • •

Boarding the train to Scotland was less dramatic, and Baillie felt weak with gratitude. Outside the train window, the more depressing industrial outskirts of the city soon gave way to miles of countryside, and she couldn't stop smiling. Various shades of green painted the fields and trees, grassland dotted with wooly sheep and stone fences. The English countryside was delightfully peaceful and tugged at her imaginative heartstrings. She leaned back and slowly nodded off to sleep.

Stepping from the train six hours later, Baillie spotted a line of miniature cabs and headed toward the first one. You could fit two of these in a New York taxi, she mused. The dialogue around her was more lyrical, more personable than when she'd left England. She'd slept through the crossing into Scotland, but the voices had changed. Dorothy was definitely not in Kansas anymore.

"Where to, miss?" The grizzled cabbie grabbed her suitcase and easily popped it into the tiny trunk.

"The Baillie Castle, please. I think I have directions here somewhere." Baillie pulled the notebook out of her shoulder bag.

The driver's pallid face paled even more. "Are ya sure of that now, miss?"

"Is there a problem? Are the roads closed?" She flipped through pages in her book. "I know I have directions from the bank somewhere. I've just inherited the property, and I have no idea what it looks like, but I do have notes on how to get there. Have you ever been to the castle?"

He nodded his head. "Aye, miss. Once." He opened the left passenger door for her, and she slid into the tiny backseat. It looked like something from an amusement park ride, disorienting, with the steering wheel on the right side.

The driver climbed in and started the car. "I took the last owner of the castle there on his first visit." His radio crackled with dispatches.

"What a weird coincidence. It must have been years ago and you remember such a thing? So you've been driving this area for quite a while?"

"No, miss," he said over his shoulder, clutching the steering wheel with tight fists.

"But the last owner, right? You said it was his first visit and all. How many years ago was it?"

"None." He made the sign of the cross. "I read in the papers the man died shortly after I took him up there." He pulled away from the station. "I pray your visit is more successful."

Baillie wished she were Catholic and had a yard of rosary beads in her hands, anything to still the tremble in her fingers. The driver must be mistaken. Maybe it was only an unfortunate accident that took a life so suddenly, maybe a heart attack from decrepit aging. Things happened.

"Where you from, miss?" The driver spoke up.

"America." She tried revving her thoughts away from the dark news. She stared at the back of the driver's head. He seemed normal enough, gray at the temples. Surely it was just a strange coincidence, getting his cab.

"Have you ever seen Mickey Mouse? My wee bairns love the silly mouse, they do."

Baillie laughed, "He's a favorite, I must say; an international star."

The driver nodded as Baillie leaned back against the soft seat and watched miles of Scotland's scenery unfold in the last vestiges of sunlight.

Was this where the soundtrack of the movie grew darker? More drums, cellos, baritone sounds? Baillie bit the edge of her bottom lip.

# Chapter Fifteen

"Isn't there electricity in this place?" Baillie sounded pitiful, whining like a spoiled American. It had been such a long journey across half the planet. The sleep in London seemed eons ago. Her stamina whittled down as the power drinks she'd used depleted in her system.

The cab had pulled up to a dark goliath of a building. Baillie wasn't sure what she had expected, but this was more out of a horror movie, with the blackness of the moat like a suffocating noose of water around the tall turrets stretched above. The cab's headlights pointed toward the side of the castle. A brief honk brought an old man holding a bright lantern through a massive door. By the time the man shuffled across a small wooden bridge, the driver had unloaded her bag, collected his fare, and had the car headed back into civilization. She refused the urge to call him back.

The wheels of her bag crunched on the fine gravel up to the edge of the bridge and then thundered, shattering the silence as they rolled over the worn planks. The lantern light barely broke through the darkness, and Baillie stayed close to the old man.

Baillie tried her question again. "Isn't there electricity in the castle?" Her voice faltered, thoughts of dungeons and torture chambers running through her mind.

"Aye," the old man answered, leading into what turned out to be the kitchen with welcoming smells and warmth from a crackling fire greeting them as they crossed through the doorway. "There is some, aye, but the banker shut the current off thinking we'd be moved out by now without an owner."

Baillie felt too tired to be indignant. She'd notified the bank of her arrival date well in advance. Things would have to wait until tomorrow. The old man pointed to a kitchen chair pulled away from a huge wooden table decked with a candelabrum of flickering light. She gladly slumped into the offered seat.

A ceramic bowl of thick, hot stew and fresh-baked biscuits appeared in front of her from the dark. The plus-sized bearer of food crossed her arms and glared down at her until she picked up the linen napkin next to the bowl and covered her lap.

"Thank you ever so much for this," Baillie got out before filling her mouth with a spoonful of the savory meal. "I can't remember the last time I ate today." She nearly groaned over the warmth it flooded her with.

Still wearing her coat—Baillie felt a chill around her legs and feet—she hesitated to take it off. It seemed impolite, but the heat she first felt from the fireplace was at the other end of the room.

After a few feeble attempts at conversation on Baillie's part, the wall of silence forced her head down over the steaming bowl. Filling her stomach pushed her over the edge of exhaustion. As she was scraping the bottom, the old woman whisked it away and growled something unintelligible at the old man.

The man stood in a doorway, holding her suitcase, waiting for her.

"Thank you for dinner. I know it's quite late, and I appreciate your waiting up for me. Truly, I do. Good night, now." Silence.

The old man picked up a thick, flickering candle with his other hand and led the way up to a large stairway. The walls were gray stone and icy to the touch. They slowly moved up one floor and walked a short landing to another set of thinner stairs. The suitcase wheels clunked against each edge, but Baillie had no energy; however he got her bag up there was fine.

"My room will be way up here?" Baillie stage whispered to the man's back. She couldn't see anything much past the candle glow.

"Aye, ye'll be in the master bedroom. Miss Putney requested it special for ye." The rest of his speech was a mumbled growl she assumed not meant for her to hear.

She had no intention of asking him to repeat anything. Baillie grabbed the name Putney, though, for future reference.

They climbed further, and the air became damper. Baillie sniffed at her own fears as they reached the top. The old codger was just trying to frighten her. Sure, they put the American lady in the tower just to scare the soup out of her and send her packing. Well, she'd show them no cowardice, no panic, no matter what they threw at her.

The man stopped in front of a wooden door, setting her suitcase on the floor. The black metal braces holding the wood together were mottled with age, probably older than King Henry the VIII. The iron door handle looked ornate and unusual. "This be your room." He handed her the candle, pulling a small tapered one from his pocket to light before starting back down.

"Excuse me? That's it? You're just going to leave me here?"

"This is as far as I go. I'll not be entering his room, I tell ye. Is there more ye'll be needin' from an old man in the middle of the night?"

Baillie stared at the wrinkled, stoic face in front of her. She couldn't read any sign of emotion or thought in the man's stubborn silence. "It's freezing up here. Does the fireplace work? Is there wood inside to build a fire?"

"Aye, no one has disturbed the room in many a year 'cept the woman. I am quite sure the wood pile is stocked, knowing her. If not, come down for some of Putney's supply."

He said he had no intention of stepping into the room, and stalling him any longer would not make it so. Baillie held the candle up in salute. "Well, good night then. I shall see you in the morning." She watched his dark back reflected in the gloom of the tiny flame as he started down the stairs.

Baillie reached for the door handle and felt a vibration so slight she thought it had to be the forceful pounding of her heart. She pushed; the handle didn't budge. Setting the candle down on the drafty floor, she tried again, putting her shoulder against the wood. Nothing. Baillie looked down the short corridor at three similar closed doors. Maybe she should try staying in one of those, but what if there wasn't any firewood? She wasn't sure she could find her way back to the kitchen. Before she could move her weight away from the smooth wood, the door opened with an unnatural force, knocking her off balance.

# Chapter Sixteen

The door creaked with a morbid, haunting sound as it swung into the room. Baillie looked at the dark dinginess inside with trepidation. She picked up the candle. How long had it been since anyone, or anything, had passed through this doorway? The candlelight illuminated massive velvet brocade drapes hanging to the floor, nearly covering one entire wall. No cobwebs, and she remembered the old man saying the Putney woman had set up the room for her.

She set the candle on top of the nearest flat surface, rubbing her shoulder, and went back for her suitcase. As she bent down to pick up the handle, she heard a whoosh, as the bedroom's fireplace burst into full blaze. Either this was some gigantic stone-laid edifice that lit the area like a forest fire in a sudden, blinding glow behind her, casting her shadow into the hallway—or her room was on fire.

"Oh, my gawd. I'm not alone, am I?" Baillie stuttered into the emptiness. Her hand shook as she grasped the padded handle and straightened. She was afraid to turn around. As long as she faced the darkness outside the room, there was still a chance of a normal life for herself. She could run down the stairs, tell Putney and the old man she'd changed her mind and would be selling the property in the morning. If they'd be so kind as to call for a cab, she'd stay the night in the nearest town, thank you very much.

However, she'd come too far and had too much invested to let a ghost or whatever this was scare her away now, if that were even its intentions, which she somehow didn't truly believe. This had to be her ghost from the shop, right? Lord Baillie had gone through a lot of trouble to break through the dimensions of time and space to warn her about the castle. And had she paid attention to his warnings? Noooo, she had thrown a gauntlet down and stated she would visit the castle, end of discussion. After the last storm of cold air, where he'd tried to scare her with titles of death, the music had stopped. She'd still felt him close by but always with a stoic distance. Now here she was in the very place he'd struggled so hard to tell her not to be.

Baillie almost laughed—probably hysteria—as she realized she was living one of her worst childhood fears, trapped in her own episode of the *Twilight Zone.* "Why do you watch this if you're going to be too scared to sleep?" her mother had complained during those years. "Go read a book."

Baillie couldn't stand the thought of missing a single episode. As long as she sat in front of the television in her own living room with her parents close by, the horror of the story happened to someone else. If she didn't watch, how would she know for certain she wouldn't be the main character in the next gruesome story?

The fire behind her began to break through the chill. Her back felt a slight blanket of warmth after the dank hour or so she'd been in the castle. Despite her fear, despite the nervous perspiration breaking out on her forehead, Baillie had to turn around. She needed to be closer to the fireplace come what may. She needed heat, and she needed it now.

She pulled the suitcase on its back wheels into the room. She'd been right, the stone fireplace took up almost the entire wall. The blazing fire gave her a better view of the room. Forgetting for a moment she might not be alone, she stared openly at the area in detail. Besides the curtained wall with thick cords, beautiful tapestries hung on the other two walls around the room. Hunting scenes and various artistic designs she assumed were of some Scottish symbols hung in muted colors.

A dark oak bed across from the fireplace took up the majority of the room. The four posters standing sentinel at each corner were thick and chiseled in a manly handicraft. She let go of her suitcase and walked to the closest pole, running her hands along the wood. What a beautiful antique. It looked between a double and queen size, she guessed, and was covered with some kind of old tarp or dust protector.

Suddenly, the hair on the back of her neck prickled, as she felt a severe cold pass by her back like the touch of someone's sleeve. She quickly faced the blazing fireplace and noticed her vision seemed blurred to the left of the stones. Illuminated by the glow of the fire, a watery quiver began to materialize, and Baillie grabbed the bed's poster with both hands, holding herself up. The image struggled to become solid, and Baillie watched in fascination.

A man of above average height and muscular build, wearing a kilt and sash of a familiar blue and green plaid, appeared. Under the plaid sash, a vest with leather strappings covered a long-sleeved shirt of a light cream-colored material. His long, chiseled legs, covered with leather leggings or boots, were bare above the knees. It was hard to see all the details from the transparent veil of the image. The man had his hands on his hips, and Baillie followed her eyes up into his face, the face of a young man in his late twenties, possibly early thirties, surrounded by wavy strands of thick auburn hair. The hair cascaded past his shoulders—shoulders wide enough to make a woman swoon. She didn't miss the perfect V of his broad shoulders and small waist. His eyes almost twinkled with the glow from the fire, and Baillie felt she might lose herself in their delicious darkness, framed with long, thick lashes. So much more than the grainy black-and-white image she had been given.

Yet the incredible sight of a ghostly gorgeous male in front of her was pushing the limits of her remaining consciousness. She could barely see the outline of fireplace stones now behind the spirit; he was standing right there in front of her, smiling, a breath of merriment in his face.

"William Andrew Kai Robert Baillie the fourth, my lady." The man bowed deeply at the waist as locks of thick curls fell forward off his shoulders, holding the chivalrous position for more than a second, then rose slowly to his full height.

"I, um, I'm glad to finally see...uh, meet you," Baillie said as she backed up a fraction more away from him. "I think," she mumbled. The vision in front of her took her breath away in more ways than one.

"Ye can truly see me now?" His accent washed over her in deep, cautious, baritone waves.

*Sean Connery, eat your heart out.* "Uh, yes." She couldn't get her mouth to work correctly. Now that the initial shock had passed, Baillie was ready to throttle herself for acting like a blushing teenager. "You're still a little watery around the edges, but yes, I can see you, sir, Mr. Baillie, uh, your majesty."

"Ye needn't be so formal, lass. Those close to me called me Kai." He nodded toward the fireplace. "I dinna start the fire so ye would not enjoy its warmth. Would ye not come a wee bit closer to ease the chill from such a long journey?"

Baillie tried letting go of the bedpost, her knuckles aching from her vicious grip. "Uh, thank you. There is quite a chill in this place, here, yes," she rambled. She couldn't break her hold; her hand may be permanently glued right where it was.

A pair of high-back, overstuffed chairs registered in her view though, and she quickly slid into the farthest one from the ghost. Closing her eyes, Baillie surrendered into the corner of the chair, splaying her fingers out in front of her. Every muscle in her body melted into relaxation as the crackling fire provided a sweet lullaby to her weary soul.

Hearing a faint noise, she opened her eyes and saw only the fireplace. She rubbed her tired eyes and looked again. Nothing. Maybe exhaustion had manufactured the gorgeous image of a man in front of her. However, she had heard him give his full name—it couldn't be all in her exhausted imagination. The noise continued and she turned her head, nearly letting out a scream as the ghost appeared behind her, poking at her bag with his foot.

"What does yer strange satchel harbor inside that it needs wheels, my lady?"

Steadying her breath, Baillie squeaked out, "That's my suitcase, and most of them now days have wheels to make traveling easier."

"Where be the rest of ye crates? Surely this isna everything ye own?" His eyebrows raised above his dancing dark eyes. A grin played around the corners of his mouth.

She laughed. "Heavens, no, but enough for a visit. I'm only here for a short while." His face darkened. "I, I didn't know what to expect," Baillie tried soothing his scowl. "I packed light for this journey. I hope this doesn't meet with disapproval?" A gruff snort was all she heard. "I must say you have the old man downstairs convinced you're real. He dumped me outside the door and disappeared," Baillie stood up from the chair. She'd had enough sitting during her travels the last two days and stretched her arms out to the fire. She turned and removed her coat, draping it on the chair.

"Aye, Robbie would no more step into this room than the devil hisself. His wife keeps it tidy now and again."

"They're married?" Baillie forgot the incredible situation of conversing with a ghost for a moment. "She growls at the man, I swear." Biting her bottom lip, she asked with careful words, "Does she see you? Is that why she keeps the room clean?"

"Nay, woman, she fears her husband's tales of bloody ghosts haunting the place but has convinced her own heart if she keeps the room up, I'll not bother her." A slight chuckle came from his direction. "Interesting that she appointed you in this room; she's kept the other owners off in the east wing."

"The others?" Baillie whispered. Her mind raced through ideas of torture and death.

"The owners before ye, though none of them female nor of the New Colony." He came back and stood in front of the fire, staring down at her. He shook his head, his eyes dark. "Ye shouldna have come. Dinna I try to warn ye 'tis dangerous for ya to be here? Have ya not the sense God gives a goat?"

Baillie stood straight, fatigue dropping away like wilted petals. "I'm here of my own free will. The bank declared I was the rightful owner of the castle, and I don't need your permission to evaluate the grounds and the castle proper." She folded her arms across her chest.

He lowered his head. "Aye, the damage be done, I will be respectful. Lass, welcome to me home. 'Tis true, the land be yours now, the place of my youth. Forgive me, I have not had the pleasure of talking to anyone in hundreds of years, let alone a lass, be ye a rather stubborn one."

Kai walked slowly, almost a glide, across the damp-darkened floor of the room. "The years of training and education took their toll on this body over the years. I'd fare make it up the stairs as a lad before collapsing in sleep."

"If your family owned the land, why did you work so hard?"

"The enemy ne'er sleeps, my lady. You must be ready to battle for your land at all times. The clans be many and not always honorable, to say nothing of other countries."

Baillie lowered herself to sit on the edge of the bed. An old dust cover crackled under her weight. "Well, looks like they left your original sheets on this thing. I think I just broke the material." She stood up and grabbed the ancient sheath. The dank odor of forgotten bare threads filled her nostrils as she yanked the cover up and off the oversized bed. Underneath was a layer of discolored maroon silk brocade sewn into a royal quilt. An embroidered family crest decorated the center of the bed. "Oh, my. How beautiful."

"Lass, ye terrorize this room like a ram in glory among a field of ewes. Be careful what you grab, you know not what lies underneath." Kai gave a sad, half smile as he looked over her shoulder at the bedraggled bedclothes of his past. "No one's been given to stay in this room nigh all these years. Putney's charm made it unpardonable of anyone to enter such a fine room of the family. Highly odd she changed that dogged will of hers for the likes of you."

Running her hand over the cold silkiness, Baillie said, "I think the dynamic duo downstairs is hoping I'll be frightened into leaving by putting me in the ghost wing."

He snorted.

An extensive yawn snuck up on her. "Excuse me, jet lag has settled into these old bones. It's way past my bedtime in one time zone or another."

His face flushed in the firelight. "Ye must be weary after such a long journey. How selfish I have been this evening. I shall take my leave then." His eyes took on a pensive sadness.

Baillie curled up next to the ornate headboard and noticed his hesitation. "What is it?"

"Introductions have not truly been completed, lass," he said, opening a hand toward her.

"Heavens, I'm sorry, it's Baillie. I just assumed you knew that from your time in the shop."

He blew out a breath. "Aye, and something has troubled me since first I met ye, lassie. Why do all the good folks around ye call ye such? Do heathens live in the New World that they can't call a fine woman as yourself by her Christian name?"

Giggles escaped before she slapped her hand over her mouth. "Sorry, I guess that's a decent question coming from, well, from your standards. My name is Catharine Baillie." She thought a minute. "My blessed mother, when a young girl, loved an old black-and-white movie called *Wuthering Heights* and named me after the leading character, Catharine. Mom thought it was an incredibly romantic thing to do. I'm more inclined to think of the concept as a curse."

"What be a movie?"

"Um, a story, like a play, you can see and hear any time. See, the storyline of *Wuthering Heights* comes from an Emily Brontë book of the same name. The actors portray the story once, and it is captured on film. Hmm, film's even more difficult to describe. Geez, like the television, the box you've seen in the house where I live. You've been upstairs in my living quarters, haven't you?" She held her breath, not sure she wanted to know.

Kai ignored the question. "Aye, you speak of the talking black box that yammers back at ye at night. Many people talking at once, blasting continual noise—it's a bloody nuisance."

"Yes, that's it, a lot of noise and not always substance to it. Anyway, back to the movie. I hate the name Catharine, have ever since I was a little girl. It sounds like some ancient, dried-up duchess. And when I got older and watched the movie myself, I didn't like that Catharine was rather mean and selfish. I made everyone and anyone call me Baillie or rue the day the C name crossed their lips."

"I kinna address a woman as yourself in such an unholy manner." Kai's beautiful eyes clouded in a mask of concern, and he lowered his long lashes. "I've seen yer wrath against mere mortals, woman, and I'll not tempt me own fate by using Catharine to address ye. I can't be callin' ya Woman now, either, when I need your attention. What is a poor man to do?"

Baillie wrinkled her nose. Who'd have thought her name would be a problem after fifty some years? She rubbed a finger gently against her nose. "Well, my middle name is Anne. I was born Catharine Anne Baillie the first, one summer's eve. Anne is rather neutral, I guess. I could live with that."

"Anne? Ye not much of a staunch Anne in my book." The man stood a moment, staring into her eyes until she looked away. "But now, Annie. Aye, that'll do. Annie," his voice deepened to a baritone as he repeated the name a second time in a husky whisper.

An unexpected heat crossed her tired face at his silky voice caressing a part of her birth name. She couldn't remember the last time a man had made her tingle with such intimacy. Where was a fan when you need one? She looked up.

"Annie, yer cheeks be looking like two sweet flowers at dawn. I kinna imagine a more beautiful color for a rose." A slow, lazy smile came to his lips. "Aye, ye be Annie Rose to me now." He reached a hand out and softly brushed back a wisp of hair from her face. She shivered under his touch. "Ye stubborn wench, now ye blush like the roses themselves."

"You are truly here." She felt herself tremble from a combination of a childish fear of ghosts and sexual wonderment at his caress. "Not a figment of my imagination after all those months at the bookstore."

"I say ye speak your heart through your eyes. Words need not be spoken to be heard, lass." His eyes twinkled with wicked pleasure as he slowly bowed deep at the waist and stepped away. "I'll bid you good night, sweet Annie," he said and disappeared.

# Chapter Seventeen

Someone had opened the heavy drapes, Baillie noticed, as the room was now saturated in weak sunlight. The fire had been fed, and the room felt toasty warm. Who had done this was the question. A tray holding a teapot and cup and saucer sat on the small table where she'd left the candle—must have been Miss Putney. Baillie stretched her arms over her head. She'd obviously slept soundly. She hadn't heard the woman come in or leave.

Rolling to her side, away from the closed door, she stared up at the three arch-shaped windows. The decorative glass was patterned in fist-sized squares set in black iron. The bottom of the window looked to be four or five feet from the floor. No worry of peeping Toms in these windows. Beyond the glass she watched the cool, gray clouds move across the sky. *I spent the night in a castle*, she mused. *I own this castle!*

A deep sigh and a long stretch followed before she decided it was time to get up. Wrapping her robe around her, she poured a cup of the lukewarm tea and nestled into the same high-back chair from last night, enjoying the fire.

She felt decadent with no work ahead of her, no store to open or customers to help. When was the last time she'd sat relaxed, curled up with a morning cup of tea? No television, no radio, not even a phone ringing. Just elegant, rich silence spiked with the snap of wood in the fire.

"Be ye decent, woman?" His soft voice tickled her ear.

She jumped, holding tight to the cup and saucer. "Unless you have both your eyes covered, you already know the answer." Baillie tried to act irritated, but her anticipation of spending more time with the good-looking spirit gave her away.

With a quick wave of energy, Kai appeared in front of her. "Good morrow, my lady. I came to tell you I shall wait for you outside the castle door for a walk among the grounds."

At first Baillie tightened her lips at Kai's casual demand. How dare he just expect her to follow at his beck and call? Then his words sank in. "I have grounds," she smiled at his startled face. "It sounds so regal, *grounds*. Not just a fenced back yard or an acre of apple trees. I have grounds." She rolled the *r*.

He raised an eyebrow, and she giggled. "This is all so bizarre, forgive me. I mean no disrespect. Truly." The giggles continued. *And I'm talking to a gorgeous, kilt-wearing ghost!*

"Hmm, so ye say. The land is quite narrow in spots, spacious for meters in others covering the moors. I dinna mean we would cover it all this day, just a walk around the moat, more a lay of the immediate area with ye. I havena had the opportunity with the others who came before ye; no one has been attuned to meself. I have much to say if ye care to listen."

"I'd like that. Give me an hour or so. I'd like to dress and unpack first."

"Aye, as you wish." After a deep bow, Kai disappeared.

• • •

Baillie blinked in the glare of sunlight from the doorway, excited for the chance to roam the grounds. Miss Putney had wrapped a warm scone in a cloth napkin and handed it to her without a word as she'd headed for the door. The pastry was crumbly and filling.

Kai walked alongside her as she ventured out the kitchen door. The air felt damp and smelled of earth and sweetness as they walked over the bridge. Everything looked fresh, inviting in the light of day, not terrifying in the least. The water below still looked dark, yet not sinister or menacing. *It's a moat*, she thought with a smile. The word almost brought a giggle, but Baillie forced herself to calm down. She popped a bit of scone in her mouth as she stared at Kai beneath her lowered lashes. *Could the man look more dashing?* His long, flowing hair moved away from his shoulders with the breeze. Time went into slow motion for Baillie, like a commercial for expensive men's aftershave, as she took in the full look of this Highlander. Thick muscles looked ripped under the material of his shirt, his upper arms bulging. His calf muscles tight as cement…she stopped her imagination from going up his legs any further.

The sides of the moat were surprisingly straight. She visually followed the straight line to the perfectly square corner of the building. Amazed at the mechanics of an exact sizing built by people hundreds of years ago, she hesitated in thought. A gruff sigh tore her back from the daydream.

"Have ya not seen a moat before? Ya stare at the water like a man dying of thirst."

They walked toward the front of the castle. Here, Baillie could see the individual mottled bricks on the outside walls, some cracked with age. She wanted to run her hand over the ancient stone. At the front corner, a turret column stood tall with dried vine branches spread like long, jagged fingers across the face.

Baillie stepped to the front area and squealed. "Oh, my stars, it really is a castle! With turrets like King Arthur and the Knights of the Round Table." She bounced on her toes.

Kai shook his head. "Do ya have bedbugs, woman? Ya canna stand still."

She strained her head back to see the top of the castle. "Not good enough," she whispered and dashed off in the other direction. Kai popped up next to her as she turned and put her fists on her hips. Awed at the brilliant sunrays bathing the entire castle in golden light, she pulled her cell phone from her pocket to snap a photo. Kai peeked over her shoulder, seeing the image frozen on the screen.

"What did you do?" he asked suspiciously.

"I snapped a picture. Like a camera." His confused face told her she wasn't getting through. "Uh, in the past an artist would paint an image on canvas. Then man invented cameras, where you could capture an image in a machine. Now, my phone can also act like a camera and take photos."

"That miniature box is a phone? Nay, woman, I've heard Putney call the mechanical box she uses in the kitchen now and again a phone. How can that be?"

"It's complicated, trust me, but I can talk on this, too." Turning her back on Kai, she continued to study the castle and sighed. "It's like a fairy tale, Kai. If I don't take pictures, I feel like I'll wake up tomorrow and all of this will have been a dream."

She snapped half a dozen more shots of the outside and one of the wooden bridge to the front gate. Then, walking with a spring in her step, she took some of the moat. She paused for a moment and sniffed the air.

"Aye, we have gardens, Annie. Ye won't find any better in the county. Some o' these shrubs go back to my mother's day, planted when I was but a wee bairn. Others are probably planted by my grandmother or great-grandmother."

"But the aroma seems rather strong for this time of year."

"Putney dries some of the blooms, as those before her have done. It may be the lavender you smell; seems the strongest of the lot."

He led her back toward the bridge to the kitchen and then veered off to the left. Baillie practically skipped to keep up with his long strides as they came up over a slight rise to a colorful patch.

"I never knew there would be such a large garden." She walked down a thin gravel path mere yards from the castle door. Kai guided her into a well-tended park. The sizes and colors of dark green stalks with varieties of dahlias dazzled her.

"Dahlias! Oh my, look at them." Baillie reached out and gently touched one of the blooms, the stalk as tall as her chin. "So vibrant with different colors! And over there, the sturdy chrysanthemums—how lovely they look. Now this yellow fellow I am not familiar with, Kai. What is this ground cover growing all through here?" Baillie pointed at the yellow petals.

"That be whin, or gorse, some call it, woman."

"Ah, and thistle, of course, what an incredible array of autumn color. I love this."

"Take care as ye walk the grounds," Kai spoke from behind her. Baillie turned. "I apologize, but I've a matter of importance to attend to this morning. Forgive my short absence as your host." His body bent into a dramatic bow before he disappeared from view.

"He comes and goes so quickly here." Stepping further into the garden, Baillie pinched herself. *Could this be really mine?* she wondered as she walked along a well-worn path between shoulder-height stalks of dahlias. The fresh, brisk air prickled her lungs—a damp chill very similar to home in the Northwest.

A piercing scream shattered the silence. Not a panicked, criminal sound—more animal than human, she felt. Horses. Curious, she changed course, retracing her steps back toward the moat, and headed toward the low-level building behind the gardens. The path dropped down three shallow steps as the ground fell in a gentle slope. Again, a horse's challenging trill cried out, and Baillie felt the call deep in her soul. Drawn by the sound, Baillie walked quickly to the stable's open wooden doors. Equestrian aromas of hay, manure and damp earth assaulted her as she stepped inside. She stood in the cold shadow, letting her eyes adjust to the gloom.

Baillie noticed a slight young man bent over, mucking out an empty stall. Between the doorway and the energetic stable hand, a glistening black horse hung its head over a stall gate. Baillie shrank against the stone wall behind her. The beast towered over the gate;

she'd never seen such a huge specimen of a horse. The puck-sized black eyes, nestled among the long, dark forelocks, bore through her like an icicle, sharp and clear. The majestic head lifted up, and the horse let out another blood-curdling cry. The noise vibrated in the barn, amplified in the enclosed space.

The young man paused, his back to Baillie, and said, "Aye, Dougal, you and I agree, but complainin' will do no good. No good a'tall with this bunch."

Baillie gasped in surprise, as the voice was definitely female. Baillie slapped a chilled hand over her mouth, but it was too late. The thin girl swung around, holding the pitchfork as a ninja might hold a vicious weapon, threatening, defensive. Piercing dark eyes glared at her.

Baillie raised both hands in surrender. She stuttered, "I…I'm sorry. I heard this sound, this scream, while walking outside. I wanted to see what kind of creature…" Her voice faded into nothing at the girl's fierce stare. Why did she seem to put her foot in her mouth with every staff member she ran into? "I didn't mean to refer to the horse as a creature. Not like some Loch Ness monster or anything. The cry just seemed so penetrating and…and Godzilla like." Baillie shrugged her shoulders, failing miserably to explain herself. She dropped her hands, palms up.

The girl, her pale face framed by wisps of short brown hair and streaked where sweat had mixed with the dust and dirt on her cheeks, stared another second or two. Then she turned back to her work. She mumbled something as the pitchfork jabbed into the debris on the floor. Baillie hesitated whether to introduce herself or leave while she had the chance.

Leaving won. Baillie ducked out into the sunshine, gulping in air and rubbing her hands together. Another fine mess she'd made on a first impression. She was batting a thousand. Might as well tattoo "American" across her forehead.

• • •

Sally picked up the phone by the second ring. "Pen and Pages, may I help you?"

Baillie felt a rush hearing the familiar voice from home. She missed her shop and people who liked her. "Pack up and send the rest of my things, Sally. I'm staying here," she announced loudly.

"Over my dead body," Sally squealed into the phone. "Oops, sorry, I didn't mean dead, you know like dead people and ghosts or anything. I didn't mean to talk about dead, uh, things." Baillie could hear her sigh even thousands of miles away. "Let me start again. How are you? How was the trip—you obviously got there all right?"

"Fine, fine, and yes. This place is incredible! You should see the gardens outside. I didn't expect so much foliage. I thought castle grounds would be stark, barren…you know, just bare ground and grass."

"Girl, your *Wuthering Heights* movie was in black and white. How would you know about color in Scotland? You are so naïve. I told you to stop watching those old movies nonstop. It's distorted any perception you have of reality."

"It is a little overwhelming. I feel like Dorothy when she first stepped into Oz and you see all this color, honest to God. They have stalks as tall as I am of colored dahlias and tons of floral-ness stuff. It's beautiful. At first it looks like somebody threw out a gallon of wildflower seeds, then as you walk between the islands, you see there are designs, a method to the gardener's madness. Somebody planted, like, friggin' patterns in the ground. Who has time for that?"

"Is there a dungeon?"

"Yeah, like that's the first question I'm going to ask when I arrive. The staff already looks at me like I have horns growing out of my head. I don't think they quite know what to make of an American for an employer," she snapped.

"Hey, I was just curious. You're my first castle baron."

"Sorry, I'm not myself right now."

"Tell me everything you can until the next customer shows up."

Baillie took a sip of tea and snuggled back against the feather pillows on her bed. She'd asked for her supper in her room, and the warm dumplings had soothed her. Comfort food, her favorite. The fire flickered in the dark room, pushing the gloom to the sides of the gray walls with its yellow glow. For thousands of years people surrounded flames for warmth and protection. The gods of fire reigned in people's minds. Kai was not a god, yet his presence affected her almost as much.

"Guess what the taxi driver told me at the train station? You'll never believe it."

Gripping the phone, Baillie rattled on about the details of her journey. She held back the story of Kai appearing in her room, though. *No way am I ready to let go of that news yet.*

• • •

Kai appeared at the end of the call just as she hung up the phone, cutting the link to home and friendly people.

"Ye sound sad, Annie. May I be of any service?"

She stared at the muscular vision in front of her. How could she focus on a wisp of homesickness with a hunk of gorgeous Scotsman standing silhouetted by the glow of firelight?

His worried look blurred in shadow; she ignored the note of concern in his voice and let her eyes drink in his beauty, soothing the minor pangs for familiar surroundings, probably from a lack of Diet Coke.

A gruff snort woke her from her imaginations. "Sorry, yes, you remember Sally, who works at my shop? Everything is okay, and I guess it's just she's doing fine without me. I didn't expect the place to fall apart, but it's like I'm not needed."

"Ye've been here a wee less than two days."

Baillie forced a smile. "Well, that's true." She played with her cell phone, keeping her eyes down. "I don't know where this melancholy is coming from," she mumbled. "Maybe it's just being childish. I don't think I've made a very good impression with the staff."

Kai turned his back to her, moving to the fireplace, his broad, still shoulders blocking the majority of light into the room. The silence was broken only by the crackle of wood.

Baillie scrambled from under the covers, wrapping her robe tightly around her against the chill, and quickly walked in front of Kai. She stared into his black eyes, seeing the flames reflected in their darkness. "Kai, I'm sorry. This is all so bizarre for me. Dang, I keep saying that to you." She slapped her hand to her cheek. "I'm famous for putting my foot in my mouth when it comes to expressing my feelings or saying the right thing. I have no tact genes. I've certainly been doing it since I got here." She reached out her hand but stopped short of trying to touch his arm.

"Aye, this must seem primitive to you," he said, his tone as cold as the room.

"Well, maybe once the electricity is back on, right? Miss Putney said tomorrow sometime." She curled up in her now favorite chair, and Kai settled across from her. He filled the entire chair. "I must sound like a spoiled brat to you. I'm used to people smiling at me; I don't mean to pout. We lose power during storms where I live, and I've done my share of camping by candlelight in the house. But it was my home. I knew all the nooks and crannies, and that the lights and heat would be back soon. You've seen how many lamps I have in the shop and my apartment—I don't like darkness.

And I didn't bring my bottle of Vitamin D." She tucked her legs under her body, enjoying the warmth of the fire. "And, you're the only one talking to me. I met a young woman at the stables after leaving the garden, and I thought she was going to bite my head off. I don't mess with angry people holding pitchforks."

Kai broke into laughter, a loud, lustful noise, and Baillie couldn't stop her own giggles. "The girl scared the soup out of me." Her odd phrase sent Kai into another spasm of laughter, dispersing any lingering tension in the room. "I heard this scream coming out of the stable and went investigating. Have you seen that horse in there? Oh my gawd, it was enormous! What did she call him, Doogie?"

"Dougal," Kai chuckled. "His name means dark stranger."

"Well, that was a good choice."

"And I apologize for the lack of introductions to the staff. The young girl be named Rogue."

"Rogue, what an interesting name for a girl. Is that wild black thing Rogue's horse?"

"He's a fine horse that belonged to the owner before you." A scowl crossed his face, the firelight showing deep crevices between his brows. "'Tis a mystery I canna understand. The man was found dead months ago, fallen, nay thrown, from the sea cliffs. I saw no boot marks near the edge. Dougal came back in as if a banshee had attacked him. Crazed, frothing from his bit." Kai's voice dropped as he seemed to consider something. "Rogue feared someone had tampered with his feed, that he'd been drugged, poisoned."

Baillie blinked.

"I must take my leave, my lady. You will be exhausted and need your sleep." He stood up, making Baillie tilt her head.

His face was still distant from their conversation, his eyes seeing something far away.

"Yes, it has been a long day." She twisted the end of her sash, wishing she could erase his concern. It made her nervous, less safe. "Will you walk with me in the morning?"

"Aye, Annie. 'Til the morrow," he said and bowed deeply before disappearing.

• • •

The soft clink of a breakfast tray on the table cut through her veil of sleep. Baillie rubbed her eyes and worked to sit up in the thick, soft mattress. "Good morning, Miss Putney."

A grunt sounded as the woman turned to stoke the fire back into life.

"Is it supposed to rain today?" Baillie fought with the sleeve of her robe. "I figure yesterday's sun was more of a fluke for my benefit." She stopped. Her words sounded rude somehow. "I mean I'm grateful for the nice weather," she added, her voice slowing to nothing.

The older woman said not a word but shuffled over and threw open the drapes. Rivulets of rain cascaded down the closed windows. She turned toward the room, her massive hands on her hips.

"Oh," Baillie giggled. "Well, there it is then. Thank you for the breakfast."

"Will ye be needing anything more?" Putney's words were sharp.

"No, thank you. This is lovely, truly. I'm not used to room service," she said as she poured milk into her cup.

"No more than respect, ma'am. The landowner has responsibilities; no need starting on an empty stomach." And with that, Putney left the room, closing the door behind her.

"That's the most I've heard her say at one time." Baillie poured the tea and took her cup to her chair.

"Aye, ye'll win her heart soon enough."

Baillie squealed at the deep sound of Kai's voice. "Don't you knock?" She tugged at the edge of her robe, covering her knees.

"'Tis a wee damp this morning, so I came to ask yer plans for the day."

Sipping the warm liquid soothed her fast-beating heart. "Well, sounds like today would be perfect to explore," she paused, "the inside." His face broke into a crooked grin. "You can show me around your castle and all the secret passageways and hidden doors."

Arching his eyebrows he asked, "I thought my lady had ne'er stepped on the Highlands. Ye seem acquainted with our architecture quite enough."

Baillie giggled before she could stop it. *I sound like a simpering teenager.* "Cross my heart, it's more like watching too many movies with castles and gargoyles, I'm afraid."

"Again with the moving pictures? What about real life, Annie?" He dropped into the facing chair, his hair tied back with a piece of worn leather. "Do ya not explore and travel in the New World of yours?"

"New world? Oh, America—no, not really. It's such a large country, literally stretched out between the Pacific and Atlantic oceans. I'm a West Coast girl. Though I visited New York once for a book exposition and couldn't get home fast enough. The constant noise twenty-four/seven drove me crazy."

"Twenty-four sevens?" He scratched his head, shaking a curl loose.

"Sorry, it's a popular expression meaning all the time, twenty-four hours a day, seven days a week. Traffic, noise, horns, people, sirens—I was exhausted from the intense city lifestyle."

Silence filled the room. Baillie finished her tea and stared at the bottom of the cup. If only she knew how to read tea leaves. "I guess I better change into something warm for my tour."

"Change?" Kai asked in confusion. She looked down at her robe, clearing her throat. "Oh, I see, ye mean dress." He stood and muttered something about scouting ahead as he vanished.

A sigh escaped Baillie. “Get ahold of yourself; you’re twice his age,” she snickered. “Sort of.” The room felt hollow and empty when he was gone.

Baillie poured water into a basin and carefully added a hot rock from the fireplace. She refused to wash in cold water. Miss Putney brought in fresh water twice a day, and Baillie appreciated the tenacity of the woman to carry food trays up those stairs every day. But while she wasn’t overly conscientious about her over-fifty skin routine, there were limits.

Yesterday she asked the old man, Robbie, for the bathroom locations. She’d used the one near the kitchen area but there had to be others. He’d offered brief tales about the renovations during the forties where the owner had installed one or two modern receptacles per floor. The rooms are easily discovered, he explained, as their doors were modern paneled wood with doorknobs.

Grabbing a bite of scone, Baillie pulled a pair of pants and a sweater from the armoire. She sniffed, picking up a sweet scent. She pressed the clothes to her nose, inhaling deeply. “That’s not my fabric softener.” She opened the carved wooden door again and noticed flower petals tucked in the corners. “Nice touch, Miss Putney.”

By the time she reached the main floor, the shadows had disappeared in the room. Lights! The electricity had returned. Baillie turned slowly and realized there were wall sconces every few feet, double candle-shaped bulbs that brightened the area and gave the castle a much more homey feeling. The ceiling, lost in the gloom before, was made of carved panels stretched overhead, now revealed from hidden track lighting pointed upward. She sighed at its beauty.

One thing she’d noticed yesterday and more so this morning was the amount of drapery. The castle architect had many high-vaulted windows in some rooms, while others had ornate and beautiful windows with wide sills at waist level. She’d found a favorite spot in a drawing room where the windows made a corner nook. Standing there, she could see the moat below and the grounds full of trees and shrubbery. A most peaceful view, she felt it fill her heart with an odd longing.

"Such a perfect view," Kai's deep voice caressed her ear. "I see ye've discovered one of my favorite spots, woman. I kept a writing desk here in my day."

Baillie didn't startle at his nearness. An intimate urge to lean back into what should be a warm, solid frame of manliness nearly swept her backward. Would he catch her if she started to lean back? She had no doubt.

"Come with me," he whispered. "Let me show ye my home."

After hours of following Kai through decorative archways of carved wood, down circular levels of stone stairs, and up short flights of wooden stairs, Baillie wondered if she shouldn't have left bread crumbs for a trail back to their starting point. Kai, swept up in the excitement of sharing the nooks and crannies of his childhood home, didn't notice the trickle of sweat at her temples. She hadn't exercised this much in years. They must have traveled miles inside these thick, cold walls. And nothing looked familiar—or different. Maybe mustier and damper at times, with different paintings on the walls, but the gray stone walls, all mixed with beautiful wood-paneled walls and walkways, were blurring together.

"Enough, stop," Baillie called out, no breath left to laugh at the absurdity of chasing a young ghost throughout the castle. "Take me outside, rain or no. I need fresh air." She ruffled her polyester sweater away from her damp skin.

Within moments Kai pulled open closed drapes to reveal a large wooden door and pressed against it to the outside world. Baillie tripped over the edge of the doorsill. Kai grabbed for her, and Baillie felt the instant cold from the shop. She gasped at the sudden remembrance of his touch. "You touched me in the shop," she whispered.

"Aye, I fought so bloody hard to get through to ye. The most I could do was lay a hand on your arm or your back now and again to get your attention. Bloody limited."

Baillie's teeth started chattering, and Kai released her, realizing she had her balance. She gulped in the warmer outside air, which felt like a sauna compared to his touch. She shoved her sleeves up to her elbows.

"Come, there's a place to sit just beyond those trees." Kai led her down a muddy path.

Baillie craned her neck to look around. There seemed to be enclosed, gray walls around them. She didn't see the moat anywhere. "Where is this place?"

"A spit of a courtyard some ancestor had built inside the castle. There is a larger one if ye come out the north side—it's a way of being outside yet protected. Though walls protect this from the outside, there was probably once a garden nestled in these walls. I hid many an afternoon here away from my studies." He pulled a long, white handkerchief from somewhere and wiped a spot for her. Slumping onto the wet concrete bench was not her finest hour. "Ye look worn, Annie. I apologize for my exuberance in showing off my home. I havena had a soul to talk to all these years, and I feel like a young boy showing off his prize. I dinna mean to harm ye."

"Just give me a minute. Harm? Heavens, no, don't think such a thing. Just winded." She pulled her hair off her sweaty neck. "Kai?"

"Aye, my lady?"

"You came through much worse trials finding your way to the shop to make contact with me. You wanted to warn me of the castle."

The man turned his broad back to her, leaning against a low, thick branch. "Aye, for the good it did."

"What were you warning me of? The staff doesn't seem vicious, except maybe the girl in the stables."

"There is evil close by." Kai's voice became low and dark, like a rumble of faraway thunder.

She shivered and rubbed her upper arms. "I don't understand. You're frightening me."

"I dinna mean to sound the bells of doom, but it is best ye keep yer wits about you. There are those nearby waiting to destroy ye."

She swallowed noisily. "Like what happened to the last owner?" she forced out. "The cab driver made it sound like he hadn't lived here very long before he died and then…was the horse deliberately drugged?"

Nodding his head, Kai came back and sat beside her. She wanted to grab his hand and plead for quick answers. Instead, she waited as Kai settled and, bending his head down close to his chest, told her stories that chilled her heart.

# Chapter Eighteen

"Good heavens, woman, the girls have been beside themselves. It's been forever since you left. Why haven't you called?" Baillie heard a distinct pout. "I should hang up on you immediately for neglecting me."

"Sorry, I've been a tad busy figuring out this castle lifestyle. I know exactly zippity-do-dah about anything over here. Who knew I'd have a motley collection of staff members? It's amazing—me, with servants."

"You own a castle, my dear, of course it should come fully equipped with all the essentials. You know, pool boy, chef, masseuse…"

"Gillian," Baillie scolded, feeling her shoulders relax. She should have called her friend earlier and deserved his sarcasm.

"How is the land of bare-legged, barbaric men in tight skirts treating you?"

"Gillian, kilts are not tight. I could see you over here praying for a windy day—which it is, by the way, every day. And you would be sorely disappointed, love. Those heavy woolen drapes with the weird thing-a-ma-bobs in front keep the material right where it covers the most." She heard a lustful sigh on the other end.

Baillie smiled as the familiar voice washed over her in a wave of everything Northwest. She suddenly felt a riptide of loneliness—not enough to drown in self-pity but enough to flounder for a moment. So many years she'd been contently rooted between the shop and her minimalist home life. It didn't take much to make her day—a glance out the window at the fir trees, a flash of blue from a Steller's Jay, or a rainbow painted on thick, gray clouds as a brief sunbreak opened in the skies. She didn't need adventure to be happy. What was she thinking? A passport would magically make her someone worldly?

"I didn't call to talk about tartan fashion. There's something terribly wrong over here. I talked with Kai and…"

Gillian broke in like a New York detective. "Who's Kai?"

Baillie frowned for a few seconds before taking the plunge. "My ghost, Lord Baillie."

"You've talked with your ghost?" Crackling noises through the phone sounded like Gillian was trying to force his way into the receiver. "Are you serious?"

"Uh, yeah. Seems I'm sleeping in his old room, like from three hundred years ago. I guess the staff thought they'd scare the soup out of me in the haunted bedroom and I'd go running back to America on the next plane. Funny, I know being an American woman has thrown them for a loop, but I'm all they've got right now between staying here and being kicked out. I guess I'd be defensive too. I can't blame them."

"You're on a first-name basis with your ghost?"

"He said to call him Kai. Anyway, he's been filling me in on some stories about this vicious banker guy who thinks he should own the castle, and it is uh-gah-ly."

"Ooh, tell me more, girl, don't hold back one delicious drop of juicy details. The girls are going to bleed me dry for this. Rafael has nearly worn a hole in the entryway carpet pacing each day waiting to hear from you."

"Do tell him and T-Cup I'm sorry for not calling sooner. I'm not used to jet lag, you know. And then when Kai introduced himself—"

"Shut up!" Gillian screamed, interrupting her. "You've seen him? Tell me what your ghost looks like this very minute. Anything like that grainy photocopied image or Haunted Mansion resident?" The phone crackled again as Gillian shifted to get more comfortable. Baillie could imagine his long legs draped over the arm of an expensive executive chair.

"Beyond your wildest dreams gorgeous. He's oh-my-gawd good-looking and more." Tall, dark and mysterious, how did she get so lucky in the phantom realm? "Listen, I don't want to tell you everything over the phone. I'm not positive this medieval castle isn't bugged for sound. Just because everything looks old doesn't mean it is."

"So there are some modern conveniences? I've imagined you next to a spinning wheel."

"Ancestors have spent millions on restoration and upgrades around here. But I'm not sure someone's not standing outside my door or something. The wood weighs a hundred pounds, but I don't have a clue how soundproof it is. Grab your computer, and I'll send you some of the unbelievable goings-on from before I got here."

"My little lost child of reality, what are you babbling about? I am always Wi-Fi-ed for action day or night, even while babysitting your shop."

In the background, Baillie could already hear the rhythm of his fingers hitting the keys on the computer. Of course he'd be online; the man made his living from programming. Relief like thick, healing syrup seeped through her, chasing away the chill of danger. She was not alone in this Gaelic mess of mayhem anymore. The briefest touch of the mouse on her laptop would link her to Gillian.

"Lead the way, my frenzied lady of the heather."

"Thanks, Gillian. Give me the net address you showed me right before we went to the Renaissance faire. We need something really secure. Then give me a few minutes after we hang up to plug things in over here. I'll send a test message to be sure I've made connection. The castle doesn't have Internet, so my connection is going to be glacier slow, modem style. I have so much to tell you on what Kai's told me." Baillie found the hand holding the phone shaking slightly at the intensity of her need for his help. The satellite link back to America and normalcy meant everything.

"Get off the phone then, dear. I'll be waiting here with bated breath for you to tickle me with your delicious Scottish flings. And yes, everything is just fine here, since you didn't bother to ask," he pouted.

Baillie snorted. "I never had any doubts. There wouldn't dare be a problem at the shop with you and Sally around. I knew I left it in the most qualified of manicured hands. Bye and keep your fingers crossed this works, Gillian. I need you to come through for me."

"Darling, I'll handle everything."

Baillie sighed as she tapped the hang-up button. She unfolded herself from the high-backed chair and bent over her suitcase, pulling out an old, worn leather case. She set the laptop up on the wooden writing table, running her hand over the polished top, wondering if Kai had written love letters by the light of a candle, words of romance to a faraway princess. She snapped herself back to the present and plugged in the international electrical adapter she'd bought at AAA. Her laptop beeped and clicked into business.

"What kind of magic is this?" the familiar deep voice spoke in her ear.

Baillie stifled a shrill scream and grabbed her chest. "Kai, can you make a noise or something when you enter the room? You scared me half to death." She immediately crossed her legs tight. Fear adrenaline had coursed through her quickly, and she'd nearly peed herself. Catching her breath, Baillie wondered how much of this was from the sudden fright or her reaction to his presence.

"Ye bring a box of lights and noise with you? Are ye a sorceress?" Kai braced his legs apart with a scowl etched into his face, and Baillie's heart fluttered at the fierceness of the look.

"Hardly. It's…" Baillie wondered how to explain without appearing more like a witch. "You've seen the electric lights installed in the castle. And I'm sure you've heard Putney's radio now and again, the box where music comes from or someone talking about the latest news?"

"Aye, times have changed greatly."

"Oh, and do you remember at my shop back home there was a monitor on the counter? A screen with lights and colors similar to this? This is a mini version of that. Sit behind me and watch. I can write to Gillian—you remember the blond young man with me at the faire and later at the séance? In Washington? He'll answer back without fear of anyone listening to the conversation. I can't trust the staff just yet, Kai, though I know you believe dearly in them. Someone here could be working with the banker."

Her fingers flew across the plastic keys to open her Internet access and email. Kai's face leaned close to her, though she felt no warmth, no husky smells of having the man so close.

"Lady Catharine?" came Gillian's first message.

"Cute. Real cute, Fashion Boy. Watch it," Baillie typed back and hit enter.

"Fashion Boy?" Kai made a guttural sound of disgust. "The man with the yellow hair was my age, was he not? You think of me as a mere boy?"

"No, sorry, it's just an expression in my country—a joke, that's all, since he called me the C name." She could feel the testosterone level rising fast in the room.

A window popped up. "Give it up, girl. Tell me everything," appeared on the screen.

Baillie dumped paragraph after paragraph of what Kai had told her onto the screen. She purposefully ignored any description of Kai himself with the spirit looking over her shoulders. Her fingers flew across the keys—thank God for her typing teacher—and it didn't take long to bring Gillian up to speed. She smacked the enter key when she finished.

Baillie rubbed the back of her neck.

Kai leaned close. "Ye remembered everything well from our discussion, woman. What will this accomplish, giving this man, Gillian, the information? He's far from our isle." His hand, which was gripping the back of her chair, felt cooling on her tense muscles as she leaned back. She sucked in a quick breath as delicious tingles ran down her back.

She tried to focus on the screen and not the gorgeous hunk next to her. "Gillian will Google the banker and run an initial investigation of him, see what we can dig up."

"Google? What form of magic is Google?"

Baillie laughed. "A very wise and powerful white magic. I'd be lost without it."

• • •

Wafts of fresh baking dough called Baillie to the kitchen like a siren's song. Her mouth watered before she crossed through the doorway. *Biscuits and cookies or scones, oh my*, she thought. But instead of home-baked freshness, the kitchen air seemed charged with an intensity she couldn't place. Rogue stood at the sink scrubbing her hands.

"Excuse me, Miss Putney, I didn't mean to intrude. I couldn't resist the aroma of whatever you're baking." Baillie watched the cook's hands as she scooped fresh scones off the pan to cool. "Those look scrumptious."

"Aye, it doesn't do a body good to go without on such a rain-soaked day." She brushed her hand on her apron. "Tea kettle's on if ye care to join us for a bit?"

Rogue glared at the cook over her shoulder, drying her hands on a kitchen towel. Silently she tossed it on the counter and walked to the massive oak table. Her plaid shirt was untucked, and a twig of straw stuck to her back. The furniture seemed to dwarf her in size, yet she yanked out a chair with ease.

The girl hunched her shoulders the closer she got to Baillie. It was like watching petals of night-blooming jasmine close in on themselves. Rogue reached for a roll, and Baillie noticed her close-cropped nails. Not broken or split as she'd expect from the labor the girl did, but taken care of. Smiling, she looked up into familiar, piercingly dark eyes. Baillie nearly gasped. She recognized those black twin pools. Rogue had Kai's eyes.

Immediately, Baillie put her head down, scrambling for a butter knife. She didn't want to alienate the girl more than she had or spook her by staring too hard. Her mind bounced around, trying to think of something to say. The weather was boring, and unfortunately, she knew next to nothing about horses. She bit into the end of her roll and groaned in satisfaction. "Oh, my." She swallowed.

Miss Putney's cheeks flushed a rare pink. "'Tis nothin', mum."

Rogue snorted. "Ye lie like the devil," she mumbled through a mouthful. "She usually—"

"Hush yourself," the cook snapped.

Leaning across the table, Baillie asked softly, "What's the story?" Conspiring with Rogue loosened those tense shoulders.

"These be none other than her famous biscuits, mum. Usually we nigh see these but for holidays." Rogue finished one and tore another into pieces, waiting to pop them in her mouth.

A string of Gaelic came from somewhere near the stove.

"So these are special, huh?" Baillie grinned.

"Aye, very," Rogue replied, as she shoved half a roll into her mouth and nosily chewed.

A couple of biscuits disappeared over the edge of the table as Rogue snuck them into her lap.

"And don't be feeding that beast any of my cooking!" Rogue ducked her head at Putney's bark.

"The beast?" Baillie remembered the gigantic black stallion she'd seen her first day. "He's enormous. What did you say his name was?" Settling into her chair, Baillie watched a transformation occur across the table. The more the girl talked about the horse, Dougal, the more she bloomed into a charming personality. The sound of her voice softened almost lyrically as she told of first meeting the charger years ago on the streets.

Baillie tried to calculate Rogue's age. She talked of the last castle owner like a father figure. They came here expecting a long, happy life together. Baillie shook her head at the incredible losses the girl had suffered so young. The cook pulled another tray from the black oven as Robbie wandered in, his suspenders a dark green against a pale-colored shirt. His white hair seemed blown every which way, reminding Baillie of her portrait of Einstein hanging back at the shop.

"And look what the wind blew in," Putney flashed a look across the room. "Aye and next it'll be the ghosts themselves coming after me food."

Baillie choked on the food in her mouth. Rogue ran around the table, pounding her back with the flat of her calloused hand.

"See now what ye've done?" Rogue spoke to no one in particular. "Frightened the poor woman nigh to death." The girl leaned down closer to Baillie's ear. "Did ye not hear the words in town, miss? The castle is haunted."

Reaching for her cup of tea, Baillie stalled answering by sipping the warm liquid, coughing against her scratched throat. Rogue continued smacking against her shoulder blades.

"Enough, child, ye'll knock her senseless," the cook barked. "You know there's no point in shaking a beehive, but what you'll get yourself stung. Let the rubbish rumors lie."

"Haunted?" Baillie squeaked out, a tear trickling down her cheek as she tried to breathe.

Robbie watched Baillie with a penetrating stare, as if she were on display. Was her face giving her away about seeing Kai? Did the old man know? "I, I don't believe much in spooks and restless spirits." Baillie swore the man was boring his way into her soul.

"I believe." Rogue nodded her head. "I seen things move in the dark stables when the ghost thinks I'm sleeping, nigh after midnight. 'Tis true, I've seen it."

Baillie's mouth dropped open.

"Enough with ye and ya wild tales," Putney braced her reddened hands on her hips. "Go and finish yer chores, ya slacker. They won't get done on their own."

Scraping her chair back to the table, Rogue marched out the back door, her head dipped between her slumped shoulders. The room fell into a thick, awkward silence.

Putney mumbled under her breath as she turned back to the stove. Baillie picked up her butter knife and tried avoiding Robbie's stare as she spread the creamy treat over the last bite.

"I'm sure I should be doing something," Baillie started. She squared her shoulders and faced Robbie. "Are there papers to read or review now that I'm here?"

"Hasna the banker not called on ye?" Putney's eyebrows practically disappeared into her gray hair.

"Havena seen a hair o' the man." Robbie leaned back in his chair. "The lass from America showing up on the doorstep seems to have caught him by surprise."

"Really?" Baillie turned toward the cook. "I sent word to his office I was coming. Honest. But I think he expected me to just sign over the family farm without a by your leave."

Chewing on the end of his pipe, Robbie watched her from the end of the table. "Does he now?"

"The first papers I received had stickers and highlight marks showing exactly where to sign for a bill of sale. I have to say, many of my friends pushed for me to make the deal."

"A deal with the devil, it would have been," Putney sniffed.

"That's what it felt like, especially when—" Baillie sat up straighter. She'd come close to spilling the fortuneteller's warning about the castle. Scrambling to change the strategy in her mind, she slowly took a deep breath. "I'd never ventured away from home so far. I didn't even have a passport. I wanted to see where my ancestors came from, you know?"

"Aye, the Baillie blood is strong." Putney nodded her head. The woman pulled out the chair where Rogue had been and settled herself at the table. "Ya seem like a scrappy one, Miss Catharine."

She bit her tongue to keep from cringing. After hearing Kai's distress about being called by her surname, she didn't feel up to explaining things to the older generation. And it was getting a little easier to tolerate the name spoken with such a thick accent.

"You're too kind, Miss Putney." Baillie smiled. "Tell me how you came to be here at the castle. How long have the two of you worked here?"

"As long as time itself, lassie." Robbie looked at his wife. "Herself was practically born and raised in these walls."

"Aye, my mother and hers before have worked at this castle. I took me first steps in this very room chasing after some nonsense or other."

Leaning forward in her chair, Baillie refilled her cup and listened to story after story. A hearty laugh broke out now and then until the couple sighed and squeezed each other's hand.

"Go on, old man, and wash up. I'm needing to get the evening meal to the table."

"May I help?" Baillie scooped up her dishes and took them to the sink. "I can at least set the table."

"If you must." Putney bustled off.

• • •

Before reaching the second set of stairs, Baillie felt Kai's presence beside her. She grinned as she went to nudge him with her elbow, only to have her arm chilled immediately in the empty air.

"That's so not fair," she laughed. "I can't do anything but get frostbite with you."

"Did ye enjoy yourself tonight?" His silky voice wrapped around her heart.

"I did. Robbie and Putney told me such delightful stories of how they met." At the door, Kai opened it for her. A fire crackled in full force inside. "Ah, this is lovely, thank you. It's been a long day."

"At your service, sweet Annie."

She stretched her arms over her head. "I had a chance to talk with Rogue a little at tea."

"Aye?"

"She mentioned she's seen the ghost of the castle." Kai stood still, a statue near the fire. "Late at night in the stables, she's seen things move. That's you, isn't it?"

He gripped the edge of the thick mantle. "I thought the wee wench be asleep. I do visit the horses. Sometimes I miss the feel of the wind in my face and the pure freedom of a good gallop. I canna take Dougal out without the girl knowin'. She practically breathes the same air as the stallion."

"What is that thing?" Baillie curled up in her favorite chair.

"Thing?" The man swelled to twice his size, his voice booming. "Thing? You dare call that magnificent beast…" He couldn't finish.

"Okay, geesh, I'm sorry. You're all so touchy. It's a nice horse."

"*Nice*?" He spat out the word like something foul in his mouth.

"What? What did I say?" And suddenly she was alone. "Kai?" She looked around, nothing. "Seriously? You pull the disappearing card? Dougal's just an oversized horse."

She slid out of the chair and started getting ready for bed. "Never, no matter what century they're from, slander a man's transportation." With a long sigh, she took off the layers of clothes and draped her robe over the end of the bed before crawling under the down-filled covers. Within moments, she was sound asleep.

# Chapter Nineteen

A hollow bell sounded in the distance. What in the world was that? Baillie perked up from a stack of paperwork. Robbie had brought her to the office, a tiny cubicle of a room off the main entry, and showed her where to start familiarizing herself with the castle books and expenses.

Footsteps clicked as Robbie slowly headed toward the front door. At least Baillie assumed it was the front; she still wasn't acclimated with the floor plan. Setting her pen down, she poked her head out to see who her first visitor was.

Murmurs came from the dim entryway. Robbie looked wooden, standing straight, with his hand firmly holding the edge of the door. The old man didn't ooze personality and would never be voted Mr. Congeniality, but he certainly didn't like whoever was on the other side of the door, which blocked Baillie's view. The unknown voice sounded more insistent as Baillie crept closer.

"I asked if ye had an appointment," Robbie snapped. "Herself is not to be disturbed at the moment. In the future, I suggest ye make arrangements before trotting yourself over here."

A moment later, Baillie heard a car door slam just before the deep growl of an engine, an expensive one from the baritone purr. Baillie expected squealing tires, but it must be difficult to make a dramatic exit on brick and gravel. She heard only the fading roar of the engine.

Finally closing the door, Robbie turned and saw her. A chill slid across her neck as she felt she knew the answer but had to ask. "Who was that?"

"The banker, Mr. Bruce," came the brief answer.

"You lied to him." Baillie grinned at the sour face in front of her. "I didn't think you had a sneaky bone in your body." They walked together back to the office. "I'm pleasantly surprised."

"The arrogant excuse of a man hasn't a shred of respect in his whole body. Demanding to see ye without a please or a warning. He'll think twice before showing up unannounced again."

"Thank you, Robbie." Baillie stepped back toward the desk piled high with stacks of paperwork. "I would like to be prepared for my first meeting with him."

"About an hour before tea, miss." He shuffled off down the hall.

A second later, Kai appeared in the room. "Ye'll not be safe here, Annie, as long as ye stay. The man is ruthless in the hunt to destroy ye. Ya should'na be here."

Baillie's heart raced at the gorgeous vision beyond the desk. Tight, toned shoulders stretched the soft material of his shirt, the neck opened wide. The man paced in a slight alley between the desk and an antique file cabinet like a lion wearing a path near the bars of his cage. But the view wasn't enough to cloud his negative words.

"I'm not running away, Kai. The man is evil from what you've told me, and I'd worry what he'd do to the staff if I leave now. Remember my first night? He'd already shut the electricity off. With them still living here!" Anger was getting the better of her.

"I dinna say ya need to run away like a cur with his tail tucked low, woman. I warned ya coming here was dangerous. The man will not take no from anyone. He kills those in his way."

"This is my inheritance." She flopped on the edge of the desk. "Somehow we need to trap him at his own insidious game."

"The fox is nae one to wonder about the chickens playing games, Annie. His cunning lets him succeed undetected." He clenched his massive hands into fists. "I am helpless to protect ye much outside these walls; my strengths do not allow me to enter his home, or I woulda choked him with my bare hands afore now."

Baillie snorted. "Just grab him by the arm long enough and the cold will stop that dark heart."

"Dinna work; I've tried." Baillie blinked at him. "I see my hands pass through him like thick fog."

"Really?"

"You doubt my word, woman?" Kai bellowed.

Baillie practically fell off the desk. "Geesh, don't yell." The man barely looked contrite. "I was just wondering why at the shop no one else felt the cold. Well, Lady Nell did if I held her hands. No one heard you playing the bagpipes or whatever, except me and, again, Lady Nell if she touched me."

"I dinna understand the ways of it meself. Sure that you are of my blood, though."

Baillie knew she blushed scarlet. "True, DNA is probably the key." Her head swirled with deep South hecklers and Appalachian rumors about falling in love with cousins and incest. The man was hundreds of years removed from her family tree branches. Her heart lusted over a familial spirit. No harm in mindful lusting, right?

• • •

Kai watched Baillie, curled up in her favorite chair, staring into the fire. He couldn't imagine the room without her. A place more than hundreds of years silent and cold, now warm and full of conversation. He delighted in watching her face when she described something of the twenty-first century. The animation intrigued him.

He cleared his throat before materializing. "Did ye mind some company tonight?"

Her eyes reflected the flames of the fire as her head tilted up. "Kai, I was just thinking about you."

"Good thoughts, I hope." He settled into the chair across from her. His eyes discreetly took in her long legs tucked underneath her, smooth fingers circling her teacup and the sweet tilt of her head leaning against the back of the chair. The glow of the firelight enhanced her timeless beauty in his eyes.

He crossed his legs and brought his hands together as her voice continued a one-sided discussion of another story about something that happened at the shop. She never spoke with pride or arrogance during her tales. He appreciated her naivety one moment and self-deprecating humor after that.

Chuckling at the end of her story, Kai leaned forward. "Ye make the life of a shop owner more a life of gaiety than struggle, woman. Ye have a rare talent with people."

"I always try and make people happy. Life is too short to, uh—" Baillie stopped.

Kai watched her face flush with color, and his heart filled with a joy, her sweetness an elixir of sugar. "Aye, woman, life is but a blink of an eye." He smiled at her. "No need to feel embarrassed for me. My time in the netherworld has been many lifetimes now."

"Tell me some of the things you've seen."

Kai stood up and tended the fire, adding wood, avoiding her face. "Nay, ye'll think me foolish. What seems impossible magic to me is but ordinary to ye."

"I will not." She sounded hurt.

He turned, seeing the emotion in her eyes, and something twisted inside his soul, cracks appeared in the ancient block of indifference of his long existence. "Ye make it hard to deny ye, woman."

The night flew by as the two talked away the hours. A tap at the door startled them both. Kai hesitated a moment. "It's Putney with yer tea tray."

"Putney? It's morning already?"

"Aye, Annie, it is the morrow. I will take my leave and apologize."

"No, Kai," she said as the door opened.

Putney startled seeing her awake and sitting in the chair. "Miss Catharine, is there anything amiss? Are ya ill?"

Kai watched from his stance against the mantle. He didn't want to leave and end their time together.

"No, no, I must have fallen asleep in the chair last night." Baillie stood and stretched her arms toward the ceiling. "Thank you, tea sounds delicious."

Putney opened the drapes with quick, experienced pulls, filling the room with soft sunlight. "Let me know if you need anything, miss. I'll leave ya to as you will." Putney walked quickly out the door.

Kai smiled. "Ye look like a fairy imp being caught in dawn's light, Annie."

"Don't pick on me, Kai; I must look a mess sitting up all night." Her smile back to him softened the words. "I will definitely need a nap later today."

"Until later then, Annie, I enjoyed the evening." Kai bowed deep and vanished.

• • •

Days later, Mr. Bruce called and made an appointment to visit. Baillie paced in the drawing room, going east and west along the high-edged windows, while Kai paced at the other side, going north and south along the fireplace, his hands locked behind him. They had talked for hours last night, and Baillie's head was buzzing with intense anger laced with fear for her own life.

Robbie knocked twice on the wooden door before opening it wide to let Mr. Bruce enter. Baillie had stopped pacing at the first knock. A quick glance at Kai for reassurance, and she stood ready, composed, to face the enemy.

The man who walked into the room, though, shattered her visions of the vicious Mr. Potter from *It's a Wonderful Life*. Sean

Bruce had the swagger of a highly confident man with the muscled body and good looks to back it up. An older Dennis Quaid had nothing on this man. Baillie barely kept her mouth from dropping open as the immaculately dressed gentleman crossed the room with his manicured right hand outstretched.

"Ms. Catharine Baillie, it is a great privilege to meet you at long last." Dressed in an expensively cut suit, the man's features were chiseled into perfect proportions. Up close, his face was breathtakingly handsome—a cross between George Clooney and Richard Gere. His thick salt and pepper hair and clean-shaven face stopped above her with a dazzling, disarming smile.

Still soaking in this surprise, she forgot to take his hand for a split second too long. His smile let her know he noticed the delay and found her befuddlement quite delightful. His hand was smooth and warm, similar to Gillian's. Shaking herself as if from a spell, she finally spoke up. "Please, won't you have a seat, Mr. Bruce?"

"After you, my dear." His movements were slow and purposefully staged as he walked to a nearby sofa, waiting for her to sit down first.

She hesitated then chided herself. *This is my house.* Where he sat was not important—she'd already chosen a high-back chair facing the sofa for herself. She wanted control of this meeting.

"I've brought a treat for us to share with our tea." He held up a small cake box tied with string. "I wouldn't think of visiting without bringing one of my own chef's delicacies." His voice practically purred as he placed the box on the end table. "I understand you haven't had a chance to venture into our fair town yet and enjoy the local sights. May I offer my services to escort you on a tour some day?"

Baillie grimaced—as close to a smile as she could muster—noting out of the corner of her eye that Kai was ready to spring across the room at the intruder. "That's very generous of you, Mr.

Bruce." She moved to ring the bell for tea. "I have much to keep me busy here, catching up with paperwork and all."

"All work and no play does make Jack a dull boy, though, Ms. Baillie," he oozed, leaning toward her. Baillie blinked at the sudden similarities of the voice and movements to Shere Khan in *The Jungle Book*. The man was used to getting what he wanted.

She was saved from replying as Miss Putney entered the room with the teacart. The woman's face could turn a heart to stone, and Baillie relaxed against the side of the chair. This devil was most charming, and it felt good to have the cook run a few minutes of interference.

"Would you please pour for us, Miss Putney?" Baillie asked, not sure her hands wouldn't shake holding a cup and saucer at the moment. "And could you set out dessert plates? Mr. Bruce has so generously brought a cake for our visit."

Baillie looked carefully to the side where Kai paced the room making fists with his hands as Miss Putney poured the tea. Mr. Bruce passed the box over to the cook who untied the string and carefully took the decorated cake from the box, setting it on the low coffee table between them.

A smile tugged at the edges of Baillie's lips—though pretty, the petite dessert looked like an oversized cupcake covered with a light ivory frosting dotted with pink slips of something and ribbons of fresh pink flowers at the bottom edge. *You call that a cake? I've seen muffins back home bigger than that.*

"I did want to inquire while I'm here if you'd made up your mind about selling the property." Mr. Bruce made his words sharp and pointed, ensuring Putney heard, too. He took a sip of tea and stared innocently over the rim of the cup. "I am prepared to offer you quite a tidy sum of money as I've stated in my letters, an inherited amount worth almost double in America with the rate of exchange right now."

"That will do, Miss Putney, thank you."

Excused from the room, Putney stomped her way out the door.

"I see you have no qualms in your offer, sir." Baillie took up the knife to cut into the cake.

"My dear, the bank completely understands the extreme costs needed to maintain this run-down facility. Your announcement to visit was quite a surprise, though I suppose your American curiosity got the better of you."

Kai lunged a giant step forward, gripping the back of Baillie's chair roughly. She struggled not to show any expression. "I haven't had a chance to finish going through the financial records yet. I am hardly prepared to discuss your generous offer in person without understanding more of what the castle and grounds entail." She sliced into the cake and tore some of the pink petals.

"Please be assured I was taken aback at your hesitation, Ms. Baillie. Surely a successful businesswoman such as you understands the tens of thousands it would take to maintain this quaint, near ruinous, relic." He took the offered slice of cake with a nod. "Why, the salaries and upkeep of the staff alone would deplete any financial accounts before you had a chance to seriously play landlord from another continent. Let alone the gouge from America's inheritance taxes."

Baillie had just realized that her knuckles had turned white with her grip on the cake knife when suddenly the cake flipped from the table and fell on top of her feet. She jumped up from her chair as the icing slid into the sides of her shoes. Lumps of cake fell on either side, crushing the flowers into a gooey mess on the floor.

"Oh, my dear," Mr. Bruce stood quickly, offering his napkin to her. Baillie noticed a flick of vicious irritation cross his face before the mask of innocence reappeared. "I didn't mean to upset you with my practical notions of selling the property for a smart profit." Baillie thought the man was going to bat his eyelashes at her. Her stomach roiled.

She raised one sticky foot, watching pieces of moist cake fall on the rug before ringing the bell sharply. "Sir, I believe our meeting for today is over. Please allow Miss Putney to show you the door," she finished as the older woman stepped in the room. Baillie wondered if the cook had been standing out there all this time.

"Please accept my apologies if I've upset you." He smiled sweetly. "I will call again in the near future for your answer regarding a tour of our fair town." The man bowed and saw himself out, Miss Putney following on his heels.

Kai materialized next to Baillie as she bent down on one knee, scooping the cake mess into the box. "Don't touch the cake, Annie," he barked. "Nor lick your fingers. Here, don't move." Kai grabbed her linen napkin and wiped the thin smear of icing from the side of her fingers. "Dinna ye notice the flowers on the cake?" He growled. "Did ya not see the pink pieces in the icing? Are ya blind, woman?"

Baillie flopped back into the chair near tears. Not only were her feet covered in goo, but this overgrown ghost was yelling at her. "Excuse me?" She kicked off her shoes and used Mr. Bruce's napkin to wipe the top and sides of her feet, smearing the icing. "I'm at fault here? You threw the cake at me."

"What else was I to do, woman?" Kai had most of the destroyed cake back in the box. "Ya looked ready to pounce on it, so I had to take measures into my own hands." Baillie stared at him like he'd lost his mind. "The flowers, Annie."

"What about the freaking flowers, Kai? They looked nice around the cake. What's the big deal?" Her own anger, already on simmer from the banker's audacity, overflowed. "You…you overgrown Sasquatch! And yes, I've seen flowers on cakes and salads before."

"They be foxglove, Annie—pretty to look at but highly poisonous flowers. It wouldn't have taken much to make you deathly ill," he said between clenched teeth. "I was trying to save yer bloody life, woman. The icing was filled with torn petal pieces. Dinna ya see the pink?"

Baillie's mouth dropped open as Miss Putney came back in the room with a dishtowel. "Who were you yelling at, miss?" She looked around the empty room. "The devil is gone."

"Aye," Baillie rubbed the back of her hand against her face then made a slight grin at using the word. Kai was rubbing off on her. "The man is a black-hearted son of a gun. I just needed to vent a little, yelling my frustrations in the room."

Miss Putney nodded her head as she cleaned up the end table and picked up the banker's dishes. Suddenly, Kai smacked the edge of the plate with the final slice of cake from her hands, shattering the china on the floor. "Why, I…" Her words came quick, flustered. "I don't understand. I have never dropped a plate, miss, not ever in the whole time I've worked here."

Baillie's eyes grew wide. Kai glared at her and pointed at the thin slice of cake. "You want such an innocent woman to fall ill herself if she made the error of ingesting any of the poison?"

"Oh, no," Baillie whispered shaking her head. "No."

"Miss? Truly I'm sorry, I am. I don't know what came over me. It were as if the plate suddenly became too heavy. I…please forgive me." The woman was on her knees, picking up the broken china and scraping the mashed cake into a pile.

"Miss Putney, listen to me," Baillie's voice came out sharper than she expected. "Be very careful. I believe the cake is poisoned. Did you hear me? Listen, the flowers, those pink petal thingies in the icing, will make you deathly sick. Wash your hands carefully after we clean up in here." She looked at her own shaking hands. "I need to, as well."

"What are you saying, miss? Poison?" The woman craned her neck up to look at Baillie and something in her expression flipped a switch in Putney's demeanor. "Why that pompous *arse* of a man. How dare he come in here—" Her voice strangled off.

Her breathing came rapid as the anger built inside. “Robbie!” she bellowed. “Robbie, enter this room now, ya old man!”

The old man shuffled into the room. “Aye? What’s the fuss? I saw the man’s car drive away.”

“Miss Catharine here thinks the cake be poisoned. Of all the bloody nerve, bringing a cake like that in this house and me to serve it. I need ya to bring a trash bag and take this mess out to the garbage and be quick about it.” She mumbled under her breath, scraping icing from the rug. “Please hand me your shoes, miss. I’ll have them cleaned up in no time.”

Kai stood near the fireplace, not taking his eyes from Baillie. “Dinna I warn ya? Ya canna turn your back for a second with the likes of him.”

Nodding, she stayed silent, numb, as Robbie came in with a plastic garbage bag. Barefoot, she took a sip of her cold tea. Villains, poison and angry ghosts. Baillie felt like a character in an Agatha Christie novel, well out of her comfort zone.

# Chapter Twenty

"I can't believe the man tried to hurt me, possibly kill me, the first time we met. The man's insane. What if you hadn't been there to knock the cake over?"

Standing against the mantle in her bedroom, Kai watched her pace in silence.

"What?" She threw her hands up. "Say something."

"I warned ye."

Three clipped words, and she felt as if he'd hit her with a bucket of ice water. Staring at him, she knew she must tread carefully against his temper, rein in her emotions. "Yes, you did."

"Ya dinna listen, ya stubborn wench."

"True, but I can't leave now, don't you see? He'll think he's won, chasing me out. The man is a murderer. Who knows what other vile things he'll do if he gets his way?" She raised her hands in the air on the last word.

"I warned ye." Cold as granite, he didn't move a muscle.

She continued pacing, too distraught to stand still and be judged. "I know, but…but it's too late. I'm here."

"And I am not." Kai disappeared.

• • •

Fuming, Kai stood at the top of the north turret, a harsh wind whipping his hair. Bracing his legs, his arms locked straight, he leaned on the damp stone, the muscles of his face appearing carved in granite as he stared out at the open land around him. The screech of a lone hawk matched the echo in his empty heart.

His anger crashed like cymbals as his mind replayed the cake-cutting scene. The woman was incorrigible in her willfulness.

Dinna he warn her over and over again only to find his words cast adrift, meaningless in the woman's headstrong stubbornness? A bull has more intuition toward the farmer than this lass has to listening to the common sense of protecting herself. Kai's hands clenched into tight fists. How can one female cause such extreme chaos in his mind?

Never had he let a woman talk to him the way Annie did, as if she felt herself an equal. No female had ever raised her chin at him, nor stepped an inch from demureness in his presence. This woman dresses like a man and announces herself knowledgeable in the ways of his homeland? The pure audacity of the woman went beyond disrespect, and yet there was something about her that caught his attention, had kept his attention since first seeing her in the New World.

The hawk above him let out another scream, and Kai looked up. A second bird now flew in matching circles, their dark outstretched wings seeming small against the backdrop of overcast skies. The female hawk kept pace with the male, catching the air drifts in patterns overhead. Kai followed them with his eyes until they vanished behind a cloud.

• • •

Baillie knew Kai was angry with her but she couldn't let it go. What would happen to him if she just signed the sales papers and walked away? What if Bruce tore down the castle and put up a shopping mall or something? What about Rogue and Putney and Robbie? Baillie bounded from her chair to the bed, back to the chair. *Think, think.* The hamster started spinning on its wheel in her brain as she drummed her fingers against the arm of the chair. She felt like she had so little details to work with, her frustration level increased until she flew out of the chair and marched over to the bed, fiercely kicking one of it's ornate legs.

She regretted her impulse the instant her foot made contact with the solid wood. Incredible pain shot through her, and she let out a short scream. Grabbing her foot, she lost her balance and fell against the bed and bounced off, hitting the floor with a loud thump, jarring her teeth together.

"Do ya always take yer anger out on unsuspecting beds?" Kai grinned down at her as he stood in front of the mantle. "I hear a lass scream out in pain and what do I find to rescue but a heap on the floor."

"I don't need rescuing." Baillie gritted her teeth against the throbbing pain. She rocked in place on the floor, cradling her foot in both hands. She didn't have a clue as to how she was to get up off the floor, however; she wasn't about to roll onto all fours in front of Kai trying to get herself in an upright position.

"Sure and yer not needin' any help from the floor, Annie?"

With an exasperated sigh, she stuck her arm straight up. "If you would be so kind, Lord Baillie, as to assist me from here."

The ghost chuckled as he bent over, put his arms around her and lifted her completely off the ground in one smooth motion. He turned and carefully set her down in her usual chair. "Now that dinna hurt ye much, aye?"

"Thank you," she pouted while rubbing her toes. She looked over at the armoire across the room then down at her foot.

"What is it now, woman? Will it kill yer stubborn pride to ask for a wee bit of service?"

"It might," she mumbled. But she didn't have much choice. She either had to hobble her way across the room at the immediate humor of Kai or ask him to help. Pain made the call. "Would you do me a big favor and bring me the blue satchel from the cupboard?"

Bending deep from the waist, Kai practically swept the floor with the back of his hand before moving to the other side of the room. Opening the doors, he reached in and grabbed the bag. It rattled as he moved it from the shelf. "What manner of potions ye harboring in here, my witch of the New World?" He turned with a wicked grin on his face. "Need I be worried about ye casting spells in the middle of the night?"

"Seriously. I have enough trouble sleeping through the night, like I would waste precious hours playing hocus-pocus. Please just give me the bag. I want to take a couple aspirin for my foot." And realizing she needed one more thing, she rushed through the request. "Plus a glass of water, please?" She had no talent for taking pills dry.

Baillie heard the stream of water from the pitcher, and he stood in front of her offering the bag in one hand and the glass from the other. "Anything else, my lady?"

As their eyes locked, Baillie felt what little pride she had left melt away. Kai was right, he had warned her not to come. "Yes, please sit down with me." She rustled through the bag and pulled out the bottle of pain medicine and balanced the glass on the arm of the chair to get the security cap off. After swallowing the pills with a large sip of water, she tucked the bag next to her. "Now I thought we could do a little brainstorming together about what to do about Bruce."

Kai blinked at her and sat silent.

"There must be some way we can stop him or expose him for what he is, don't you think? There has to be an end to his madness."

"I dinna think ye can march into the guards in town and explain about tales ye heard from a ghost? They'd be declaring ye a drunkard and locking yerself up."

Leaning back in her chair, Baillie stretched her legs out toward the fire. The throbbing had eased, and she gazed at the flickering reds and yellows, hoping in the maze of colors to come up with some kind of idea. "You know who's really good at this?"

"Hmm?" Kai sounded far away.

"My friend, Gillian." She watched Kai suddenly sit up straighter, and for some reason she started babbling fast to get the words out before he objected. "Really, Kai, he's worked on computers and security technology for years. I'm sure he'd come up with a marvelous plan of revenge."

"Revenge is not the Baillie way, Annie." His voice sounded stilted. "We live by justice and honor."

She hesitated a second. "Same thing, isn't it?" and grabbed her phone. "This guy is truly old style, pure evil." Baillie cradled the phone and tapped her good foot on the floor.

"Who calls hysterical at eight in the morning?" She heard rustling in the background. "Oh, that's right, the woman who inherited a castle far, far away who was told to sell." Gillian was not at his best sans coffee.

"Oh, please, if you didn't stay up all night playing on your laptop, you'd be awake at a decent hour."

"Meow, the lady doth be a witch in her own right. Who stole your cookies this morning?"

She explained the cake fiasco with the banker and how Kai had rescued her. She didn't mention the arguing and fight.

"What do you need, Baillie? I've given you what little gossip I could find on Mr. Bruce. The gray-haired boy has kept a lily-white profile, albeit a rather popular one in the local area. You know my talents are always available to you."

"I was actually thinking of different talents." She bit the edge of her lip. "This guy is too smart to get caught up in anything typical. But maybe a little American razzle-dazzle gaiety will be the ticket. Right?"

"Gay-ity?" Gillian sounded intrigued. She heard him call out, "Brutus, bring me coffee, stat."

• • •

Their conversation wound down, and she thought for a second. "Hey, in all your travel preparations, don't forget to ship my package you promised. I have a gut feeling Rogue is part of the family. The girl's eyes are identical to Kai's, so distractingly dead on. The family resemblance can't be just arbitrary."

She stared over at Kai who was leaning against the mantle like a statue. Baillie felt the chill of his displeasure across the room.

"I've pulled a few strings, love, and my man assures me he can analyze family DNA with quite extraordinary results. He's extremely talented and owes me quite a few favors. Just send me the samples; he'll do the rest."

"You're awesome."

"Speaking of awesome, how is your kilted hunk doing?" Baillie closed her eyes staying silent. "Hello? I asked about your Lord of the Ghosts. Seriously, is he everything you imagined?"

"I, uh, guess so. I can't really say anything right now."

"Ah-ha, he's there, isn't he? Well, I told you the age difference might be a big problem. He did work tenaciously to warn you away from there."

"And I didn't do as I was told. There are a lot of ruffled feathers about that; I hear it often."

"Ouch, sorry about that. Too bad I can't have a man to manly ghost talk with him. Well, I'm sure Sally will have a list of eligible possibilities for you. The woman is quite annoying about the subject of your lacking social life. I can't wait to board the plane and see this mansion of yours. I'll take care of everything once I get there." Another long pause. "Are you feeling better, Baillie?"

Baillie realized exhaustion had caught up with her. "Yes, thank you. Knowing you're coming is a nice sedative after this crazy day." Baillie didn't see the dark scowl plastered on Kai's face as she ended the call.

"*Ciao* then, *bella*. We'll talk later."

• • •

Kai paced near the stables in the night's rain. Both hands clenched into fists, he growled into the wind. "She practically melts like heated wax when talking to that Gillian." Dougal let out a penetrating scream from his stall. "Aye, and what good would it do to tell the vixen anything of my feelings? She looks at me, and I think there may be something in her heart. But when I see her talking to this man who has been a friend to her, supporting her, what am I to think but that he is the only one for her?"

As if in empathy, the skies opened up, and the rain became a drenching storm. Kai lifted his face to the heavens and let out an emotional howl of pain. Dougal thrashed about in his stall, letting out a similar scream until Rogue appeared at his door.

"Shh, shh, ya warlock from the dark. What's gotten into you today? Canna you see it's raining? You're not going for a run in this weather. Ya feel brethren to the storm, maybe?" Rogue calmly held the horse's enormous head against hers and rubbed her hand down his jaw line.

• • •

On the second sunny day of her visit, Kai and Baillie took a walk outside. The ground was moist, even soggy in places, but though the smell of Putney's dried lavender and potpourri was wonderful inside the castle, nothing compared to fresh air after days of rain.

"I love these country paths." Baillie poked her hands in her coat pockets but raised her face to the sun. "How much land did I inherit?"

Kai swept strands of auburn curls from his face. "'Twas a time I owned as far as I could see from the top turret." Baillie turned her face to the top edge of the building. "But now it's probably half the area."

"Is there a current map for me to review? I didn't see anything in the paperwork but markings and longitudes."

Kai pointed toward the stables, his eyes sparkling. "I have a better idea. Let's go for a ride and I'll show you the lay of the land."

Baillie stopped. "Ride? Like on a horse?"

"Aye, one of the gentler ones, Annie. We'll ride together."

"I haven't been on the back of a horse since I was six or seven years old. Rogue is not going to let me take out one of her horses. She's not very fond of me."

"Annie, ye own the horses and the stable. Rogue will do as ye ask of her." He smiled, his hands on his hips.

With a heavy sigh, Baillie turned and headed toward the wood and stone building. Her equine memories consisted of her grandfather helping her astride a pony and hooking her feet into stirrups raised for her short legs. How tall she'd felt with the horse's mane in front of her showing a line to follow. She had rocked back and forth as the horse stepped across the pasture toward the woods beyond Grandfather's farm. How tough could it be? Like riding a bicycle, eh?

Kai walked next to Baillie as they stood in the open doorway. "Tell her you'd like to take the mare out for a ride, if she would saddle her for you."

Baillie cleared her throat. "Uh, Rogue?" She waited for a response.

From one of the back stalls, Rogue poked her head out. "Yes, mum," came through clenched teeth.

"Would you be so kind as to ready the mare for me? I'd like to take her out for a nice ride."

Kai raised his eyebrows. Obviously, she wasn't being as assertive with the help as he expected, she mused. *Get over it.*

"You ride, mum?" Rogue walked out, brushing her hands on her jeans.

"Uh, yes, I used to ride my grandfather's horses. I was thinking I would see more of the property while we had a sunbreak today."

Rogue grabbed a harness set but looked back over her shoulder. "What's a sunbreak?"

Baillie laughed softly. "Sorry, that's an expression we use a lot back home. Where I'm from the weather is more likely to be overcast or raining. So on days where the sun peeks out for a short time between cloud banks, we call it a sunbreak."

Rogue led a beautiful roan out to the open area where Baillie was standing. She finished with the straps and looked Baillie up and down before offering a leg up. Baillie grabbed her gloves from her pocket and thought of scraping her shoes before stepping into Rogue's linked hands, but there was nothing around so she grabbed the edge of the saddle, set her foot, and Rogue pushed her up. Baillie felt Kai immediately behind her as he patted her arm.

Rogue adjusted the stirrups. Baillie glanced down at the girl. "Thank you, Rogue. This feels good. I'll probably be out quite a while."

With a surprised look, Rogue nodded as Baillie felt Kai's hands cover hers and shake the reins. The horse lifted its head and walked out into the sunlight. Kai maneuvered the horse to the right, and they headed away from the castle. Baillie tried relaxing in the English saddle, but with no horn to hang on to, her legs were tight against the sides of the horse. Her butt slapped up and down as the horse broke into a trot. She could feel Rogue probably shaking her head as she watched Baillie ride away.

"Dinna ya learn to post, Annie?"

"Post what?" she tried to talk without biting her tongue.

He laughed hard in her ears. "Heigh," Kai called out and slapped the reins. The horse rocked into a gallop, and Baillie almost sighed at the smoothness of the ride.

As the land and stone fence flashed by, Baillie's nose tingled with the biting cold air in her face. Her eyes began to water, and she blinked often, clearing them without taking a hand off the reins, though she knew Kai was in control of the horse. She felt him pull softly on the reins, and the horse slowed to a canter and then a brief trot before slowing to a walk. Baillie snuck the back of her glove up to her dripping nose.

"Have ya seen yer cattle?"

"I have cattle?" Baillie twisted a little to see Kai behind her.

"Your cheeks are red as sweet roses, Annie. Yes, you have quite a herd." He clucked and turned the horse toward a stone fence and stopped. "Check out there."

Baillie followed his arm and noticed fluffy four-legged animals with horns standing together near a bare tree. "Uh, Kai, those aren't cows. Look how long and curly their hair is."

"That be Highland cattle, Annie." She heard the laughter in his tone.

After a minute, three started walking toward them. She was captured by their round, dark eyes and long bangs, which fluttered to the side as they moved their heads. Even their various hues of brown intrigued her. "I love them. Can I pet them?"

"Ya sound like my mother. She, too, found the cattle most charming in their presence. She was never allowed to become too attached to the calves, or we'd have starved come winter."

Baillie slid down and realized the cattle were a lot larger than they looked from the saddle. Still, their faces pushed over the top of the fence as they studied her. She moved slowly, with her arm outstretched, cooing softly to the animals. "Oh, you are a lovely bunch. Look at these faces." They snorted, ears flickering as she approached. "Kai, these are mine? Truly, mine?"

"Aye, Annie, and I see ye'll need to be separated from the herd come butchering time. Yer worse than my mum. They be animals, woman, not wee *bairns*."

"They're so beautiful. Especially this one." She rubbed the ear of the largest of the trio. "I shall call him Ferdinand. Yes, Ferdinand, watch over the herd until I come back. I'll bring an apple or carrot or something."

Kai patted the horse's neck. "Come on, there is much to see."

Dragging herself away from the herd, she stretched her arms over her head before bending slowly toward her toes. Her body creaked, and she groaned. "Not use to bouncing on a saddle, I guess. Things are feeling a little stiff." He cupped his hands and lifted her leg up easily.

Kai pulled the left rein and guided them away from the pasture at a comfortable walk. They followed a dirt road quite a ways in silence. Baillie leaned back a bit, enjoying Kai's arms on either side of her. The beautiful land made an excellent backdrop to her daydream with Kai.

As the road curved, Baillie heard a sound off in the distance, a beat with a long pause between the sounds.

"Is that the ocean?" She stretched her neck upward, standing in the stirrups, but saw nothing but land in front of them.

"Aye, and ye must be careful in this stretch. The cliffs are a sheer and vicious drop to the water below."

"I didn't realize the ocean was so close. And we're still on my property?"

"For another good mile or so."

"And then what? What's next door?" Silence came from behind. She asked again with no response. "You'll have to tell me sooner or later. Give it up."

"The Bruce manor," he growled.

"Nooooo." The word stretched out. "You're kidding? He's my neighbor? I gotta see this. How close can we get?"

A hard squeeze covered both her hands, and they galloped off, away from the cliffs. Over to the west was a rise, and Kai urged the horse to the top. Turning the horse, he stopped, giving them a clear view across the area. Beyond the trees sat a grand, ornate palace with manicured lawns and neatly trimmed shrubbery both in the front and back. An elaborate maze of dark green hedges filled an entire corner of the property. Baillie marveled at the austerity in front of her.

"Oh my gosh, are you serious? One man lives there? The evil banker?" She felt Kai nod behind her. Her head swiveled back and forth taking in the unbelievable details—cement driveways, topiary that from here looked like a collection from Point Defiance Zoo. "That is ridiculous. And the man is obsessed in grabbing your, uh, my land." She growled to herself, "Men!"

The throat clearing got very vocal behind her.

"And why didn't you say something before?" The mansion's perfectionistic beauty irritated her. "Take me back, Kai. I don't want to see any more of this." She tightened her hands on the leather as he turned the horse back down to the road.

# Chapter Twenty-one

"Miss Putney, I've, uh, invited guests to come stay with us for a week or so." The cook froze in mid-stir, a statue. "Three gentlemen are flying in next week from Washington, and I'd like to have rooms available for each." No response. "I'll make a list for the market; we'll need a few extra supplies brought in. The guys are not really used to home cooking. They are a rather flamboyant group." A snort sounded, and Baillie smiled. "I must admit it's going to be quite entertaining around here for a while."

As Baillie walked away, the grumbling started. "Blooming Americans…a bunch of single men…a list she says, as if I haven't done the shopping…"

Baillie snickered as she rounded the corner and nearly knocked Robbie to the ground.

"Woman!" he straightened his cap. "Oh, it's you. What the devil is going on? I'm not liking what I hear from the kitchen."

The man had ears like a wolf. "Sorry, that would be my fault. I've invited some friends to help me catch—" a sharp jab of cold poked her ribs. "Uh, celebrate, I mean, my good fortune in inheriting a castle." She rubbed her side and noticed Robbie paying close attention to her movements. *Suspicious old fool. It's like he knows.* "I asked Miss Putney if we could make available three rooms for their visit." A soft chuckle from the old man eased her mind.

"Been many a year since the missus has had to cook for more than a handful. You are shaking the cobwebs lose, Miss Catharine." Another chuckle. "Aye, she'll be much to live with for a while." He puttered off to the kitchen.

"Are you trying to get me in trouble with the help?" Baillie hissed in the hallway once the coast was clear.

"Ye be trouble all on your own, woman." Kai visualized as they walked. "What might wee Robbie think, ya blaming a man ya barely know of murder? He's still concerned about the cake but not convinced you weren't overreacting over a mere pastry."

"I heard my mistake; you didn't need to give me frostbite in the ribs." Kai threatened to touch her again, and she yelped at his tease. "I think Robbie suspects something. He stared really hard when I jumped."

"The wee man has believed in me since the first day he got involved with his woman, Putney."

"But he can't see nor hear you?"

"Nay, just a notion he has from the stories she heard tell from her mother and grandmother. The woman badgers the old man unmercifully."

They stopped in a spacious room where dramatic floor-length drapes were opened to weak sunlight. "Where are we? I don't remember coming here before."

"The library." He stared at her with a wicked grin. "You tend to wear out during my tours. There be many rooms left to explore."

Breaking away from his gaze, Baillie saw the floor-to-ceiling bookshelves packed with old volumes. Her heart pounded as she moved to the books in a trance. "Why didn't you bring me here earlier?"

"I feared I'd lose your company to the books and you'd never come out," he chuckled.

Baillie flashed a grin before absorbing the quality in front of her. She reached up and ran her fingers along the spines, reading titles and author names.

"See? Yer already bewitched." He gently took her arm and escorted her to a side where, hung on a monstrous cord, an enormous painting encompassed most of the wall.

Her breath caught in her throat. It was an eight-foot likeness of Kai standing next to a beast of horseflesh identical to the monster in the stables. The artist had caught the intensity of Kai's eyes, with his auburn hair framing his face as the bitter winds blew against him and the horse, entwining locks of hair and mane.

"I'm afraid Putney sees me like this in her heart. A towering man of power mixed with unresolved childhood fears."

"Look at you," Baillie whispered. Had he not been standing right next to her she would have needed a towel for the drool. "Wait 'til the girls see this."

"Girls? What girls?" Kai's head shot back. "Dinna you tell me that motely group from the séance was coming?"

"I did, and I don't know how to explain my last remark to you." She ran her fingers through her hair. Might as well break it to him now. Walking over to an antique loveseat, she plunked herself down and wiggled into the corner against the stiff bristles of the furniture. She should have chosen an overstuffed chair. Kai refused to sit; instead, he planted his legs apart, as if bracing for drastic news.

Mentally flashing through various ideas on how to explain the girls, Baillie spotted a complete shelf of Shakespeare's work just beyond Kai. Hmmm, the Renaissance Faire had those hilarious Shakespearean skits on various stages…maybe that was the place to start. "Did you ever see wandering minstrels acting out a play? Actors who travel from town to town to entertain?"

"Aye, now and again, I'd say." He glared down at her as if challenging what a bunch of foolish actors had to do with her friends.

"And who played the parts of women? Who dressed up and painted their faces, donning long-haired wigs?"

"The men, of course." Baillie let this soak in, sitting quietly. "Ya mean these men are actors? They act as women?"

"Extremely well. They look better than I do, I must say, when in full glamour mode. But they don't use a script, as they're not in a play during their performances. They enjoy two lives in a way, though they do perform some weekends as famous singers."

Kai's expression of shock made her double over in laughter. "Just wait and see. It's more impressive and easier to understand when you see them decked out." She wiped a tear from her eye. "I'm counting on their delicious feminine talents to bring the villain Sean Bruce down."

"Down? Down where, woman?" he barked. "You're talking nonsense."

"Sorry, it's just an expression of speech, to bring someone down, like have him arrested. Down off his high horse of terrorizing this family."

• • •

"A package arrived for you, miss." Putney pointed at a box on the table near Robbie's elbow. He reached over and gave it a slight nudge.

"Great, it's here. Excuse me." Baillie dashed off to the privacy of her room with the package in hand.

"Such a wee bit of a box to get you running like a colt through the castle," Kai said, leaning against the mantle as she carefully took out the kit.

Baillie nodded, her nose buried in the directions. "I asked Gillian to call in a favor and send over the kit. It may just be my imagination, but I could swear Rogue has your eyes. Like she's part of the Baillie family tree somewhere, and this will help answer the riddle."

"Annie, how can it do much of anything?"

She looked up. "This is just for taking the samples. Gillian sent enough for two, one for me and one for Rogue. They'll be sent to a laboratory where the magic actually happens. They can test to see if Rogue and I are related through our DNA."

Baillie snapped on a pair of plastic gloves. Pulling a cotton swab from its clear container, she rubbed the white head against the inside of her cheek. Carefully, she put it in a plastic tube and sealed it. Ripping the gloves off, she grabbed a pen and wrote her name on the label.

"How do you get the wee lass to stick something like that in her mouth? She'd as soon slap your hand away if you try."

"True. I'll wait 'til she's asleep maybe and visit her then."

Kai stared without conviction. "She may be a light sleeper if she noted me at times in the stables."

"You must come with me and keep Dougal quiet. He'd sound the alarm against me as soon as I stepped one foot inside."

"He senses your fear and makes fun of ye. The animal is verra smart, Annie. He's quite gentle."

Baillie snorted. "Sure, a gentle giant ready to trample me to dust."

Kai built up the fire and smiled at her worried face. "Tonight I will be by your side as you wish."

Baillie moved to the bright flames, spreading her hands in front of her. "Will you wake me sometime after midnight? Or should I set my alarm?" She pulled her cell phone from her pocket.

"The tiny box can even tell the time to wake up?"

"We evolved from roosters and dawn-breaking a hundred years ago. We live by the clock—where to be, what to do."

"Time has become your task master."

"In a way. So much to do in so little time is a mantra of the twenty-first century."

Kai shook his head, a flush of curls falling across his shoulders. The fire created a glowing outline of his features—strong jaw, classic cheekbones. "What an odd concept, the twenty-first century." His eyes glazed in a faraway stare.

The silence grew in the room, broken only by the soft pop and crackle of the fire. Her eyes traveled slowly over the still figure.

Her heartbeat skipped to a quicker speed, creating a warmth in her heart. How strong yet gentle the rugged face, ageless now and forever. His kilt draped to his bare knees. Baillie watched him draw in and wondered what he must be thinking.

"I canna believe I have wandered these rooms nigh on three hundred years, caught in a medium of not here nor there." Kai's voice was low, pensive. "Helpless against the restoration of the castle as electricity and this wondrous indoor plumbing arrived, modern conveniences invading the halls of my ancestors."

Why had he come to warn her? How difficult it must have been leaving the security of his homeland to reach out to her a continent away where, to him, we lived a whole new lifestyle of absurdity. *He struggled through unknown processes to contact me. What must he think of my friends, especially T-Cup's vivacity and mannerisms at first glance.*

"Annie?"

"Hmm?" The smile lingered as she came back to the present to find him staring at her.

"Who brings such a bewitching smile to you this hour?"

She dropped her head. "Uh, you, actually." He moved closer to her, an eagerness in his eyes. "I was thinking back to the night of the séance and your first meeting with Gillian's friends, especially T-Cup."

"The little rapscallion is like a horsefly of annoyance." He crossed his arms. "I've seen his type in power, bringing a nation to near ruin."

Baillie's giggle caught him by surprise. "You think what I say funny, woman?" His eyes flashed in anger.

"No, honestly, I just remember history classes where a few of the smaller kings were considered 'poofters' or less masculine," she explained quickly, "a perfect description of T-Cup." Baillie pulled on the cuffs of her sweater, covering her fingers. "How I wish I had known you in your time." Her voice dropped low. "And watched you as lord of the manor, protector of your people."

"Aye, many a family lived here, working the fields or minding the mill. The area bustled with new generations popping up in late summers. The bounty of life kept me whole."

"Then what happened? To you?"

"The Bruce clan waged war on my people. Their brutish strength and larger numbers thought it gave them enough to invade us. I wouldna budge and armed my people."

"What happened?"

"Not a very honorable story, Annie." He sighed and refused to look at her. "I believe ye shall think less of me."

"Please," she whispered.

"A young girl came to me in servitude; I wasna aware of whence she came. She spent many an hour trying to catch my attention, offering more than her assigned duties. I shoulda kept my guard up, but I was weak and one night invited her to bed. During the dark of the moon, she killed me in my sleep, a single stab wound to the heart. By dawn she had disappeared, and no one ever saw her again."

She brushed a single tear from her cheek. Kai refused to turn his face, his shoulders stiff with shame. He took a deep breath. "My grandfather had told me stories at his knee of the Bruce clan poisoning the wells and the cattle to drive us off our land."

"So this feud goes way back?"

"Beyond myself, aye. The Bruces felt entitled to the land, and their bitterness and anger have not slighted over time. Sean is the last of his line, and his determination to avenge his ancestors is fierce."

"But his mansion is twenty times more opulent and extravagant than yours. Why continue the violence?"

"We Scots be stubborn, Annie. Now it be the principle of the thing. For Sean to go to his grave with his fist wrapped around the deed to our land is his only goal in life."

"What a miserable outlook. No wonder he's crazy. He's obsessed with an ancestry of greed."

• • •

"Annie?" Kai whispered. "Annie, awake, my lady." The lump under a pile of quilts moaned and moved. Kai chuckled, and grabbing what he hoped was her shoulder, shook it. "'Tis the hour you wished, Annie." He shook again, his hand lingering, his grip steady.

"Me and my bright ideas," a voice murmured from underneath.

Kai whipped his hand away, though his heart wished it could linger on this wild woman in his bed. "I've built a fire for ye."

A light snore came from the bedding. Kai reached out and squeezed, the pressure sinking into the softness of quilt and her upper arm. He stared at his hand, fingers curled, and closed his eyes for a moment. He broke loose of his thoughts and shook the lifeless body again. "I'll wait for ya outside, if ya are truly awake."

"Yes, I'm awake, Prince Charming. I'll be down shortly."

Reaching again for the lump, his arm outstretched, Kai let a silent sigh escape before disappearing.

• • •

Baillie struggled into jeans and her boots. A feeling of a strong hand gripping her shoulder lingered in the back of her mind. Was that Kai or her imagination? She lit a small stubby candle, snapped on the other pair of Latex gloves to avoid creating a noise later in the stable, and made her way quietly to the kitchen. The smell of spices and fresh bread met her before her eyes adjusted to find the door.

"Kai?" she whispered in the cold blackness.

"I be here, Annie," he said, revealing himself. "You should know the way by heart, aye?"

"Sure, but it is bloody dark out here." A soft chuckle caressed her ear.

Kai went ahead and stood sentry with the beast. The other horses stayed quiet as long as the stallion was calm.

Baillie slipped inside, set the candle down, and felt her way to Rogue's room. A serenade of snoring guided her and eased her mind that the young girl was fast asleep. Pulling the tools from her pocket, Baillie felt unsure of getting a sample from inside the tiny mouth. The girl's lips were barely apart, and she feared opening them too wide would disturb the girl. Just then she noticed a slight glint of reflected light at the corner of Rogue's mouth. *Perfect! She's drooling.*

Baillie carefully brought the swab to the edge of Rogue's lip and slowly swirled the white cotton against her skin, coating it thoroughly. Two seconds later, she dropped it into a plastic tube, sealing it tightly, and carefully made her way back to the candle in the stable area.

"Are ye done?" came a whisper through the dark.

Baillie saw a brush moving across Dougal's black neck. "Yes, all done."

Soft whisperings for the horse floated to her before she saw Kai next to her. His devotion to the horse warmed her heart.

"I enjoyed our ride together, you know," Baillie whispered in his direction.

"So ye'll be up to riding again soon?" He smiled in the darkness. "A daily ride, perhaps?"

"Don't push your luck."

Baillie made sure the kitchen door was secure by pressing her hands against the wood. She picked up her candle and started back to her room, touching her pocket to ensure she had the sample.

Dropping her jeans on top of her damp boots in front of the fire, she blew out the candle and scampered under the covers. The sheets felt freezing after her short escapade. She rubbed her feet in quick, short motions against the sheets, trying to warm them.

She felt the quilt suddenly tuck tight around her. "Excuse me?"

"Did ye mind me being here, Annie?"

*Do I mind having a gorgeous man next to me? Hmm, let me think about this.* "No." She faked a yawn, trying to show she couldn't care less what he chose to do. "Maybe it will help me get warm. Funny, I didn't feel any cold when we were on the horse together and nothing now with your touch through the quilts. I guess if there are enough layers between us the cold doesn't get through."

"As I'd hoped." Kai made himself comfortable stretched out next to her and wrapped a muscular arm around her waist, drawing her close against him.

Baillie's heart pounded in her chest. It wasn't a solid feeling truly, yet she felt him there with her, near her. Only her imagination? She didn't care at this point.

"I dinna mean to frighten ye," Kai said quietly. "Yer heart's beating like a wild colt."

"No, that's not fear, trust me." She tried to relax with his body next to hers. "It feels good, Kai," she answered to the room.

His arm tightened as Baillie melted into the hold. "Good night, Kai."

"G'night, my Annie."

## Chapter Twenty-two

In the morning, Baillie gave the DNA kit to Robbie for mailing, wandered into the library—her favorite room now—and opened her laptop. She checked the time and did the math; one am back home. She was emailing the tracking information to Gillian when a ping from Instant Messaging told her he was still awake.

"How are the travel arrangements going?" She typed.

*Ping.* "Making decisions is not their best skill set."

Baillie chuckled. "Let me know when you have definite dates and times. You are gonna die when you see this place. I practically pinch myself twice a day."

*Ping.* "You'll be the second to know once we get things settled. I saw the castle photo you posted, girl. Impressive. *Ciao, bella*."

"I guess it's good night to you, Gillian." Baillie closed the laptop and looked out the windows. Stretching her legs, she walked over to an alcove and sat on the wide window ledge. She loved the windows and their pattern-making ironwork. She watched the moat outside. With a sigh, she relaxed and soaked up the soothing beauty. Gillian and the girls were coming. The peace and quiet soothing her chaotic thoughts would soon change.

• • •

Slamming the lid onto the kettle, Putney viciously threw the coated ladle into the sink, splattering sauce on the sides. "Her high and mighty wants me to cook for that scoundrel of a penny pincher. I will not put my decent food in front of him, I tell you."

Robbie hid his face behind the newspaper.

"First she says she's bringing in a carload of Americans and now a party for the devil. I'll not hear of it, old man. How dare she invite someone so despicable to this place? He tried to hurt her not that long ago. Has the woman no shame?"

"Calm yourself. Has the lass done anything during her stay for us to doubt her ideas?" Robbie set the paper down and started cleaning his pipe at the big table.

"No, but I wanna know what's going on. One minute we have guests coming and now we have the devil hisself invited, to a party no less, with some famous stars from Hollywood? It's madness."

• • •

"Always keep your enemy in sight, Putney," Baillie spoke to the woman as she broke off a piece of bread to dunk in her soup. "Better to see what he's up to." She slathered sweet butter on the bread. This was getting to be a caloric habit but so delicious she couldn't help herself. "Putney, you spoil me. This is heavenly. Better not serve it Saturday night or I'll make a pig of myself in front of company." She had arrived late to breakfast; all the others had eaten earlier.

"Company, indeed. The man is walking evil in a tweed business suit." Putney snorted as she turned her back.

"We have lots of those in the Olympia area. They're costumed as lawyers, bankers and politicians. Evil suits are alike no matter what country or what fabric they're made out of." Baillie had trouble swallowing. She didn't like keeping things from Putney, but the details of her plan to wring answers out of Bruce needed to be kept secret from the staff.

"My friends should be arriving in a couple days." Baillie looked over to Robbie for a moment before talking over her shoulder to the one that mattered most. "Please let me help in getting things ready. I can do laundry and make the beds. You only need to point me in the right direction. I am quite handy with sheets; I make mine all the time." She took a sip of tea. "That was a joke. But seriously, please let me help."

"Tell me more about these friends—ya say the leader is named Gillian?" Robbie pulled a chair out, and Putney came over, wiping her hands on her apron.

Baillie knew she needed to prepare the couple more than she had at this point but hadn't a clue how to start. "Well, there are three, as I've said, and all three are gay." She didn't wait for any remarks. "Gillian and I have been friends for quite a while. He helps out at my bookstore if I need to be somewhere. He's quite handsome—tall, blond—and extremely smart. He works with computers and helped bring my shop into the computer age."

"Never used one myself," Robbie commented. "I hear they have some in town; the younger folk seem eager to have one."

"True, most everyone I know in the States has at least one in their homes. Now the other two friends are quite, uh, colorful."

"What do these other two young men do, Catharine?" Putney wrapped her red hands around the fresh cup of tea Robbie had brought her. He lifted the teapot and warmed up his own. He offered to add more to Baillie's cup.

"Yes, thank you. Well, they are very talented entertainers. They travel the West Coast and perform from Seattle to Hollywood, including my home city of Olympia."

"Being entertainers is why they have such unusual names?" Putney asked.

"Exactly. I don't think I even know what their birth names are. T-Cup is quite the live wire, and Rafael is sass and spice but the steadying force of the two. He's the one booking their acts in various places."

Both servants stared at each other, clearly trying to understand what she'd just said. There was no help for it; she'd have to keep talking.

"Now, I must warn you they are eccentric, bordering on spoiled, sometimes. But I know they would sell their souls to help me. I trust them explicitly."

"Eccentric entertainers?" Putney kept a straight face, her composure broken only by her fingernails tapping the side of her cup.

"You mentioned Hollywood singers before. I thought you had additional people coming," Robbie questioned.

"Yes, well. Rafael and T-Cup are actually going to perform for Mr. Bruce. In America, they're known as drag queens, and the two are very talented." There, she'd let go the main event of their visit.

Silence. Baillie feared one or the other would explode, but they sat stone faced, blinking the only movement between them. Baillie swore she could see a wall going up in front of Putney. She'd crossed a line of respect to the older woman.

"Excuse me." Putney stood from the table and walked out of the room.

Robbie rubbed a hand through his hair. "Lassie, I fear for your soul this night." A door slammed somewhere.

Baillie was surprised as tears welled up in her eyes. She had become quite fond of the cook and keeper. "Robbie," she said, as she reached for the hand closest to her. "By the stars above, I am not doing this out of flirting with evil. There is a method to my madness. I just ask you to give me time to prove myself. I need my friends' help. I have learned deplorable things about Mr. Bruce that need to be stopped. His blatant approach at bringing a cake laced with foxglove proves how overconfident he's become in gaining this property. I won't be forced out by his arrogance nor let him threaten any of you."

Her tears did the trick. He leaned closer. "And where did you find this information, lass?"

"I can't tell you, I'm afraid."

The man stared at her as if she were almost invisible, as if he could see through her into her mind, into her heart for the answer she wasn't revealing. "Ye can't explain where you came by this information that makes you believe you can do something about the serpent who lives next door?"

Baillie nodded her head, not trusting her voice to speak.

"And the missus and I should trust you and this band of merry men to come in and take care of everything?"

"Sounds rather pompous, doesn't it?" She released a giggle from stress. "I know it sounds like I'm turning the castle upside down, and I wouldn't suggest such a detestable thing if I didn't feel I had a definite purpose, a real goal when it was over. The less you know right now, the safer you'll be, though. I just need you to trust me." Baillie inhaled deeply. "But when my friends get here, it's going to be a daily circus and seem even more bizarre than you can imagine."

Robbie rubbed his nose and stared at the tabletop. "A circus? I dinna think the missus is going to be happy having performers and pride running through the floors. But it's important to ye somehow?"

Baillie couldn't hold the back tears that now trickled down her cheek. "Ah, Robbie, it's very important. This place has captured my heart. And I know it's only been weeks, but it feels like home. I want a future here with you all, a chance to make decisions on my own, not frightened and hunted down by a mad man. He has no right to threaten people. This is Baillie property!" She nearly slammed her fist on the table.

He nodded. "Then I will do my best with the wife. And ya promise to explain all this to me some day."

Baillie jumped out of her chair and threw her arms around the old man, and he reared back in surprise. "Yes, I promise! Thank you, thank you, Robbie!"

# Chapter Twenty-three

"Isn't this marvelous?" Baillie bubbled over. "I can't believe the sun is out for their arrival. Their first view of the castle will be breathtaking." Baillie had been pacing outside for the last half hour, finally spotting a car coming down the drive. "They're here!"

"I should hope so," Kai growled, standing planted in one spot, his arms crossed. "Ye act like you're waiting for the bloody queen."

"Plural."

"What?"

"Queens. More than one queen, technically. It's a long story."

"Queens? That motley crew from your shop?"

"I know I haven't described my friends very well. They're modern, extreme, X Games wild. You'll have to trust me on some of this. But I'm counting on them to get the dish on Bruce."

"Baillie!" T-Cup bounced out of the back seat right behind Rafael, who needed a desperate stretch himself, and bent, touching his toes.

"Really? You have to do that now right in front of me?" He waved both arms. "We're here, we made it."

Baillie rushed up to the car. "Gillian, I'm so glad you're here!"

Gillian wrapped her gently in his arms. "I'm a total mess, darling; please don't linger. This is truly out in the country." Seeing as how he was dressed in a designer suit, tailored fit, Baillie laughed at his remark. He turned to the driver, flicking his hands toward their matching patterned luggage Rafael was hauling out of the trunk. "Will you please take those over the moat for us, up to the door?" Only Baillie saw the driver roll his eyes.

Suddenly she was enveloped in two sets of arms. Rafael stepped back from the group hug and stood in a pose, checking her out. "You look marvelously happy. Shabby chic, and what have you done to your hair? That smile, though, is priceless." He gasped. "You love it here, admit it! You're glowing."

Baillie felt a chill touch her shoulder; Kai had stepped to her side. She shivered, a movement Gillian's careful eye caught. They locked eyes, and Baillie nodded ever so slightly. Gillian's face brightened with a quizzical look as he stared to her side. His eyes flickered around, then he shrugged and stepped back.

"Girls," he clapped. "Be aware, staff is in their late nineties waiting at the bridge. I want each of you to take at least two bags and begin bringing some order to this welcoming. I need a shower desperately." Gillian pulled his wallet from his suit pocket and counted a large quantity of pounds into the driver's hand, whose eyes widened at the wad of colorful paper.

"Let's step up and introduce ourselves first, ladies." Gillian waved an arm, gathering them together.

The three walked in a straight line toward the bridge in matched steps, and Baillie felt goose bumps down her arms as she swore time shifted into slow motion. The beauty of the men filled the moment, and Baillie watched Putney's cheeks flush pink. The cook felt it as well.

"Am I to be impressed by these male peacocks?" Kai snapped.

"Sarcasm doesn't become you," Baillie said calmly.

Gillian stopped first and bowed slightly. "Please accept our deep appreciation in welcoming our group to stay in your home. We are delighted to meet the people in care of this glorious castle." His voice purred. "I am Gillian Nation," he stretched out his hands and wrapped them around Putney's, "and you must be the incredible Miss Putney. Allow me to introduce Rafael and T-Cup." He turned a slight degree to Robbie. "And you, sir, must be Robbie. I am humbled in meeting you." The two behind him bowed.

Flushed, Putney played with the edge of her apron, at a loss for words. "Catharine?" she called for help.

Gillian raised his left eyebrow dramatically, turning to look at Baillie. She glared briefly and shook her head.

"Yes, these are our guests; I promise they won't bite. I would like to introduce Miss Putney and Mr. Robbie, who have been taking excellent care of the castle for years and of me for weeks." She approached the gathering, and T-Cup wrapped her in another hug. "Missed you, too, T. Let's get your luggage inside, gentlemen. Miss Putney has made some delicious treats for you."

Each of the men went back and hoisted a shoulder bag, then took a bag in each hand, barely putting a dent in the quantity on the gravel. Chatter and voices filled the area.

Just inside, Baillie pointed up the nearest stairs. "Follow me. You're staying in the east wing."

They moved as one away from the front door, whispering and giggling, heads turning side to side and up and down, trying to soak in as many details of the castle as possible. Putney moved into the kitchen, shaking her head. Robbie set the bags down inside the door and turned with a sigh, watching his help disappear.

Looking up at the three windows in the first bedroom, Rafael said, "Obviously they had problems with jumpers back then. Who puts windows by the ceiling? But look at this room!" he squealed. "I'm in delicious shock. A whole wall of velvet! How medieval." Rafael closed the floor-length drapes and opened them again.

"Okay, Rafael, sit for a minute." Gillian patted the bed before stretching his arms up over his head. "Spill everything, Baillie. This is a real castle. Those little photos you sent through your phone seemed so Robin Hood and Maid Marion. This is like a Paramount movie set."

Baillie bobbed her head up and down but couldn't speak, as a wave of tears strangled her. T-Cup appeared at her side and handed her his handkerchief. "Ssssh, we're here. It's gonna work out."

"Speaking of here," Gillian moved to the carved mantle in the room, struck a pose, and paused for dramatic effect. "Is he here?"

Baillie burst into giggles, still dabbing her eyes. “I, don’t think—” She stopped in midsentence as Kai materialized in the room. “Uh, as a matter of fact, Kai just arrived.”

“Really?” Gillian let the word out slowly. “I knew instantly by the change in your eyes. And since you’re looking in this direction, I assume the kilted prince is close by.”

Kai glared. “Aye, Annie, I remember the lot. Ye believe they will help us against the villainous Bruce?”

“Yes, Kai, I do. Let me make introductions so you have names to faces. This is T-Cup, the heart of the group.” She moved around the room while everyone else stood with their mouths open, staring toward Gillian. “Rafael is the energy. And, of course, there is Gillian, manager extraordinaire. We have a lot of work ahead of us, but this is a very talented group.”

T-Cup squealed. “I am so happy to meet you, Mr. Ghost, sir, your highness.” He focused toward the mantle, clapping his hands together then dropping into a fast curtsy.

Despite the odd introduction, Kai brought his heels together and bowed from the waist. “Please pass on my welcome to Castle Baillie and deepest appreciation for their attendance.”

Baillie beamed. “Kai is bowing and says he welcomes you to his home. I have a fabulous idea, if all of you will come with me.” She bounced to the door. “Come on, I have something special to show you.” Running out the door, the men followed without question.

At the bottom of the stairs, she pushed them to the left, down a darkened hallway, around two other turns, and stopped in the library. “Ta-da! This is the magnificent Lord Something, Something Kai Something Baillie. Well, he has a lot more names than that, but I can’t remember them.” Baillie stretched her arms out doing her best Vanna White next to the painting, enjoying their stunned silence. “T, here’s your hankie back; wipe your drool.”

Gillian stood farthest back, hand under his chin, critically scanning every dramatic inch. His eyes pierced the colors, angles and facial features. Kai appeared next to him, looking from Gillian to the painting and back, the same glare still on his face from upstairs. The others stopped and stared at Gillian, waiting.

"Please have this moved to my room immediately," Gillian finally said.

Rafael and T screamed. "You have to share!"

"Okay, so when I talk about Kai, to him or say he's in the room," she did another sweep, "this is what he looks like…well, without the horse." The two screamed again. "Except right now he has his hands over his ears." Laughter filled the room.

• • •

Kai couldn't get away from the squealing group fast enough. He grimaced as he replayed Gillian holding Baillie in his arms. Each second of the long embrace had pounded in his head as he clenched his fists. "The yellow haired one adores Annie, ya can see it in his eyes. The woman practically sparkled when he came toward her today."

Kai walked the south parapet, his hands behind him. The wind whipped around him, but he felt nothing. Mother Nature had no power over him. Rain, storms—nothing got through. But he was beginning to think there was one woman who could affect him. He snorted and turned, walking back. *Impossible! How could I have these feelings for Annie?*

Annie. They dance around her like a goddess, a trio of powdered men. He turned his back from the land, taking a deep breath. *She says they be necessary in stopping the Bruce.* Wiping his hands on his kilts, he fought the emotions boiling inside him, a jealous rage as feelings for the woman surfaced from somewhere long unused.

# Chapter Twenty-four

"Thank you for making time for me on such short notice, Mr. Bruce." Baillie smiled. The butler had led them into a dramatic ballroom where it looked as if Sean had just finished his fencing lesson.

With his face still flushed, he wiped his hands on a white towel held by another servant. "Not so formal, my dear. Call me Sean. And I see you didn't come alone—who is this fine, young gentleman?" Sean nodded his head toward Gillian, who was standing next to her in a well-cut suit, looking as if he'd stepped out of a fashion magazine.

"Mr. Bruce, my name is Gillian Nation. I am the manager of a stable full of A-list celebrities out of Hollywood and a close, dear friend of Miss Baillie's." He stretched his manicured hand out and accepted the dried hand in a strong shake.

"Celebrities? Would I know any of your clients, by chance?" Bruce rubbed the towel across the back of his neck, but Baillie noted his panting interest at the word *celebrities.*

"Oh, I'm sure you have, sir. I only handle the finest divas in the music world." Gillian played it candidly. "I've invited some of my sweetest clients to stay at Miss Baillie's castle for a week or so."

The man flinched but regained his composure, staring directly at Baillie. "How charming. I assume you're still in a quandary about my bank's offer?"

"I am, sir. Gillian is here to help me with his quality opinion. And since he owed a few of his more famous clients a respite, he turned his trip into a healthy tax write-off."

"A true benefit for you," he purred. "Might I have a chance to see your clients during their stay? As a neighborly gesture, of course." He leaned toward Gillian.

"Why, certainly, I will do my best to bring them over incognito. I must protect and limit their exposure over here. The reason I requested Miss Baillie to schedule a meeting with you was to warn you of the possibility of paparazzi swarming the immediate area should any errant notice of their arrival leak to the media. It can be quite inconvenient and chaotic in that case. All precautions will be taken, of course, sir."

"George," Sean addressed the butler who'd handed him the towels, "please escort my guests to the parlor and fetch them some delightful refreshments while I run upstairs and change." Baillie raised her hands to object. "Now, now, it's my fault for scheduling you so close to my lesson. Please, let me make it up to you," he pouted. "I won't be but a few minutes."

Gillian dropped his head in agreement, and Baillie nodded as the man dashed off. The two followed the older servant in a slight maze to the parlor. They relaxed in twin, overstuffed chairs.

"The bait has been set and quite easily, as I suspected." Gillian scoped out the room and sniffed at the overzealous decorating. "It looks like the tooth fairy threw up in here."

Pastels overwhelmed the furniture and walls of the room. Baillie twisted her neck in looking around as the servant returned from the kitchen with an antique teacart filled with pleasures. Picking up a cup and saucer, the stiff-backed man turned to Baillie. "One lump or two, miss?"

"One, please, with a splash of milk."

"I'll have the same, kind sir," Gillian said before turning his attention to Baillie. "You will remember to order in a case of her favorite bubbly, won't you? She demands a bottle be chilled and prepared every evening should she wish to partake in a glass. She goes into freaking hysterics at room-temperature alcohol."

"You emailed me the list of demands last week, Gillian, a list nine pages long, I might add. I never thought having divas under one roof would be so difficult and dramatic." She raised her voice to ensure the help heard everything. “I thought the women were coming over for a respite, a chance to meet together over a possible combined album without the nosey American media peeking over their shoulders. This seems like a circus.” She sipped at the strong, delicious tea without hesitating about its safety. She felt sure Gillian had hooked Sean by mentioning celebrities, so he wouldn’t be stupid enough to pull something.

“There you are.” Sean waltzed in with a chilled bottle of water in his hands. “I do hope the tea is satisfactory. Nothing for me, thank you. I still need to cool down.” He took a sip as he sat gracefully across from them. Crossing his legs, he leaned forward a bit. “Now, Mr. Nation, you caught my attention with your delightful profession and this upcoming visit.”

“Please, call me Gillian, sir.” A Cheshire cat grin pulled at his lips. “It is not often I can offer my girls a chance to spend some relaxing time in the Scottish countryside. Hollywood can be quite insufferable this time of year.”

Sean looked dumbstruck. He couldn’t soak in Gillian’s words fast enough. “You call them girls?”

Gillian set his cup and saucer down and lowered his voice. “Not just any girls, Sean. The crème de la crème of Grammy winners.”

Baillie watched the show from her chair, carefully sipping the tea and nibbling a biscuit to hide her smile. Once Gillian got into character, there was nothing more brilliant on Broadway. She loved watching him in action, whether closing a sale at Pen and Pages or getting what he wanted from the girls.

Holding her saucer on her lap to keep her hands from shaking, it was time to say her part. “Mr. Bruce…uh, Sean, I can’t believe I am going to host these incredibly talented women in your country. I’ve never met a D-list celebrity, let alone the caliber of stars coming to stay at my castle.” She pretended to fan her face. “Over the years I’ve sold a few rare first editions to Gillian through my shop but have never had a chance to dip my toe into his star-cluttered world."

Baillie gasped suddenly, opening her eyes wide. *Hope I didn't overplay that. What did Gillian tell me? Excess within control.* "Gillian, Mr. Bruce has been so generous in assisting me with the mounds of paperwork on the Baillie Castle and quite diligent ensuring me of a prompt and profitable sale of the property should I wish it so." She nodded to Sean. "Couldn't we do something special for him while these fabulous women are here?" Baillie thought the man would fall off his seat. "I know it is a once-in-a-lifetime event for me, and I am more than flattered to offer them a place to stay. But this important man is also risking the possibility of being harassed by swarms of low-flying helicopters and imposing hoards of media trespassing on his property."

Gillian checked the cuticles of his right hand as if contemplating her request. Baillie hoped she had sounded innocent, sincere enough. Gillian had coached her on these key lines over and over last night. She felt like Oliver asking if he could have more.

"What did you have in mind, dear?" Gillian sounded guarded, like Baillie was an autograph hound ready to annoy his clients.

Baillie batted her eyes—she'd throw up later. "Couldn't they do a few songs, like a private concert type of thing after a light dinner some evening?"

Gillian stared at her as if she had stepped into a warm pile of something disgusting. "You want me to ask my girls to perform on their vacation?" His voice chilled the room. Sean sat mesmerized, breathless.

"Gillian, think about it." She set her cup and saucer down before she dropped them. "How often are they going to get a chance to sing in an old castle? It's unique, exotic, and we'd keep it down to like one song apiece," here she glanced conspiratorially at Sean with twinkling eyes, "right? It wouldn't have to be a huge extravaganza." Sean's head nearly rattled as he shook it. "I think these insanely talented women would think it a hoot singing, well, *performing* actually, in a real medieval castle, especially after a few glasses of that expensive bubbly you had me order."

"A hoot, Miss Baillie?" Sean's voice cracked. "What does that word mean?"

"Like having silly fun. And they'd get a chance to meet a real Scottish manor lord or such." She pointed both hands at Sean.

Gillian sniffed again, studying his cuticles. "I suppose I could propose something simple, though it would totally be up to them. I don't want a drafty, cold room to damage their sensitive vocal chords."

Sean found his voice. "I can assure you, Mr., uh, Gillian, the castle was remodeled decades ago. The multimillion dollar renovation I heard my grandfather speak of back in the late forties, early fifties brought in electricity and heating into the rooms." He smiled like a child bartering with his parents. "I could loan some of my staff and portable heaters if you wanted, or better yet, I offer you my home itself for the performance."

Baillie thought the man was going to faint. Gillian needed to pull the batteries out of this guy before he took over the whole event.

"Now, that is quite generous of you, Sean. This exquisite home is more of what the divas are used to—five-star penthouse suites, multi-floored homes of pure elegance." He flipped a hand out. "But Miss Baillie has a rather unique point, if you will, of the opportunity of abiding in more of a medieval theme abode, a carnival trick of living in the past that I think they would enjoy."

Sean masked his disappointment well. "I suppose I understand the rustic appeal." A sly smile pulled at the corner of his mouth. "Then it sounds like you will allow me the delightful opportunity to hear your clients sing. Lovely."

Baillie blinked, unsure of how quickly the decision was made. Well, that was what they had come here for. "Gillian, thank you ever so much." She clapped her hands together. "I don't wish to take up any more of your time, sir…uh, Sean." She stood, and both men rose from their seats. "I believe once Gillian has any news for you he will be in touch directly. I have your card at home, of course, with phone numbers and will share it with him."

Gillian nodded. "I will do my best with the request and will let you know in advance."

The men shook hands, and Baillie smiled at the banker as she followed the butler to the door, her hands twisted together in front of her. She didn't want them flying around in excitement.

Bruce baited and hooked? Check.

# Chapter Twenty-five

T-Cup stared around the room. Open suitcases stashed in various corners had exploded with pieces of outfits and accessories. A knock at the door brought a sigh. "Come in."

Baillie stood with a couple of cold bottles of water. "Need any help in here?"

Clapping his hands together, T stepped up and took a bottle. "You're a savior. I need about thirty-two light bulbs around a good makeup mirror. How am I supposed to get fabulous in this dungeon of a bedroom?" He twisted the cap from the bottle and drank deeply.

"Hmm, hadn't considered that. But remember, there are no spotlights tonight. You don't have to layer on the cosmetics for bright lights. You're going to be singing by candlelight. Things are gonna work out just fine."

"You are such a jewel, Mama. How is my favorite witch, Rafael, doing? She has gotten so jealous of my junk while you've been gone." He turned and paraded his backside. "Nothing jiggles here, girlfriend, check it out. Great padding is the key, and I don't want to hear any catty remarks tonight."

"Have I told you how much I appreciate you guys being here?"

"About a dozen times, love. You know we'd do anything for you. We girls stick together." T took a critical look at Baillie's face and then a long, slow look down to her shoes. "Girl, you better get started on your own self. You are not showing up to this premier performance in flannel." He stomped and gave a vixen snap.

Baillie let out a long sigh blended with a giggle. "Yes, I hear Gillian is in charge of dressing me for tonight, which I guess is a very good thing."

"Thank goodness. Now *ándele, ándele*!" T pushed her toward the door, practically skipping.

"*Si*, Speedy Gonzalez," she laughed.

Baillie wandered down the hallway, and Kai appeared next to her. "Woman, these tiny men are not my vision of rallying the battle cry for help."

She stiffened her shoulders and forced a smile. "True, but trust me, sometimes you fight the enemy with candlelight and glamour, not swords and steel." She wished she could stab her finger on his chest for emphasis without her finger going *through* his chest. "Tonight is important, and I believe in Gillian's idea. They're going to wear wires, and I'm hoping the girls can get some kind of confession or information out of Mr. Bruce."

"Those wires you speak of..."

"It's a tiny transmitter, a little machine that records voices, so whatever is said can be played back over and over. In this case, something we can play for Scotland Yard and get this guy arrested. Gillian brought the equipment from Seattle."

"Ah, Gillian, a man of many talents." Kai's voice hardened. "Again, it's Gillian."

"Yes, oh crabby one, he has quite a head for details and how to pull things off in style." She swished a few steps for emphasis. "I wouldn't be able to do any of this without him."

A disgusted noise came from Kai. "I dinna know why you won't let me take care of the devil here in me own way. Invite the villain over and leave me alone for a few minutes with him."

"Oh, sure, and how would I explain a dead body in the parlor? This is the twenty-first century, Kai. I would end up in jail with that great plan of yours. Bashing him on the head with a candlestick in the library isn't a game at the end of the day; it's a crime scene investigation."

"He seemed to have no hesitation in feeding ya the poisonous foxglove, Annie."

"Well, that's true, and I'm not sure what explanations he would have come up with to authorities if I only got violently ill from the cake."

"Ill? Woman, you'da died at his evil hands." His voice barked. He stopped, and Baillie felt the frosty bite as he grabbed her arms. "You shouldna come here, ye wild stubborn one. I couldna bear your death, Annie."

Despite the cold, she stared into his twin dark pools, almost seeing her reflection in his eyes. Her heart pounded at the closeness of his face, his chiseled features right in front of her. Her knees felt weak until she pulled up her resolve. "But I am here, and I don't regret one minute of my decision." She refused to turn away. "Not a single minute."

Kai cleared his throat and let go of her. Taking a step back, Baillie realized they were standing in front of her bedroom door.

He reached behind her and opened it. "I shall be close, Annie. I'll not leave your side this evening." He bowed deeply and disappeared.

Standing in the doorway with her hand against her heart, she didn't hear Gillian come up.

"Am I interrupting anything?" he whispered.

Baillie squealed, "Don't sneak up on me!" She grabbed the doorjamb with one hand and flipped a stray lock of hair with the other. "He, uh, he just left."

"Looking at that face, I could have guessed as much. The lady doth wear her heart on her sleeve for a certain Highlander," he teased.

She punched him in the arm in quick response. "Well, I must be the only one. Don't mess with me, I'm a nervous wreck."

"All the better to start getting ready for tonight, my dear." He pointed into the room. "I had Putney press some of the wrinkles from the dress after its long trip in my suitcase. I think you'll be quite pleased with the fit."

Baillie stared at him, confused, then looked over at her bed. Yards of emerald green fabric draped over the side. "Oh, my, goodness, you didn't. It's utterly breathtaking."

"I took the liberty of purchasing the dress you wore at the Renaissance Faire and had it updated a bit in design." Gillian looked like the cat that drank the cream. "How else could I assure the dress would fit? And I knew you hadn't brought anything decent; nothing you packed was respectable." He stepped into the room. "Sally gave me the shoes you wore that day. Let's see your kilted friend deny his feelings after seeing you tonight. Now what am I going to do with that hair of yours?"

Baillie put a hand up to her recently washed hair, not taking her eyes off the dress. "I thought I would just wear it up. It's a night for the girls, not for me."

"*Just* nothing. You are the host and heiress tonight and must look the part. I'll have Rafael come in once you're dressed to curl your hair and whatever hocus pocus she can with your makeup." He flipped his fingers in a slight goodbye. "Do bring large and gorgeous with you tonight. I don't want him to miss this." He laughed as she shut the door in his face.

Baillie hummed as she slipped out of her jeans. She avoided looking in the mirror. Tonight she was young and beautiful, not middle-aged and gravity challenged. Swirls of sweet Disney princesses danced through her head. She grabbed a tube of hand lotion and slathered a bare leg. "I swear my skin is a bottomless pit of dryness." She hummed something from *Sleeping Beauty* and started on the other leg as a cool breeze caressed the back of her neck.

"Seriously? You snap at me, practically picking a fight, and then sneak in here when I'm half naked?" Baillie talked to the air. Nothing. She couldn't decide if she should be flattered or furious. She wasn't twenty-something anymore, and nothing stayed smooth and flat anywhere on her body. No wonder he didn't seem interested.

She rubbed her hands up and down her arms, soaking up the last of the lotion before picking up the neckline of the dress. Stepping into the opened center, she pulled the folds of green slowly up her body. The material felt cool and wonderful. Slipping the shoulders up, she twisted her arms behind her to find the zipper when it started rising up her back by itself. Chills ran down her spine, and not from cold. "Kai," she whispered, tilting her head.

A knock at the door made her jump, and for a moment she was disappointed before she slipped to the other side of the room. The dress swayed and swished perfectly as she walked. T-Cup stood on the other side of the door in a brilliant red silk robe cinched tight at the waist.

"Oh, good, you're dressed. Come with me, Little Mama, we found the perfect hideaway and made it into our dressing area. We brought all the candles and mirrors we could find, and it helps in the tiny space. This place is archaic, girlfriend."

"It should be; it's a castle." She laughed at T's flustered tones.

"That's no excuse; it's been remodeled, though whoever did it had no imagination for real conveniences."

They turned a corner, and Baillie blinked at the bright lights reflecting from the various mirrors. Rafael was seated, laboring over layers of makeup, wearing a skullcap. Gillian had his cell phone out, texting.

"Good, you're here. It seems I have news about the DNA samples." Gillian remained glued to the screen, his finger scrolling through the message. "My friend said the lab results came in this morning—well, his morning. This all-day time difference is thoroughly annoying."

Baillie stopped gawking at the makeup area and stared at Gillian. "I don't care about the freaking time difference! What did he say?"

"Chill, woman." He scrolled down and tapped the screen. "Seems your intuition was correct about the young waif. You two are a match." He looked up. "She's a Baillie, Baillie."

"What madness is he saying?" Kai materialized at her side, barking the question right near her ear.

Baillie spooked, which caught everyone's attention. T whispered, "He's heer-rrre."

Embarrassed with all eyes—multiplied inside the various mirrors—in her direction, she said toward the empty space, "Remember the kit Gillian sent where I needed to get a sample from Rogue?" While she talked to a blank spot in the hallway, the girls stared past her, trying to see anything different in the air. They looked in the mirrors and back to Baillie—searching for a ripple, a slight shimmer, she supposed.

"Aye, I remember the night quite well, my Annie," his voice dropped, deep, silky. He leaned toward her, his eyes flashing.

Gillian smirked. "My, our friend must have said something delicious. I've never seen you that specific color of deep red. How I wish I'd been a fly on the wall during that night."

"Shush, Gillian," she snapped, hating to be the center of attention, about ready to stomp her foot at someone. Kai stepped closer, and her eyes moved up to adjust. The girls leaned forward, watching closely as the tension in the area increased. "See what you're causing me?" she chastised her ghost, who seemed to be enjoying himself.

"Annie?" He waited patiently for her answer.

"The tests came back; Gillian just got the results." She folded her arms across her chest like a shield against the news. "Rogue is a Baillie, too. Her DNA, her sample, matched mine. And since she is, she must be a more recent bloodline."

Her mind couldn't wrap around the results, though she had started the process and understood the consequences. If Rogue were a Baillie, she would be the true heiress of the castle. Baillie had zero claim. It wasn't hers. She bit the edge of her bottom lip, and a silence settled over the area, a damp cloak of understanding about the announcement rippled around the group.

Gillian broke the depressing silence first. "Well, we'll need to do more research on this. He'll overnight you a copy of the results. But for now," he clapped his hands, "we have a performance tonight. We still have a killer to catch, girls. That hasn't changed."

Baillie nodded her head, but her heart wasn't in it. She tried to keep her face steady as she stared up at Kai. "She has your eyes, Kai. I recognized them when I first got here. It's hard to deny she's not family. I had to know, and we found she's an immediate branch of the family at that."

"Annie, the man found the lass in the streets of Edinburgh, a runaway orphan she was. I heard him talk the tale a few times with Robbie and Putney. Nothing but the stallion brung 'em together years ago, and he committed his life to the care of her as if she was his own wee bairn. Now you tell me she be a Baillie?"

"I realize the impossible odds, but look at us." She brushed a single tear away. "This is just as impossible, our communication, our…friendship. But it happened; is happening."

The girls turned back to their mirrors and dozens of makeup brushes, glitter and paints. Baillie was thankful for this token of privacy. But in the silence that followed, Rafael sighed and stood up. "Baillie? Excuse me, Mama, but you need to get ready. Come, sit here, let me do my work." She reached over and led Baillie to an empty seat; her eyes followed Kai until she sat down. Rafael stuffed a few tissues in her hand. "Girl, no tears or the makeup will run. You'll get spots on the dress." She dug into a nearby case and wrapped a hand towel around Baillie's shoulders.

Kai bowed before disappearing, but only Baillie knew.

• • •

Kai retreated to his former bedroom. He hated to see Annie in tears. Scanning the room, he noted her things scattered about and relaxed in the feeling of the new normalcy he had grown to enjoy.

Her cell phone sat on the bed, her laptop on his writing table, clothes she'd worn this morning bunched in a corner.

He picked up her robe and held it against his face. The idea of her leaving the castle left a hollow void. But there was much to do, and Annie needed him. Despite how mad her scheme seemed to him, he would stay by her side and pray her friends would succeed in their venture. He must keep his Annie safe this evening.

## Chapter Twenty-six

"We have about an hour before Mr. Bruce arrives." Baillie checked her watch. The girls had scrunched and pulled themselves into their costumes. "We need to go down and introduce you to the staff." *Isn't this where a person crosses themselves before going into the lion's den?* "We don't want you to give Robbie or Putney a heart attack from your magical transformation."

Gillian tugged on his tuxedo sleeves. "Girls, let's go now and break the news. You can put on the finishing touches when we come back upstairs."

Dragging them away from their mirrors brought grumbles and complaints, a flurry of powder, and heavy sighs. The group moved together to the stairs and headed down toward the kitchen.

"No slouching," Gillian snapped.

Baillie almost slipped on the stairs. "What?"

"Walk like a lady, head up, shoulders back." Gillian demonstrated. "Watch the girls and imitate the best you can."

The two divas glided down the stairs as if the bottom landing were teeming with photographers instead of empty space. Robbie came around the corner and gasped. The women continued down the stairs, now waving in queenly style. Baillie's strained nerves caused her to giggle. Robbie looked terrified—he blinked twice and dashed off toward the kitchen calling, "Woman!"

"And the carnival begins," Baillie said out of the side of her mouth to Gillian.

Putney shuffled out in front of Robbie, urging him to move faster as they came around the corner. Wiping her hands on her apron, she didn't see the glitter and glamour immediately. But as she looked up, everyone heard the loud inhalation of breath. Robbie's face lit up with a silly grin.

"I said you won't believe your eyes, woman, dinna I not?" he chuckled.

Putney just gaped.

Gillian moved through the sequins easily and put his hands out to the cook. "I'm so glad you're here. I'd like to introduce you to the girls for tonight." He stood tall and, stepping beside her, draped an arm around her shoulders. "First, I present the very talented and saucy Jaello."

Gold lamé and glitter shining from head to toe, Jaello stepped quickly toward Putney, a long fringe of gold beads swirling and swinging with each step. "*Muy bonita, senorita.*" Jaello slid her back leg behind her in a deep curtsy, blatantly winking at Robbie before moving to the side.

"And no fantastic show would be complete without the frenetic, fabulous spitfire, Beyawncee." Gillian moved his arm out like the ringmaster at a circus.

Beyawncee, dressed in a nude-colored body suit sewn with crystals and sporting pieces of black lace and beads swirled in patterns in significant places, danced in quick, vibrating steps across the floor. Five-inch heels helped the petite diva look Putney right in the eye. "Darling, all the single ladies are here." She flung her arms over her head, shaking the wig of wildly flying blond curls.

Baillie still stood at the bottom of the stairs, her hands clasped in front of her. Gillian leaned his head down and softly said, "And you've met the hostess for this evening, Miss Catharine." He winked at Baillie, who rolled her eyes and walked carefully with her shoulders back and head up as if balancing a stack of books. She stopped in front of the couple.

"Child, I don't know what to say," Putney said. "I've never seen such a spectacle. Celebrities here, performing, tonight." Each word choked its way out.

"The girls have to finish getting ready," Gillian spoke up. "Dinner will be in a half hour so be at your best, all of you." He bowed to Putney. "May I escort you back to your delightful gastronomic palace, my dear?"

The woman stared at him, speechless, and nodded. Robbie scratched his head, watching the girls going back up the stairs as his wife walked away with a tuxedoed man.

A gong sounded behind them, and Robbie rolled his eyes. Baillie put her hand on his shoulder. "I'll get it. You relax and keep Miss Putney calm as best you can."

She rushed to the door, skidding her feet across the floor. Kai materialized by the door in a strong barricading stance, fire practically shooting from his dark eyes as Baillie braked sharply at the vision.

"I willna let anything hurt you tonight."

Baillie nodded before opening the door. "Mr. Bruce, right on time. Please come in."

"My dear, where is Robbie? You shouldn't be answering the door like a commoner, especially as ravishing as you look this evening." Sean stepped inside with a flourish, his black, floor-length cape swirling around him.

"Why, thank you, sir." She lifted her hands. "May I take your coat?" The silk lining hissed as he draped it over her arms. He tugged on his cuffs, and Baillie detected a slight nervousness about him, which increased her confidence. "Follow me, please." Baillie led the way.

As they walked into the drawing room, Gillian stepped forward, his hand outstretched. "Sean, a pleasure to see you again." They shook hands while Baillie draped the cloak nearby.

Baillie wondered who outshone whom between this dynamic duo of ultimate men's fashion. How many zeros were included in the bottom line of their combined outfits?

"Have your clients enjoyed the beauty of Scotland?"

Gillian handed the man a glass of wine. "Exceptionally, quite in awe of the quaint countryside. They will be down shortly. You know how women are; now multiply that a hundredfold for celebrities."

That was her cue to go. Gillian didn't need her at this point. Before she could sneak out, Kai popped up beside her.

"I fear you are taunting the bull."

Baillie kept a smile on her face. "Can we move this conversation? And speaking about bull, you're blocking the door, cowboy," she said through clenched teeth.

Kai stepped aside and followed her into the hallway.

"Don't sneak up on me tonight. I know you'll be close by, but I don't need to be caught talking to thin air."

"I do'na feel I can trust this Gillian character of yours. The man looks more like a weak-wristed woman."

*He picks now to bring this up?* Baillie needed to get to the stairs and herd the girls down. "He's extremely intelligent, Kai, experienced. He knows what he's doing." She checked her speech as Robbie stepped out and nodded his head. Dinner was ready.

"It's time." Baillie turned and dashed up the stairs. Wafts of hairspray and sweet smells hit her halfway up the second level. Giggling, she burst into their sensational company. "You're dazzling! I need sunglasses up here. Ready?"

Jaello stood up first, the strings of beads flowing with her moves. "Girl, let's go kick some banker butt."

"Okay, I'll go start the music." Baillie slipped back down the stairs and grabbed a fan from a tabletop. *Bloody stairs*, she thought as a trickle of sweat tickled the back of her neck. Lifting her arms away from her dress, she fanned her face vigorously and dabbed the back of her hand against her damp upper lip. *I hate stairs.*

Fingers of ice trickled against her bare arms. She tensed, then relaxed at the refreshing chill. Kai moved his hands to her neck and brushed them under the ringlets of her hair. She closed her eyes and leaned into the coolness. "Thank you," she whispered. One minute she felt like kicking him in the shins for his childish behavior and the next he was taking sweet care of her. The most delicious feeling soothed her damp neck while something else creaked from lack of use inside her heart, growing, glowing. His touch awakened more than she was ready to admit. Baillie took a deep breath and noted the girls waiting at the top of the stairs. She jumped and punched the play button of the sound system.

Instrumental music played a seductive beat as the girls started their walk one at a time, Rafael a few steps behind T-Cup. Gillian ushered the banker into the hall for the full effect of the divas' entrance.

Sean leaned over, whispering to Gillian, who looked like the cat who'd swallowed the canary. The girls sauntered past the two men, swishing their hips, and into the great hall. The long table glimmered under the candelabras, with the best dishware and silver decorating each seat.

During dinner the men were allowed only minimal chitchat as the girls commandeered the evening telling bawdy stories of Hollywood. Sean sat flushed from the attention and endless wine. He had barely touched his food.

"Someone please take this plate away before I blow a side seam in this outfit." Beyawncee swooned back in her chair, shoving the plate. "We don't want a wardrobe malfunction tonight." She smiled sweetly at Sean.

Baillie rang a silver bell, and Putney came out in a starched uniform to clear the table. "If you all will excuse me, I think I'll freshen up a bit before the performance." The men stood as Baillie rose from her chair. "Sean, please enjoy another glass of champagne."

"Yes, I'll go check the sound system and be right back," Gillian excused himself.

Beyawncee nudged off a shoe and ran her toes up the banker's calf as she rambled on about the insufferable nuisance of being chased by the press night and day. She winked at Jaello across the table.

Gillian came to the door and clapped his hands together once. "I'm sure you two already chose who is going first, so I want the other to sit close to our guest. And behave." He raised his perfect eyebrows, and the girls laughed merrily as they stood from the table.

Gillian led the way to another room set up with high-backed, overstuffed chairs. Candles flickered everywhere, creating a soft, romantic glow in the room. A delightful corner was decorated for their stage, draped with yards of lace and silk with a microphone and stand ready.

As Beyawncee began singing, Jaello leaned over with a wicked smile and whispered, "Do make an excuse to leave early, handsome, and I'll meet you at your place for a private party."

Sean couldn't wipe the grin from his face. The loud music, quality wine, and a gorgeous woman at his side had obviously fogged reality.

Beyawncee snapped her fingers from the makeshift stage and whooped, "You go, girls! Let's rock this party!"

Baillie refilled Sean's glass and barely nodded at Gillian, pouring a splash more in his as well. During dinner, Putney had swapped glasses all night, taking Gillian's half-filled ones and leaving an empty one behind. He needed a clear head to orchestrate the night's events.

Baillie found herself swaying, her dress swishing. She felt like the intimate event was going well. Gillian had cautioned her earlier that they probably wouldn't get anything from Bruce during dinner or the show. These hours would lay the foundation, and then the party would move next door.

Sean baited, intoxicated and awed? Check.

# Chapter Twenty-seven

Jaello slid her gold-sequined rear closer to Sean on the couch. The banker had eagerly taken up her request to sneak away from the castle early, ditching Beyawncee. She'd flipped the switch on the recorder and turned on the full charm before slipping out of her coat at the door. "Now why do you want to harass that pitiful woman next door? She hardly seems worth the breath to fret over, darling."

Sean practically preened at her closeness, but his eyes took on a steely look. "Miss Jaello, you have no idea what a clansman will do for honor and respect. My ancestors had claim to that land, and a debt is owed."

Purring, she leaned closer. "You look so powerful when you talk about the Bruces. Tell me more about this delicious debt." She spread her fingers wide and placed a hand on her chest. "Is this like *West Side Story*, where the last man standing wins?"

"I'm afraid I'm not familiar with that American reference, my dear. The honorable Bruce clan deserves the property, and I'll do whatever I have to against any who try to stop me. It's my legacy passed down by my father and his before him. That woman is the last in her pitiful lineage, and it won't be long before she is packing and heading back to her homeland. Or else." The last two words slipped out quietly.

"Or else…ooh, look at how manly and powerful you are. A man who knows what he wants and goes after it," Jaello purred.

"Aye, I'll not allow a mere American woman to stand in the way of what's rightfully mine."

Jaello picked up her empty wine glass and Sean quickly poured the white wine until it was half full. "I know so little about the old woman—just a mere acquaintance of my manager, you know; I've barely met her before, a Hollywood kiss-kiss type of relationship. But I'm tickled to death to have accepted this invitation. I've discovered you and this darling cottage."

Sean practically giggled at her attention. "You are quite delightful, Miss Jaello."

"Now would you be as gruff and mean if I moved in next door?" she teased. Jaello froze at the cruel mask that suddenly came over his face. She felt afraid to breathe.

Suddenly he laughed heartily. "Oh, your American humor is refreshing." Jaello giggled nervously. "Curious, though," he took a deep drink of his wine, "there was almost an impossible piece to the puzzle that would have spoiled my game altogether. I hadn't thought about that in years until you just mentioned moving in."

Jaello batted her long lashes and said softly, "I love playing games, especially mysterious ones. Tell me more, you wicked hunk." And she snuggled deeper into the corner of the couch, playing her long fingers along the stem of the wineglass.

Sean glanced up behind him, over by the fireplace. "See the paintings along the wall?" Jaello looked over the man's shoulder at the various portraits. "The one on the right was my baby brother, Patrick, the black sheep of the family, a dire mistake by my parents one drunken night. He spent his entire youth defying our father and his bloodline.

"After turning eighteen, he disappeared one night, and years later I heard rumors in town that he had married a young Baillie. Utterly ridiculous I thought at the time. Though knowing my father, he wouldn't have discouraged any such foolishness. Patrick had the man's soul wrapped around his little finger. If they'd had any children from this ridiculous union, my plans would have been ruined. My grandfather, of course, would have drowned their offspring like a litter of kittens down the well."

Jaello stared wide-eyed at the cold facade of humanity across from her. She sipped at the wine before speaking. "And where are these errant lovers now?"

"Killed, an accident on an icy highway in northern Scotland a few years after they married, thank goodness. The detective I hired assured me there were no living Bruce relatives except myself. So let the games come to a glorious finish against the American stranger, and the castle will belong to the Bruces once again." He raised his glass in a toast, nearly sloshing the liquid.

Jaello clinked glasses with the insane banker, but she needed more of a confession than veiled threats for Baillie. She'd watched enough television episodes to know the culprit needed to be specific in what they planned. She scrambled around for a question, something to keep the conversation going in the right direction to bring this man to justice. Little Mama was counting on her.

A deep-toned bell rang, and Sean nearly growled. "I'm sorry, my dear, I gave staff the night off so we wouldn't be disturbed. I will check the door and chase the intruder away."

Jaello smiled with her eyes half closed. "Of course you will, darling. Hurry back to me."

Sean unlocked the door and pulled it wide. "Beyawncee? Uh, my dear, I, uh…"

"Where is she? Where is that man-stealing burrito? You said you were not feeling well." Beyawncee flounced her way past the dumbstruck banker, flipping a bright white boa in his face. "I went to her room, and it was empty. Where are you, my slutty Chiquita?" Her stilettos clicked across the marbled entry and then slowly came to a complete stop. "Oh my, gawd, this is gorgeous! All this outrageousness is yours?" She spun and flew her arms out. "I love it. But there's a certain alley cat I need to throw out, first." Snapping her fingers, she swished her hips around. "Here kitty, kitty."

"My dear, please, no need to react so negatively. Come with me." Sean nodded his head in respect and walked a little tipsily to her side, offering his arm.

"I go absolutely weak for a good-looking gentleman," she purred. "I'll be good, Brucie, just for you."

They entered the room together where Jaello was waiting next to the gray mantle, watching the entire entertainment. "Darling, I wondered if you and I would be sharing a duet this evening." She walked slowly toward them and the women kissed the air, cheek to cheek.

"You delicious tramp, coming over here without me. I saw the sweet charmer first," Beyawncee batted her eyes, stripping her coat off to flash her outfit. "Didn't I, Brucie?"

Sean couldn't look back and forth between them fast enough. His cheeks brightened in color as the girls took each of his arms, snuggled against his sides, and led him to the couch. "I am quite pleased to see you both again so soon. May I offer you a glass of wine, Ms. Beyawncee?" Sean moved toward the table.

The girls leaned back carefully and winked at each other behind him. Beyawncee said, "Just lovely, thank you. Is this a Scottish variety?" She giggled after taking a sip. "Do they make wine in Scotland? I thought you all were known for the fine whisky, single malt-type sweetness of the gods."

"A *lady*," Jaello sniped at the word, "enjoys this delicious local Oak and Elder." Jaello took a sip from her glass. "Why do you bring up whiskey, trampette? This sparkling white is quite wonderful. Are you trying to get this handsome man drunk to take advantage of him?"

Beyawncee blinked and spoke carefully. "Meow. This is my first time in Scotland, and I want to try the local brews." She hitched her shoulder as a sign without Sean noticing.

His soft chuckle made them both relax. "I apologize for not being a better host. Of course, you may sample a bit of our best.

Please excuse me for a moment." And he stood from the couch and walked over to the bar. "As a matter of fact, I've always fancied having a vineyard of my own someday." He poured the golden liquid into two stout glasses.

Touching her eyelashes carefully with the tip of her little finger, Beyawncee spoke up first. "A vineyard owner? Oooh, wouldn't that be romantic fun? A few acres of grapes—such a wild adventure, Sean. We could walk together between the rows during the dusk of day." She accepted the glass of whisky and downed it in one gulp. "Dee-lish, Sean. Would you be ever so wonderful and pour me another? Well, once you've finished your own, first." She saucily licked the edge of the glass for the last drop.

Sean swallowed his quickly. "Certainly, my dear."

Jaello pretended to sip at her glass, wrinkling her nose. "Where would you plant the vineyard, love?"

Sean rubbed his forehead. His face looked flushed, as the girls had hoped. He turned toward them both. "Hmm? Oh, where would I plant the grapes? I am hoping to gain a large parcel of property soon," he winked at Jaello, "which would be quite acceptable for a private vineyard."

"Ooh, would you name a spicy blend after me?" Jaello flirted.

"How gauche, demanding this lovely man name a private label after you." Beyawncee puffed up like a tiny peacock. "He's obviously more likely to name something sweet and saucy after me."

"My ladies, please do not quarrel between you. If my project comes through, there will be room enough to name something after both of you." Sean laughed, not his quiet chuckle but a loud explosion of laughter, an empty glass in his hand.

The girls broke into a stream of giggles. "Drink up, drink up, the night is young," they both sang. "Jinx!" They squealed and scrambled off the couch to raid the drink cart.

After a few more quick shots, the conversation went back to the possible vineyard. "So, you poor darling, are coming into some money soon?" Beyawncee leaned in, staring up into Sean's face.

"Soon, I hope, once I get your American friend to sign over the estate."

"He told me all about how the castle actually belongs to his clan," Jaello spoke up. "Hey, maybe we can get the old broad to sign the papers over in her sleep." She turned to Beyawncee. "I hear she snores dreadfully. We could be in and out of her room in moments." She snapped her fingers.

"Who does she think she is, keeping us from our own private label? Sean, Sean," Beyawncee called over her bare shoulder. "Seriously, let's plant some grapes together. What do you need us to do?"

Sean looked stunned at their positive energy. "I have struggled my entire life to gain that property. No one understands its importance to me." He poured more whisky in the glass and downed it quickly. He poured from the near empty bottle to replenish his glass. "I've been loyal to my clan as my grandfather before me."

"You tell 'em, handsome. A man has to clan up in this neighborhood," Beyawncee said.

The man didn't hear her. "I have slaved to the clan, foregone decency at times to ensure the land would come back to us, to its rightful owners."

Both girls raised their eyebrows and moved back to the drink table, closer to him. "Tell me, tell me all about it." Jaello ran her hand along the arm holding his filled glass.

"I have worked my fingers to the bone researching and doing all possible against the thieving owners, the lowly class of generations of scum who had no right to our land."

"Darling," Beyawncee scrunched her nose. "If you're such a clan man, why don't you have an accent like your neighbors?"

Sean sniffed. "I studied in London and lived there until my father died. You can change your diction; you can't change your loyalty to your clan."

"Ah, were you close to your daddy?" Jaello asked.

"Father was a pansy," he spat out, taking the girls by surprise, "allowing the Baillies to keep the property all this time. He never pulled a sword against anyone. But I'd heard the stories of my ancestors, especially from my grandfather. The land is rightfully ours." He swayed slightly at the cart.

The girls stared at each other. Jaello broke the silence. "What happened to your father?"

"I came up from the city to celebrate my father's birthday and gave the staff the rest of the day off. Father sat in his wheelchair here is this room, mumbling how wonderful the Castle Baillie was. I brought him one of my special homemade cakes," he paused, looking at something far away, "and old age caught up with him hours later. His heart gave out. Natural causes, of course, for a man of his age."

Both women snuggled close, making sympathy noises.

"I knew it was imperative to gain control of the neighboring castle quickly. Too many years had slipped away from my father's naïve actions."

"What did you do?" Beyawncee gripped her glass.

His face took on a malicious grin. "I very solicitously took over another one of my special cakes to my neighbor. I wanted to thank him for being such a good friend to my father. I knew they were close. Unfortunately, the next day I heard the man had died, quite sudden, though he was of similar age to my father."

The girls caught each other's eye. "The same type of cake you brought for your dad?"

"I am a humble baker; I know only a few recipes, though I do love one with a most secret ingredient."

"A secret ingredient? What is it?" Jaello didn't think she wanted to know actually, but she had nothing on tape yet but speculation.

"Red rum," Sean Bruce chuckled, a dark sound that sent chills through Jaello's spine. "My dear ladies, red rum."

"Red rum," Beyawncee rolled the *r* then started giggling. "How delicious that sounds, really. But that's not much of a secret. Why, there are lots of rum cake recipes in America." She stopped rambling and released a breathy giggle. "Hey, did you know that red rum spelled backward is murder?"

"Does it, my dear? How interesting," Sean slurred. "I took the challenge passed on by my ancestors and am now within mere millimeters of having the deed in my hands." He made a fist in front of him. His face transformed into anger. "An American as owner? No one would blame me for any harm that might fall on her. There is no respect in these moors for Americans, especially a disgusting Baillie."

Jaello's cell phone rang at the same time a pounding was heard at the door. All three jumped, and the girls started laughing, releasing the tension.

"Excuse me," Sean said, a stern look on his face as he walked out of the room.

Jaello answered her phone singing, "Heeeellllllo."

"Are you two okay over there? What's going on?" Baillie barked.

Still smiling brightly she hissed, "We need to get out of here. The man is totally creeping us out."

Gillian walked into the room behind Sean. "Thank gawd, the cavalry has arrived," Jaello muttered before loudly announcing, "Never call me again, you idiot fool, I will not waste my vocal cords talking to such a miserable person." And she tapped the off icon with a flick of her finger.

"You naughty, naughty girls. I am shocked. What are you doing sneaking out on me? What if *The Sun* had photographers surrounding this place as I speak, or the London tabloids?" Gillian pronounced each word sharply. "Imagine your fantastic photos splashed all over the United Kingdom, both of you alone, half naked with this honorable banker? You'd ruin his reputation, destroy his career! For shame."

The girls ducked their heads, giving them time to paste bewitching smiles on their faces for the old man. Jaello blew him an exaggerated kiss.

"Are they out there? Reporters?" Sean paled, his eyes wide.

"I ran into two picture-taking creeps at the front of the drive and told them Jaello had to be rushed to the hospital for exhaustion." Gillian snapped his fingers at the girls. "That's my job as manager, to control the chaos that follows these girls incessantly. I apologize completely, my dear man. Come along quickly, you vixens, before more paparazzi shows up and storms the door."

The girls grabbed their full-length coats, threw the rich fur hoods up and waved saucily to their befuddled host before rushing out the door in a dramatic swirl of fabric and perfume.

Bruce set up, played and stung? Check.

# Chapter Twenty-eight

"We got him!" Gillian wrapped his arms around Baillie after the trio triumphantly strode into the warm kitchen. "Jaello's got everything on tape." He squeezed her tight, and the girls rushed over and joined in. "Group hug of celebration."

Beyawncee stuck a painted nail under her wig and scratched. "If you don't mind, I want to change into something more comfortable before we continue this party. I'll be right down."

"Me, too," Jaello cooed, and the two disappeared down the hallway holding hands, their high heels clicking on the stone flooring.

Kai materialized in the kitchen once the girls left, but Baillie's back was to the open area. Still wrapped in Gillian's arms, she didn't see him come into the room nor the devastated look on his face catching her embraced in the other man's arms. The sweet look on Gillian's face made him furious, clenching his fists against the urge to punch the man viciously.

The jealousy took hold of him like a steel vice and ripped apart any rational thought in his mind. A deep growl slipped from his lips, and Baillie, hearing the noise, turned around. Before she could exclaim that the operation had been a great success, Kai vanished abruptly.

"Kai?" Baillie reached out her hand but the ghost was gone.

"Is he here?" Gillian asked. "Tell Lord Gorgeous the good news. He should celebrate with us."

"He's gone." Baillie took a step into the kitchen. "He looked… angry. How can that be?"

"Depends on how long he was standing there. Oh, Lucy, you have more 'splaining to do!" Gillian chuckled, putting his arm around her shoulders.

# Chapter Twenty-nine

"You seriously think in that 17th-century brain of yours that there is something going on between Gillian and me?" Baillie screeched at Kai. Her fists clenched at her sides. They'd been arguing now for hours in her room. "He plays for the other team!"

"The man had ye wrapped in his arms, quite cozy. He couldn't let go, and I dinna see ye pushing him away. The man was beaming, I saw it with my own eyes, woman. He is forever touching ye, his hands on ye, undressing ye in his thoughts."

"You bloody moron, the man is a good friend, one who has gone through a lot of trouble to secure an ending to this Scottish fiend next door." She stepped closer. "You come in here and accuse me of, what? Nothing is going on between us. And you're pouting because, why? He hugged me? Big deal. He's only thirty years old."

Baillie had never seen such a hue of red, almost purple, in someone's face, and a pale one to begin with. Kai looked ready to explode—he couldn't seem to catch his breath, that is if he actually breathed anymore.

"Ye dare scream at me like a common fishwife? I am not the one courting another under me own roof. Ye arse of a woman! The wilted lily is the same age as myself and obviously suits yer fancy more than I ever could. I'll not stand here another minute with you acting like yer an innocent maniac. Good day to ye." And he vanished.

"You coward! I don't bow to your will, simpering for forgiveness of something I *didn't* do, and you run away?" She didn't care who in the castle heard her.

"Ye are no lady." Kai materialized within inches of her face. "Go back to the New World, Miss Baillie, ye are no longer welcome here. Nothing here belongs to ye." Gone, again, as quickly as he came.

Baillie felt like someone had smacked her in the face with vicious force, her muscles numb from the punch. She knew he'd left for good this time, left behind a wall of pride. The stubborn, pig-headed brut wouldn't listen, and she wasn't about to beg for his attention. He could just go to Hades if he thought she'd leave because some pompous ghost demanded it.

Nothing belongs to me. Nothing. Nothing.

A sharp stab in her soul bent her in half, sending her to her knees against the threaded carpet, the muted colors near her face. This wasn't her castle anymore—everything belonged to young Rogue, the real heiress. In all the excitement of the night and the girls' success, she'd forgotten about the DNA results. Kai was right. She would have to go home, back to the shop, back to Olympia. Leave Kai forever. She fell over on her shoulder, curling into the fetal position. *As if he'd notice I was gone.* Flashes of their walks on the grounds, riding together through the pastures and moors, the sparks in his eyes refused to be pushed away, forcing a new wave of anger to wash over her.

Red-hot rage forced her up from the floor. She grabbed her coat and stomped down the stairs, mumbling to herself. She passed Putney in the kitchen and kept her head down. She was too close to tears and prayed the woman wouldn't say anything. Fate was on her side or Putney had great peripheral vision because she paused in stirring the sauce in front of her but didn't utter a sound.

Baillie stuffed a couple biscuits in her pocket and barely caught herself before slamming the door behind her. Crossing the bridge with heavy thuds, she didn't stop to enjoy the weak sunbeams glistening in the water below. It wasn't her moat anymore. Her boots thumped off the bridge, and she headed away from the stables. The last person she wanted to run into was the stable girl, rightful heir now to everything.

After a short time, she let the tears loose, large salty ones that trickled down her face, deflating the anger with each step farther away from the castle. She dug around in her pockets and realized too late she didn't have any tissues. After wiping her nose against her coat sleeve, she pulled out a biscuit from her pocket and nibbled the sweetness.

"How dare he think there is anything romantic between Gillian and me. The fool is just jealous, he's bloody jealous. And, and…" Jealousy meant feelings—without feelings he wouldn't care, right? She had more than mere feelings. For her it was a deep well of longing for the man who practically stole her heart with his dramatic bow that first night in her room. She stopped in the path and wrapped her arms around her waist as a sharp pain wrenched through her. She loved him. In the bittersweet, intoxicating, heart-breaking emotions roiling through her, the simple fact was she loved Kai. What good did her love mean now? Kai didn't care about her, was obviously done with her, his precious pride bruised by Gillian's attention. What a crock.

She kicked a rock with the toe of her boot and looked up to see where it landed. It didn't go far, but Baillie recognized where she was and headed slightly off to the right with purpose in her steps. Over the next rise should be the pasture of Highland cattle. Ferdinand's sweetness would soothe her fury. This was one male that wouldn't yell at her over some stupid ego thing.

Baillie came to the fence and climbed up to sit on top of the stones. The meadow looked inviting despite the chill sinking through her coat. Six of the hairy cows looked up as she tried to make herself comfortable on the cold rocks. Could she have one of these incredible creatures in Olympia, she wondered? Maybe she could talk Rogue into selling her one of the young calves next spring. One of the largest broke away from the herd and slowly started toward her—her favorite, Ferdinand. Gazing into its dark eyes though brought back images of Kai, and she growled under her breath, pain squeezing her chest like a band of steel.

"That pigheaded poltergeist has dark dreamy eyes just like yours, Ferdie, and what the heck am I doing falling for him? First time my heart gets molested, and the guy's a ghost. And can you believe it? I find out I have no claim to any of this because I forced the DNA testing. Well, fine. If Kai wants me gone, I'll leave with the girls."

She looked over the sparse pasture, the overcast skies creating a ceiling of soft gray cotton among the dotted herd. Baillie loved the peacefulness of watching the wooly, long-haired cattle. "I think I'm going to miss you most of all, big guy."

Ferdinand took another step or two closer when Baillie heard something sharp and high-pitched. She stared at the bull. "Was that you? Have you suddenly gone soprano on me?" The animal stopped. Baillie listened. Nothing but silence.

Pulling the other biscuit out of her pocket, she started to offer the bull a piece when a heart-breaking squeal of pain broke the silence. She dropped the pastry and scrambled off the fence. Baillie listened closely as she moved across the road, certain she heard a soft whining somewhere in front of her. Some kind of young animal was in pain, poor thing. The ground rolled in dips and gullies on this side of the road, so it could be anywhere. Bare trees dotted the area, some in fragments, shattered by lightning decades ago.

There it was again. She wrapped her coat tighter against the wind whipping at her face and headed out slowly, taking quiet steps, listening. Something let out a thin yelp and she rushed toward a crag.

There she found, out of sight from the dirt road, a tied burlap sack jerking, moving. She stared at the filthy bag and heard soft whimpering coming from inside. She knelt in the mud, her hands shaking as she tried to untie the frayed rope. She was concentrating so hard in loosening the rope, she didn't hear anything around her until a shadow crossed over her. She fell on her hip, bruising the soft skin, and a man stood in front of her.

"Well, well, here I thought my day only held the welcoming disposal of this worthless, four-footed noise maker. Bloody thing woke me up this morning with his incessant racket. And before I can throw a rock down on its head, I hear your beautiful voice up the road. What an incredibly fortunate surprise.

"I knew you'd come all super woman to help some pathetic runt not worth seeing another moment. At least the blasted cur managed one good thing in its short pathetic life. You are such an obnoxious, American, bleeding heart." He clenched his fists. "And I'm going to make sure that useless heart stops right here, right now."

"Sean," was the only thing she could spit out. Her head pounded from crying the last hour and now her stomach rolled over in fear. She fought hard not to throw up, taking in thin, shallow breaths of air. She refused to advertise how scared she was to the devil. "You won't get away with this, you know. Hurting me isn't going to give you the property. It's game over, Sean. I've got you on tape confessing to your murderous ways. If I were you, I'd be working on an immediate plan to get out of the country."

He didn't move—not a twitch, nothing—just a cold, icy glare pulling the energy from her soul. "You have *what*?" The corner of his mouth pulled in a grimace, a glaze of insanity grew over his eyes.

Angering the bull probably wasn't her best move today. Seemed she couldn't help antagonizing anything male around her. She tried to scout for anything to use as a weapon—a rock, a dead branch, anything but the burlap sack, now completely still. A gray pup's nose had edged out of the burlap sack, tiny, forlorn, lying between two quivering paws. Baillie's heart twisted at the sight.

Unfortunately, Bruce noticed her distraction and lunged, bowling her over into the wild grass. Her head snapped back at the force and knocked the wind from her. With no time to throw up her hands in defense, she was helpless as the banker straddled her body and wrapped his long, cold fingers around her neck.

"All you had to do was sign the papers and go home, but no, you were too stupid, too stubborn. You should never have come."

*Gee, great,* she thought through the overwhelming panic and fear. *Where have I heard those words before?*

# Chapter Thirty

"Rogue, have you seen Baillie this morning?" Gillian called out toward the stable, his hair still damp from a long morning shower.

"Nay, I have'na seen her since last night." Rogue stood with a curry comb in one hand her other against the neck of Dougal. The two stood outside the stable enjoying the bit of weak sunlight.

A cold sweat broke out on Gillian's neck as a bitter frost iced his cheek for a brief moment. Curious. Something didn't seem right in the tranquil view around him. "Kai? Kai, is that you?" He blinked in the sunlight, heading toward the wooden bridge by the propped open kitchen door. He called out, "Putney, have you seen Baillie today?"

"Aye, she tromped out of here about an hour ago madder than I've ever seen the woman. She looked like she needed a long walk to settle her fierceness." The cook wiped her hands on her apron.

"I don't think she'd leave the area angry, would she, not without taking one of us with her. It's not safe for her out there," Gillian said. His hand rubbed across his brow.

"You mean from the Mr. Bruce next door?" She clenched her apron. "On account of what you told us last night? When I saw her, she was fit to be tied, she was. Near exploding with tears. I dinna think much of it but to leave the poor thing alone."

"What would make her angry enough to be so foolish?" Another chill struck the side of his face. Odd. He had a sinking feeling. "T! Rafael!" he yelled, though he didn't think either was in hearing range. Was it really Kai causing the chills, the icebox feeling on the bridge? "Baillie's missing, man. Have you seen her?" Holding his hand to his cheek, he looked like he was talking to himself. "Do you know why she left, where she might have gone? Kai, if this cold is you, listen to me, the woman loves you with all her heart and soul. I'm frightened, truly frightened if she's left the castle. Help her!"

Putney stared at him as if he'd lost his mind. "Who are you talking to out there?"

He raised his voice. "Has anyone seen her come back?"

Suddenly Dougal reared straight up, his mighty head towering above Rogue. His scream echoed in the wind, and Rogue, having instinctively stepped out the way, now tried to calm him. His giant front hooves clawed the air as a second intensely pitched scream ripped from his throat and Rogue covered her ears in protection.

The stallion bolted clear of the girl and threw gravel everywhere as he furiously galloped away, his mane and tail flying like thick black flags in his wake.

The girls dashed out of the castle with Robbie not far behind and almost collided with Gillian. The group of men stepped off the bridge and moved quickly toward Rogue.

"What was that?" Rafael shivered, his face pale. T-Cup made the sign of the cross.

"I don't know what got into him. One minute he's gentle as a spring lamb and the next he acts like Satan himself pinched him. He tore off and I," Rogue put her hand over her mouth as tears sprang up, "I couldn't stop him."

"Shh, sweetie," Rafael wrapped her in his warm arms. "Where's Baillie? Why isn't she here after that call of the damned?"

Gillian stiffened. "He's gone after her," he whispered. "He's really going after her."

"What are you talking about?" T-Cup looked at him, flinging his arms about. "Who is he?"

"If she'd been anywhere close, that wild animal screech would have brought Baillie running like us, right?" Gillian snapped at T. "I think that crazy ghost just rode off to find her. But in case I am totally wrong, spread out and circle the castle quickly. Robbie,

Putney, we need everyone looking for her." Time was the enemy now.

"Did you just say a ghost rode off on my horse?" Rogue's mouth hung open, a tear glistening on her cheek.

Gillian ran a frustrated hand through his hair. "Yes, that's what I said, and I don't have time to explain. We need to search the area immediately. That maniac Scotsman next door might try anything to hurt her."

"Baillie!" Rafael yelled.

T-Cup echoed, "Baillie!"

They fled from the area, calling her name.

Gillian stayed rooted to the ground. "The crazy kilt-wearer does love her. He's gone to rescue her." Tears welled up in the corner of his eyes as waves of goose bumps rolled down his arms. "Hold on, Baillie, hold on for your hero."

• • •

Thundering hooves shook the ground as the stallion flew over the first knoll, his flanks damp. "Annie!" Kai screamed, his auburn hair waving wildly behind him. "Annie, where are ye? I'm coming for ya, Annie!"

Sean's face glared above her in a mask of hatred, frothy spittle collecting in the corner of his mouth as he strangled Baillie. Her hands gripped his wrists. Fingernails digging against the soft skin did nothing to ease the pain of his hold around her neck. As her eyelids fluttered, a gale of artic wind battered against her. The ends of her hair flew in tangled chaos around her face and Sean's hands around her neck. The banker blinked at the oddity but didn't loosen his grip.

An eerie, primal scream shattered against her ear as she slid into unconsciousness, away from the pain, where breathing didn't matter. She welcomed the dark.

• • •

Sliding off the horse in a panic, seeing the banker's hands wrapped around Baillie's neck, Kai realized too late that the connection between the two, Baillie holding Sean's arms, allowed him access to the murderer. He let out a vicious war cry and slammed every particle of energy against the banker's chest with a mighty force, breaking his hold on Baillie. Sean flew through the air, a girlish scream loosed, before landing, impaled on a broken branch, killed instantly.

Carefully Kai knelt down and lifted Baillie's head to his chest, her limp body still warm. Tears trailed down his ruddy face. "Annie, my Annie Rose, forgive me, I dinna mean to leave ye." He rocked her like a child as wracking sobs broke loose from his chest. A moment later, he lay her down and put his fingers to his lips to whistle as if his life depended on it.

"Whoa, boy, shhh," Kai grabbed a fistful of Dougal's black mane. "Thank ye, I need your help again. I canna carry the lass back home myself. Ye must take her for me."

The horse dipped his head to the ground, bending his front legs, moving down low. Kai carefully lifted Baillie's body and draped it over the broad back. He kissed her cheek once more before stepping to the horse's head. He leaned against Dougal's damp, warm muzzle, and his tears dripped on the dark fur.

The horse stayed in step as Kai walked him back to the castle.

• • •

Gillian stood between the castle and the barn, rubbing the back of his tired neck. He could hear the others calling out her name. "Come on, Kai. Find her, man, find her in time for us." He caught a movement in the corner of his eye, a speck of black in the distance. Squinting, he watched the speck and decided it was moving closer.

Cupping his hands around his mouth, he let out a yell as best as his tight throat could handle. "I see something. Spread the word."

One by one, people ran up to Gillian as the call of the sighting went around the grounds.

Rogue was the first to recognize the black spot. "It's my Dougal; he's come home," she whispered.

"Child, do you see Miss Catharine?" Putney scrunched her apron in her hands. "Can you see if he has a rider?"

No one spoke as time froze, waiting for the horse to come closer. Rogue took a step away from the crowd, a sound of mewing from her throat as she bolted across the garden. Gillian dashed after her, his heart pounding, fearing the worst. The rest followed at a run.

Rogue eased up the last few feet when she saw the stallion spook at the crowd running toward him. "Shh," she encouraged, raising her arm high to stop those behind her. "It's awright now. Bring her to me." Her face damp from crying, Rogue stared at the limp body, hair hanging down. "Thatta boy, ssh. Ya done good, Dougal."

Running her hand down the damp black mane, Rogue buried her face into the horse's wet neck as Gillian quickly moved forward to slide Baillie's lifeless body to the ground. Bile rose in the back of his throat seeing the large, dark bruises around her neck, her closed face a mask of discoloration and death.

• • •

"Kai?" Baillie asked, standing next to him, his eyes rimmed in red, his hair wild and clothes disheveled.

"Ah, my Annie Rose," Kai enveloped her in a smothering bear hug. "Annie, I'm so sorry, it was all my fault. Me foolish pride got the better of me. Instead of telling how much ye mean to me, I lost my bloody temper. Can ye ever forgive me for leaving ya?"

"Uh, Kai?" Baillie forced her head away from his crushing chest. "Kai," she said louder.

He loosened his arms and stared down at her pale face. "What, Annie?" He smoothed her hair from the sides of her face, leaving his hands on either side. "My Annie Rose," he whispered and leaned his head down, placing his lips roughly on hers. A sigh escaped as he tightened his arms around her, the kiss escalating in intensity.

Baillie leaned into his kiss, soaking up the dizzying feel of his passion. They remained that way for long minutes, rarely breaking the seal of their lips. Baillie melted in his warm, sweet embrace, matching his intensity with each thrust of his tongue. Her mind held no memories, no thoughts other than Kai. He filled everything around her.

"Kai," she breathed. "I think I've loved you from the first night you visualized. I couldn't say anything. I was afraid you'd think me a desperate old maid from America lusting after the gorgeous Highlander." She couldn't hold her hands still as they caressed his chest, her fingers enjoying the bare skin in the V-cut of his shirt.

"Annie," he chuckled. "I'm hundreds of years old. I—" He didn't finish but instead pressed his lips to hers.

Gently releasing the kiss, Kai stared at her. "Can ye forgive me, my Annie, for being such a fool? Yer friend, Gillian, sounded the alarm that you might be missing, and I struggled to contact him. He told me how much you loved me, and I know now his feelings for you are pure and innocent." Kai dropped his head, and a moan escaped before sealing his lips to Baillie's.

Kai's breath grew ragged and urgent, filling her ears with his sounds of need, until a slight hiccup caught her attention, followed by a strange mewling behind her. The trance broken, she brought her hand up to his strong, solid chest, forcing his lips away from hers.

"Wait, Kai," she tried stopping him as he kissed her cheeks, her face, and nuzzled her neck. "Kai, wait." And he brought his head up with a soul-wrenching sigh.

Slowly Baillie turned and gasped at the sight of her bruised body stretched out on the ground. Her eyes locked on the cruel, purple marks circling her neck. Gillian knelt beside the body and held one of her hands. T-Cup and Rafael stood off to the side sniffling and wiping their faces with the ends of their sleeves. The small group included Miss Putney, sobbing into her apron as Robbie shook his head, rubbing her back. Rogue, head bent to her chest, leaned against Dougal, who was pawing the ground.

Baillie blinked, trying to absorb the sorrow, but her attention kept dragging her back to Kai standing behind her, a magnetic draw pulling her like a metal doll away from the body on the ground. Kai's lips burned on the back of her neck, no longer patient. She smiled at the warmth. Suddenly it clicked—heat, burning kisses. "I'm dead?" The words didn't make sense. "I don't feel dead."

"Dinna question the fates, my sweet Annie Rose, my love. You're here with me now. I willna let you go, ever. You belong to me now and forever." Kai squeezed his body to her back, fitting perfectly in place.

"Kai?"

"Shh, my love. Don't talk. Stay with me."

"What did you say? Stay? I have a choice?" She stiffened at the idea. "Kai?"

"What, woman?" he sighed with rejection.

"Talk to me. What did you mean by 'stay with me'?"

Kai rubbed his hands over her arms and shoulders as if memorizing her feel, her body. "That little heathen in tights over there is about to ruin everything." He kissed her neck, increasing the length and duration. A breathy "stay with me" echoed in her mind.

"How long have I been dead?"

"How long? Time doesn't exist here, Annie. A blink of an eye to them can be days, months for us."

"But is this forever? Me here with you?" He stopped and his silence spoke volumes. "Kai?"

"There will soon come a choice, Annie. I want you to stay with me, here in my arms where you belong. We love each other."

She turned and stared into the eyes that had captured her heart on a cold dark night. She stood on her tiptoes and kissed that incredible face. Kai groaned but held still. Baillie savored the softness of his lips deliciously touching hers.

"I'm not ready, Kai." She kissed him gently. "I need, I want to help Rogue…she needs someone like me. With my business skills, I can help this little thing run the castle. Look at her, Kai, she has no idea what's ahead of her with the inheritance and who she really is. I want to be there for her."

"Aye," he chuckled softly. "She has the Baillie spitfire to her, I must admit. Why I dinna see the resemblance before, I'll not understand." He rubbed his hands along her back.

Baillie placed her head on his solid chest, enjoying the strong cocoon of being in his arms. Hesitation screamed in her mind. *Do you really want to leave this, leave him?* "Will you, uh…" she stuttered.

"Will I wait for ye? Is that your question? My Annie Rose, I'll haunt you night and day until you're back in my arms for good." He bent his head, and strands of curls cascaded down her cheek, silky in a caress.

"Promise?"

"Ye be a vixen, my Annie. Dinna torture me." His arms squeezed her tight as he kissed her one last time.

• • •

T-Cup rubbed his swollen eyes with his fists. A low guttural sound grew until his face balled up in a deep red and he yelled, dashing toward Baillie's body, knocking Gillian aside and throwing his less than five-foot frame on Baillie's chest, pounding her heart with the crushing fall. "No, don't leave us," he cried. A quick inhale followed underneath him, and he screamed in terror like a little girl.

The body under him convulsed as he scrambled off and watched her draw a painful breath. Baillie coughed, trying to gulp in air through her damaged windpipe.

"Baillie!" Gillian cried, flipping his hair from his damp face. "Girl, fight! Hang in there! Stay with us."

"Suddenly I'm Miss Popular," she croaked from her aching throat, before she slipped back into unconsciousness.

# Chapter Thirty-one

Baillie woke up in her bed, the decorated quilt over her, a roaring fire of reds and yellows decorating the blurry view beyond her feet. Kai paced in front of the fire, his hands clenched. She blinked, trying to focus. Her head pounded, and she hissed, closing her eyes.

"Ah, there she is," Putney patted her calloused hand on Baillie's arm buried under the covers. "Ye've given us quite a scare, Miss Catharine. I must go tell the others ye're waking up."

Baillie groaned as she swallowed; her throat burned as if it were full of glass shards. How had she ended up in her bed? She moved her bare toes across the cool sheets. The edge of a nightgown tickled down by her ankles. She tried opening her eyes again just as the door swung open, letting a gang of people with worried faces into the room.

"Toto, I think we're back in Kansas," she whispered.

T-Cup started crying as Gillian put an arm around his shoulders. "Ssh, she'll be all right thanks to you, my littlest heroine."

Baillie struggled to pull her arm out from under the covers then reached out to T, making him sob louder. "Thank you, sweetie," she whispered. He dropped his head on her hand, holding a lace handkerchief to his nose. Others wiped tears away. Rogue was tucked next to Rafael, in her arms a wiggling gray bundle of fur.

"Do ya remember this little thing, Miss Catharine? I named her Diva for ya. And she and Dougal are getting along just fine." Rogue held the pup closer to the bed. Baillie could only summon a tired but sincere smile in return.

Robbie dropped his arm around Putney as she stepped to the bed and pulled T away with care. "That's enough, wee one, let's give her some peace and quiet." T stood and wrapped his arms around Putney's neck still crying. She patted his back and walked him to the other side of the bed.

"Kai," Baillie whispered. She blinked once, twice, patting the edge of the bed. Kai sat carefully next to her and let go a sigh of relief.

Everyone else froze, looking at each other before casing the room around them.

"Do you see him? Anything?" Gillian asked.

"Kai?" Putney went pale. "Why does she call my Lord Kai's name?"

"Because he's real. Aye, she sees his ghost, she does," Rogue answered. "Lord Baillie hisself took Dougal, he did, riding swift as the wind, going after her at Gillian's urging."

Robbie came around and stared at Gillian, not saying a word, just staring at him. Gillian broke under his direct stare. "I believe the ghost to be real, sir. She talks to him constantly."

Robbie folded his arms, his eyes glaring. "You're sayin' the ghost of Lord Baillie be real?" Robbie put a hand on Gillian's arm, who tensed at the contact but nodded. "I suspected as much. I've seen the woman talking ta air since she first came here."

"Annie, how is my saucy wench feeling this morning?" Kai said, brushing his cool fingers across her forehead. "Ya had these people scared of your deep sleep for such a long time."

"Kai," she whispered. "You came for me." Everyone looked at her.

"I should'na never left you," Kai's voice cracked. "What a bloody fool I was."

"Is Sean…?" She closed her eyes. Her breathing was shallow, quick.

"Aye, he's gone, Annie, in hell where he belongs."

"As he should be." The last word faded as she ran out of breath.

Putney took command. "Everyone out! If Lord Kai is truly here, he needs his privacy with Miss Catharine."

"Listen to ya, woman," Robbie chuckled. "You always did believe the ghost haunted this ol' place."

"Ye'll not talk ill of the dead, old man. Now out." Putney fluttered her apron like chasing chickens. "Let her rest."

Baillie snored lightly as Kai stretched out next to her in the bed. He curled his arm around her waist on top of the quilt and pulled her closer. "I promised I willna leave ye, my Annie Rose. Now ye must find a way to stay with me. I canna bear to lose you to the New World." A tear glistened in the corner of his eyes. "Stay with me, Annie."

"Kai," she whispered before the snores commenced.

• • •

Days later, Baillie felt well enough to sit up in her favorite chair. She was listening to an adventurous story of Kai's childhood when there was a knock on the door.

"Come in." Baillie turned in her seat.

Miss Putney brought in a tea tray and placed it on the small table. "Miss Catharine, so good to see you up from the bed."

"Thank you." Baillie accepted the cup of tea from her. "Would you do me a favor and ask Rogue to come upstairs to see me?"

"Certainly, Miss Catharine. I may not be able to pull her away from that pup, though."

"Oh, it's all right if she brings her up, too. I haven't had much time to get acquainted yet with the newest family member."

A light tap a few minutes later brought Rogue and the pup into the room. Kai had moved to stand by the mantel, and Baillie pointed toward the seat across from her. "Come, Rogue, and sit down. I have quite a bit to talk to you about."

"Me, mum?" She held the gray scamp on her lap. "Have I been in any trouble?"

"No, nothing like that."

The pup turned its nose toward the mantle, wagging her tail quickly, pawing at the open space. "Is Lord Baillie here, mum?" Rogue asked.

"Yes, we both wanted to tell you something very important. When I first came here, one thing I noticed right away was that you and Lord Baillie have the same eyes. If you go down to the library, really look at the painting on the sidewall for yourself. Well, this made me suspect that maybe you were related to the Baillies somehow. There is this a technology now that can analyze your DNA between us, and they matched."

"What is this DNA?"

"Everyone is made up of DNA, like a set of instructions, and don't ask me what the letters stand for, but it's like a genetic code that makes us who we are. They can be analyzed by science programs that can verify your lineage across generations. Once the tests came back positive, I had Gillian contact Mr. Wallace's legal services here in Scotland to investigate your parents and how you ended up in foster care. It took quite a bit of effort, I must say, as your parents tried to keep their love and union secret."

"Why did they keep their marriage a secret?"

"The findings show that your dad was a Bruce—Patrick Bruce, Sean's younger brother. And your mom was a young Baillie maiden, an only child. They were forbidden to see each other though loved each other fiercely. They changed their names a few times to stay under the radar and moved to northern Scotland. Rogue, you were very young when they died and would never have known any of this."

"That's where they died in a car accident," Rogue whispered, "Mummy and Da."

"Yes, dear, I'm sorry." Baillie gave her a moment. "So you see, you and I are related; however, it works out that you are not only the true heiress of Castle Baillie but the Bruce manor as well next door."

"What?" Rogue went silent, denial draining away. She tucked her head into the puppy's fur.

"Sean Bruce was correct on one point in his confessions. He had no other surviving relatives; no one other than you, my dear."

She took a breath. "Does this mean I get to keep me horse?" She looked up with tear-filled eyes.

Baillie chuckled, "Absolutely. That Dougal beast is all yours."

# Chapter Thirty-two

"Rogue, you're wearing a path in the floor," Baillie pleaded, sitting at the kitchen table, stirring her tea. "You're giving the pup a neck-ache. Putney, tell her to sit down; everything is going to be fine."

"Mum, I can no more get her to sit than get ye to stop clanging yer spoon in that poor cup afore ya break it." She glared at the both women with her hands on her hips. "You, over there, sit down; these papers willna bite. And you," pointing a finger at Baillie, "drink yer tea. Nothing can be accomplished if you two dinna sit together. Ya both be Baillies, and I ken much has happened a wee too quickly with the news of the castle and inheritance. Ya must sit and figure out ya futures, discuss yer dreams between ya."

Gillian wandered into the kitchen in jeans and cashmere, catching Putney's last words. "Dreams, ah, my favorite pastime, love them dearly. Whose are we talking about and when can I tweak the conversation to mine?"

"What's yours now?" T-Cup asked, waltzing into the room dressed in a soft flowing dress of teal. Her blond wig of curls bounced. "And why is the conversation always about you? We are just as fabulous as you are. The world shouldn't always be about you."

Rafael filed in right behind, clothed in similar feminine comfort and stylish wig. She stage-walked into the kitchen.

Rafael squeaked and bent down in her heels to scratch the pup's ears. "Who's a good Diva?"

The girls each took a chair at the table, smoothing their skirts before they sat down. "Rogue, come sit with us. We're going to talk about Gillian, his favorite subject." T-Cup rolled her painted eyes, using laughter to break the earlier tension.

"Actually," Baillie started, "before you all sashayed in here, we were trying to talk to Rogue about her inheritance"—the word caught in her throat—"and her choices ahead." Baillie looked down at her cup with a sigh. The reality still smacked harsh on her soul. She took a deep, slow breath, trying to hold back the wash of tears threatening to overflow.

And she did it all under Gillian's watchful eye. "Oh my gawd, you don't want to leave the castle, do you?" He flipped an errant lock of hair over a shoulder, his voice soft. "I knew it, you've lost your mind and fallen in love with that ghost of yours." Mouths dropped open everywhere, and heads snapped in her direction.

"Kai and I do love each other," she managed to get out before a single tear trickled down her cheek. "And, no, I'm not ready to go back," she whispered. Her heart felt trapped in a vise and someone was cranking the handle. She twisted her head to face Rogue, who had finally moved closer to the table. "I know I have no claim to the castle, anymore." Tears fell freely now. "I've no right to ask you, but I'd really like to stay on for a while if you don't mind, if you'll let me."

Rogue rushed to her side and tightly grasped her arm with both hands. "Mum, I would truly love you to stay. I have'na slept in days." She ran her fingers through her short hair, tufts now standing on end. "I worry about how ya look so sad, betrayed, and here so soon after getting back on ya feet from death's door." The girl gulped for air. "I worry about the being in charge of the upkeep of the castle lands. I canna do this. It's madness, I tell ya. A lass like me running anything besides the stable is pure madness!" The young girl plopped herself on the floor next to Baillie's chair and shook her head. "Ya worked so hard, Miss Catharine, to go against the devil Sean Bruce. Ya risked your life for this castle, for all of us.

"And have ya seen the bloody stack of papers the bank wants me to sign?" She clutched her head with a moan. The puppy snuck up and nosed her arm, hesitant, whining, ready to dash away. "Inheritance taxes the man talked about alone give me nightmares. I need you here. The castle's heart belongs to you." Her bottom lip started to tremble. "Please stay with me."

T-Cup dashed around the table, carefully snapped a linen napkin out to full size, and laid it on the floor before dropping down daintily to sit next to Rogue. "Baillie, behave, you're upsetting her." She put her tanned arm around the young woman, comforting with gentle pats. Diva wagged her tail and dropped next to Rogue with a sigh.

Baillie broke into low-throated laughter, wiping the wet tracks on her face. "You did not just sit on a napkin. Are you implying Miss Putney's floor isn't clean?" She raised her eyebrows and turned toward the cook.

Miss Putney brought her apron up to her own damp face and started giggling behind it, breaking the tension as a wash of relief rippled around the table.

T-Cup scootched closer to Rogue, tugging her skirt over her knees. "Just ignore the insane laughter. She gets this way now and again," T said, fluttering her pastel-painted fingers in Baillie's direction. "Something about the change, you know, hot flashes, mood swings. Are you sure you want just her to stay here? I'll volunteer to take care of the castle with you. Girl, I am awesome in motion." Her hands swooshed in the air.

Rafael raised her hand high in the air with a flippant wave. "If Rogue is taking volunteers, I should get a vote, too. I'm fabulous at numbers and managing. We were the cavalry, you know—Baillie brought us over specifically to help, and we did a fabulous job, didn't we?"

"Yes, you did. All of you have been so important." Baillie bit the bottom of her lip. Time paused. "I don't know what to say, Rogue, other than I want to stay with all my heart."

# Chapter Thirty-three

Kai appeared in the kitchen, leaning, relaxed, against the counter. Baillie's face lit up like a prism in sunshine at the sight of him. "I see ya have quite a crowd around ye this morning, my Annie," he chuckled. "I'd say ye are loved more than ya think. Ya bring laughter and sweetness to everyone around ye."

"And here we go with the brilliant blushing, which means you-know-who is here." Gillian smirked as he nonchalantly looked around for a glimpse of the spirit.

"We love you, Kai!" both divas yelled together. "Huzzah!"

Kai covered his embarrassment with his hands, groaning. "What sorcery is this?"

Baillie laughed and shrugged. "You're their hero. You've won them over with your gallantry and bravery."

"Not to mention the man is hot," T said, fanning her face. Rogue stared at her. "Have you seen his portrait in the library? Ooh, girl, what I wouldn't do for that kilted hunk."

"See?" Rogue looked up at her and then to the empty area of the kitchen where Baillie had been looking. "I canna come between you and your first true love. I'm not an ogre to true love. You must stay here, Miss Catharine, for me and for Lord Baillie."

"My first what? True love?" Baillie stared over at T-Cup, wrinkling her nose. "And just what have you been telling her about me, you short gossip monger?"

"How you're celibate back home in America, not a hint of a date in eons of years, and you're turning into one of those ancient cat women," Rogue repeated from memory counting on her fingers. "What's a cat woman?"

"I own one cat, T!" Baillie barked and then looked, startled, at the other end of the room. "Stop laughing at me, you kilted clod!

You have no idea what a cat woman even means." Kai doubled over, his face bright red from lack of breath, a hand on the edge of the counter, his auburn curls falling across his face. *How can he be so gorgeous and irritating at the same time?* "T, you are so out of my will." She snapped her fingers. As Kai continued chortling, she laid her head on the table. "Just kill me now," she mumbled against the wood.

Everyone shouted, "No!"

Sitting up quickly, she said, "Oops, sorry," as she touched the fading yellow bruises on her neck. "I just meant it as an expression, you know, like of insane embarrassment. It's not every day I get humiliated by a gorgeous ghost."

Gillian rapped his knuckles on the table. "People, people!" He waited until things settled. "Naturally I've been giving this situation quite a bit of thought since I was the logical one running around getting lawyers and paperwork together during Baillie's return to us." Gillian paused for dramatic effect. "I've known most of the puzzle pieces the longest and have come up with a perfectly brilliant solution."

T-Cup clapped her hands together. "I love his plans." She leaned against Rogue. "They are fab-u-lous," stretching the word into three syllables.

"Yes, they are," Gillian agreed, crossing his legs. "I have toured this lovingly refurbished castle quite a bit in the last few days. I've taken measurements, counted rooms and the number of stairs." Gillian turned slightly. "And, of course, sampled the fine pastries and meals from this excellent kitchen," another long pause.

"You're driving me crazy," Rafael squealed flapping her hands in front of her face. "I can't handle the suspense. What is your exquisite idea?"

"I decree," Gillian placed a hand over his heart, "the castle would make a delicious bed and breakfast. Set up six sweet, romantic rooms and serve deliciously tasty fare," Gillian leaned back in his chair and snapped an errant lock of hair over his shoulder. The room stayed quiet, soaking in his words.

"Seriously?" Baillie was the first to speak. "You think so? What an incredible idea. Rogue, what Gillian's suggesting is an exclusive, romantic hotel, a money-making idea to help cover the costs of maintaining the castle."

"Darling, you have everything to make the perfect getaway. People would pay top dollar for a medieval stay in the moors. You could have a copy of *Wuthering Heights* in every room." Gillian closed his eyes. "You have stables for riding the grounds or out for a hike to the cliffs. And as the hostess, you could dress like you did at the Renaissance Faire and be in character."

Kai moved across the room and stood with his hands on her shoulders. "Annie, you took my breath away in your green dress. Ye have the perfect figure to wear the fashions of my day."

Baillie giggled, leaning against his arm, and Gillian, watching her, snapped his fingers with an idea. "You could tell stories of the castle, give tours, and Kai would be right by your side to answer any questions. How more authentic could you get?"

Baillie looked up at Kai, drinking in his beauty. "What do you think of Gillian's idea? A bed and breakfast offers just that, a sweet place to sleep and group meals. Six rooms, six couples, wouldn't overrun the place but would bring in a nice income to help toward upkeep."

The longing is his eyes gave her all the answer she needed. He stood tall and nodded. "The sooner you get these bloody people out of here, the sooner we can be alone and discuss this further." He winked at her.

She sparkled. "I think it's a wonderful idea. What about you, Miss Putney? Will you stay on as our chef extraordinaire?"

"Did ya mean your words true about my biscuits, Gillian?" She had her arms crossed.

Gillian smoothly slid out of his chair and put an arm through hers. "Anyone staying here cannot leave without gaining at least a pound or two from your scrumptious biscuits."

"Eh?" Robbie came into the room, spotting Gillian and his arm. "See here, young man. What's the meaning of flirting with me woman? I go out for a wee moment, and behind me back you're cooing up ta her." Putney couldn't wipe the giddiness from her face.

Gillian backed away carefully, his hands up.

"Aye, Gillian has a knack for this, Annie."

"Doesn't he, Kai? I told you he was full of ideas and such."

Gillian ignored her. "The great hall seats twelve nicely, another reason for just doing six rooms. Enough to make money, but few enough to make it fun, not grueling. You'll be booked up in no time."

After a few mumblings around the table, the room went silent, each in their own thoughts.

"Since I've stunned you all with my brilliance," Gillian continued, "let's add to that B&B concept with the ultimately perfect spot for medieval weddings, including rooms for the bridal party."

"I love weddings," T-Cup said. "What if Vera Wang herself came to visit and designed a whole line of gowns for the castle?"

Raphael swooned. "I would love to meet that woman."

A Cheshire cat grin spread across Gillian's lips.

Putney looked ready to faint. She turned toward the stove and lifted the hot kettle of water, taking it to the counter. Her hand shook as she filled a teapot, splashing drops of boiling water. Putney brought over the fresh teapot setting it down near the chattering group and went back to her post by the stove.

Rogue tilted her head toward Baillie. "Aye, wouldn't it be grand to work together on weddings? Especially when ya are so much in love yerself."

Gillian leaned closer to Baillie. "You do realize there is a slight, uh, problem with the circumstances of your relationship." He batted his innocent eyes at her.

"What kind of problem do you mean?"

"You do know the man is only, like, twenty-seven-years old."

Baillie rolled her eyes and raised her nose. "I'll have you know Kai is hundreds of years old and doesn't mind that I'm the younger woman."

A voice growled behind her. "You tell him, me wee spitfire. I'll be waiting for ye to catch up. Day by day, Annie, you're mine. You'll always be mine."

## A Sneak Peek from Crimson Romance
## (From *Cloaked in Fur* by TF Walsh)

The door to the underground bunker rattled, sending twitches down my spine. I threw the books back onto the shelf, blew out the candle, and froze in the darkness. It might be Radu, coming to help with the research. Or it might be Sandulf, who'd be less than impressed with my presence. That'd be just my luck for the alpha to bust in on me.

The door clattered again. My hands fisted as I silently prayed it wasn't Sandulf. If he found me here, I'd never be able to explain it away. He'd see right through any excuse I made for being in the pack's library. I was the outdoors kind of girl, not the studious type. If he guessed I was researching the lupul elixir, I was dead. Or as good as dead.

For the third time, the door shook on its hinges. The smell of rain teased my nostrils, along with the earthy fragrance of trees, but no Sandulf. I released a long breath. A storm was coming, and the gale continued to pummel the entrance.

I hurried up the stairs and slipped outside into the cold morning. With the door locked, I brushed foliage over the entrance with my foot. Lofty trees crowded the forest around me with minimal sunlight breaking through the canopy above. I inhaled the crisp, pine scents and took off. The wind tore through the area, tugging my blouse and pants, tossing brown hair over my face. Another night spent alone where I'd lost track of time searching for secrets of the potion. Later that night I'd be back doing more research, though Radu's help would make it a lot easier. He'd missed our catch-ups three days running. That wasn't like him. He was never late. Maybe he'd given up on helping me?

I pushed the trepidation down, knowing it wouldn't do me any good to think about it, and Connell Lonescu came to mind: his strong arms wrapped around me, loving whispers in my ears, and kisses that melted my insides. If I didn't find the potion before the next full moon, everything with Connell was over.

A loud footfall on the forest floor iced me over.

I held my breath. Darkness filled the gaps between trees where the sun didn't reach. A shadow flitted behind the broad trunks. I sniffed the downwind: timber, car fumes from the city of Braşov, and a barnyard scent.

The woods fell silent.

*Stop freaking out.*

I rubbed the chill out of my arms and kept moving. The crunch of foliage beneath my boots echoed.

I had just forced my legs into a jog when a prickling sensation slithered down my back. I wasn't alone.

The moment I whirled around, something massive and dark struck, hitting my chest. I screamed. It knocked me to the ground. I threw my arms up in defense, expecting to be bitten, and scrambled backward. My body pinched with pain. My heart thumped against my ribcage. The foul stench of wet sheep and dung smothered my senses.

A black wolf the size of a sedan crouched several feet from me—ears flat against its head and lips peeled back over pointy fangs. Rumbling growled from the animal's chest. Hot air steamed from its mouth, and it eyed me as if I were a free meal.

I couldn't breathe. A man-eating dracwulf, the same unstoppable animal said to eat entire villages, was in the Carpathian woods. The urge to transform into a moonwulf wriggled over my skin. But it wasn't my time of the month, yet I swore I sensed my inner wolf rising inside me.

In slow motion, I climbed to my feet.

The beast lunged.

I threw myself sideways into a roll, leapt to my feet and ran. The dracwulf was on my heels, swift and heavy, crashing through the underbrush. Each tree offered an obstacle to dodge around and stop the creature from jumping me from behind. Low-hanging branches snagged on my clothes and hair.

We were too far from the pack house.

Too close to the city.

The forest floor flew under me.

The pack's bunker, perhaps? If I wanted to trap myself. Terrible idea. A hint of panic crawled forward. What if I couldn't shake it? What if it caught me? What if…No more stupid fear.

Around the next tree, I swiped a hefty branch off the ground and spun to face the dracwulf, ready to finish it my way.

The animal collided with me, headfirst into my hip. I was thrown backward and crumpled to the ground like a broken tree, muscles and bones in shock from the impact. A horrid suffocating sound gushed from my lips. The beast came at me in a blur of speed, giving me just enough time to swing the branch out in front of my face. It was on me. Teeth latched onto the weapon and ripped it out of my grip.

Two things happened at once. I threw my fist into the side of its head as a shrill whistle sounded from a distance. The huge wolf jerked up, muzzle creased. Unfazed by my punch, the animal bounded over me and dashed into the woods like it had caught sight of better prey.

That was my chance to escape.

I pushed myself up, but my body seemed to weigh a ton. My hip flared in pain each time I put weight on it. Where had the dracwulf come from, and where had it gone? Dracwulves were not meant to exist and this one damn sure wasn't scared of me.

With clenched teeth and stumbling steps, I hurried toward my Jeep.

I took deep breaths and shoved my fists into the pockets of my pants, touching the coolness of the key to the bunker.

Connell.

Five days until the Lunar Eutine, the next full moon—the pivotal moment when a moonwulf like myself would transform into a full-blown wulfkin forever. Except I had other plans: to become human with a little help from the elixir I still hadn't found and stay that way.

My palms stung. I glanced at the red, crescent shapes indented into the flesh from my nails. The chill had returned to my bones by the time I reached the vehicle. I was surprised my body didn't ache worse. Instead, it just felt bruised.

The pack needed to know a monster lived in our woods, so I'd pay them a visit. I climbed into the Jeep and drove along the curving track toward the pack house.

My cell phone rang.

I snatched it from the passenger seat. Connell. Something tingled in my chest. I wanted to answer and hear his voice, listen to the way he said my name, but not right then. I'd call him back after I visited the pack house. I let it go to voice mail. The phone revealed he'd already called six times.

The cell rang in my hand. Connell again. I answered this time. "Hi there."

"Daci, are you okay?" Fear threaded his words, and that scared me.

"I'm fine. What's going on?"

"I called you all morning and no response. You're not at home or work. Where are you? I've been so worried."

I swallowed the dryness in my throat. "Out in the woods tracking deer for work." I hated lying. "Sorry, I missed your calls. Did something happen?"

He let out a loud sigh, and my stomach clenched. "This morning, a jogger found a dead girl in an alley behind your apartment. And the investigation team has been waiting for you before they clean up the scene. That's why I was trying to get hold of you."

My insides turned to mush. "That's awful. But why do you need me?"

"Your boss said you'd help us with identifying the animal, since we may need to issue a hunting permit to track and kill it. Please hurry back. I'll meet you in front of your apartment, okay? Drive carefully." He hung up.

The day was growing worse by the second.

A strange sensation flared inside me. I'd assisted police in the past on multiple animal attacks, since I specialized in animal behaviors—but on domestic livestock, never humans…unless… The dracwulf attack poured through my mind. My next breath caught in my throat.

I slammed on the brakes and did a quick five-point turn on the dirt track. Soon, I left the woods behind and sped into the city. Renaissance-style houses lined the thoroughfare, showcasing fashionable clothing boutiques, cafes, and restaurants. People wandered along the footpaths, oblivious of the monster stalking the Carpathian woods.

I arrived on my street in no time and slid out of the Jeep, rubbing my sore hip. Potted plants adorned the balconies of the concrete apartments along the road. Despite the bright flowers twirling around the metal railings, the rusted drains running down the cold white walls reminded me of the stories about families losing farms and livestock to the government in Communist times, then being forced to live in tiny apartments. I took hasty strides up the footpath and grimaced at the pain lacing through my side.

In front of my place, Connell leaned against the wall, staring at his cell. Despite the circumstances, the excitement of seeing him made me giddy. Blond hair fell over his sun-bronzed face. Those broad shoulders filled out a tailored pinstriped suit, and his well-muscled physique would make anyone think twice before taking him on.

Connell glanced up with chocolate eyes that made me forget what I was thinking. He pushed off the wall.

I ran up to him and threw my arms around his neck. My body molded into his perfectly. This was what I had never experienced whilst hidden in the woods with the pack—tenderness and love with a man.

"I missed you so much." Connell's arms swept along my back and pulled me tight. "Daci, I was so worried something had happened to you." There it was again, the terror in his tone.

I took a sharp breath and pulled back, unable to stop my defenses from rising. "I'm fine."

He scanned me head to toe. "Your blouse. It's ripped."

Peering down, I found gashes in the white fabric over my shoulders and arms. I poked a finger through one of the holes. Another favorite shirt destroyed. Great. "I fell over in the woods, but it's all good." In that moment, a flare of sharp pain throbbed down my leg, and I smiled through the ache.

Connell raked fingers through his hair and tucked his cell into the inside pocket of his jacket, revealing the gun holster at the side of his belt. "Are you sure?" His hand caressed the length of my arm before stroking my cheek.

I nodded, leaning into his touch, and wanted nothing more than to fall into his arms. No more talking.

"I love you so much." He plucked a twig from my hair. "But I don't want secrets between us."

Something hitched in my throat. I'd told Connell so many lies to conceal my identity as a moonwulf, I had lost track of them. "What do you mean?"

Only the wind swept past. Connell's gaze flickered around the place—everywhere but on me. "For over a week I've been calling you, and you never bothered to call back. Not even a text message to say you're busy. Nothing." He searched my face for an answer. "Then today I needed you for work, and you weren't anywhere. This whole time I thought I was giving you space because you were going to be busy at work for a while, but what if something had happened to you? I would never forgive myself."

A shudder ran through me and heat crawled through my chest. Had I really let days pass by without calling Connell? I was certain we'd spoken just yesterday. Or was it the day before? "I'm so sorry I didn't call you right away. Time got away from me."

He dug his hands into the pockets of his tailored pants. It was obvious they were fisted into knots. "All I ask is that you let me know you're okay, where you are sometimes, and that you're still alive."

My response came pouring out. "Why do you need to know where I am all the time?"

"That's not what I mean." He pinched the bridge of his nose. "Shit, Daci. I thought you wanted to be with me forever. I don't get what's been going on with you lately."

I shook my head in disbelief. Everything I did was for Connell. For us. I'd never felt this way about anyone, and I was ready to leave my pack for him. Even if it was unheard of. That was why I needed the elixir. "Of course I want us to be together, and I love you."

"Are you sure?" His voice shook.

"I can't believe you just asked me that."

The front door of the building creaked open, and an elderly woman with a bag on wheels shuffled outside. With pursed lips, she shook her head before hurrying down the street. Great, my whole neighborhood probably knew about my love life.

Connell glanced up to my apartment and back before loosening his tie from around his neck. "I know you haven't been spending the nights at home."

My breath quickened. "And you know this because…"

"I've driven past your place the last few nights, hoping to catch up with you. To see you. But you're never home. Where do you go every night?" His incredulous stare pinned me on the spot, and right then I was certain my legs would give out.

"Are you stalking my place?"

I couldn't tell him that I spent my time in an underground bunker searching for a potion that might turn me into a human for good. Or that if I turned into a wulfkin, I'd be forced to live with the pack, mate with one of them, and lose him forever. It would make me sound like a crazy person because, in his world, moonwulf and wulfkin didn't exist.

He drew in a quick breath of air. "Of course not. We haven't caught up for weeks, and I missed you. Daci, tell me what you want from me, or am I an idiot for believing something serious was happening with us?"

I reached out for him and took his hand in mine. "It's only you I want. Nothing else is going on. I've been working extra hours for a huge project at work. That's all."

His hand slipped out of my grasp. "Part of the problem with being an inspector is that it lets me know when someone is lying." His voice held a ragged edge. "After my ex-wife, I never thought I'd be able to love again. Then I met you. But now I'm getting that same feeling I got when I realized she wasn't telling me the truth." His gaze held onto me. "I don't want to go through that again."

He might as well have pulled the ring from a hand grenade because my heart stopped beating. "I'm nothing like—"

"Why can't you—"

"Let me finish," I said through gritted teeth. "I'm not like your ex-wife. I would never cheat on you, so don't compare me to her, ever. How could you even suggest it?" Pain squeezed my throat. "What do you want me to tell you? Something that isn't true so you can say all females are liars?" I struggled to hold my composure and hugged myself. "That's not going to happen."

Connell shut his eyes, his lips pressed tight together.

"All I ask is for one week to finish a project at work. Then you won't be able to get rid of me. I love you so much." I couldn't think of anything else around my trembling limbs and numb brain.

He opened his eyes slightly, and a shade of brown flashed, reminding me of his sexy look just before he had his way with me. My body tingled. I'd never wanted a man as much as I did Connell.

He pushed his shoulders back, and a hard expression slid over his face. "I don't want to talk about this now. We have to go to the crime scene." An edge of bossiness crept into his voice. He turned his back to me. "Ready?"

I couldn't speak.

A dracwulf had attacked me.

Connell hinted at breaking up.

Somehow my day had managed to suck even worse.

Printed in the United States
By Bookmasters